Tiger

S J Richards

TIGER BAIT

Published worldwide by Apple Loft Press

This edition published in 2025

Copyright © 2025 by S J Richards

S J Richards has asserted his right to be identified as the author of this work in accordance with the Copyright, Design and Patents Act 1988.

All rights reserved. This book or any portion thereof may not be reproduced or used in any manner whatsoever without the express written permission of the author, except for quotes or short extracts for the purpose of reviews.

www.sjrichardsauthor.com

For Kirstie and Lily

The Luke Sackville Crime Thriller Series

Taken to the Hills
Black Money
Fog of Silence
The Corruption Code
Lethal Odds
Sow the Wind
Beacon of Blight
Tiger Bait
Mr Killjoy

Chapter 1

Diana sat back on the bar stool and surveyed her all-white kitchen. It was the stuff of dreams with its hand-crafted cabinets, Corian worktops and top-of-the-range Wolf appliances.

She smiled as she recalled returning from the Costa del Sol, a holiday paid for by her dad as a present for her fortieth, to find him waiting at the front door with a bunch of flowers.

"I've got another surprise for you," he'd said with a twinkle in his eye.

"They're lovely," she'd said, taking the bouquet from him and assuming the roses were what he meant.

He'd laughed. "Not those. Close your eyes."

She'd closed her eyes and he'd grabbed her hand and led her into the kitchen, while her then-partner Pierre had followed meekly behind.

"Now open them."

She'd cried when she'd seen the transformation to her kitchen.

"Wow, Dad. It's lovely."

He'd smiled and kissed her on the cheek.

"Nothing's too good for my precious."

Little did either of them know that the cancer had already taken hold of his body. Three months later, he'd been diagnosed with leukaemia, and soon afterwards the oncologist revealed that there were cancerous cells in his spleen and liver.

He'd survived for almost a year, but then her dad had always been a fighter.

She wiped beneath her eyes, took a deep breath and tried to steady herself. Hardly a day went by without her thinking of him, and of the inspiration he'd been, but she needed to remain positive and reflect on how proud he would be of her plans for the family business.

This new endeavour was risky, but it also had the potential to be the most profitable since she'd taken the reins.

But only if her planning was meticulous.

Diana started checking through the fifty-odd actions on her notepad, and was halfway through when she realised she'd omitted a crucial element. It wasn't much on the face of it, a phone call to Flynn to check he was in situ, but success required that she dot all the I's and cross all the T's.

It was disappointing to have missed something so obvious. If she wasn't thorough, everything she'd been planning for weeks could come to nought. Although she had a lot of faith in the people working for her, coordinating their activities so that they functioned as a team wasn't easy. They were strong-minded individuals, and success required excellent timing and seamless execution, but above all that they worked as one.

And also, although she hated to admit it, it required an element of luck.

One more run-through and she decided the plan was comprehensive. It was important to start phoning around the team, but she couldn't do that until her son was out of the house.

She looked up at the kitchen clock, then walked to the hall and called up the stairs.

"Roma, are you ready yet?"

There was no response.

She raised her voice.

"The match starts at eleven. You need to leave in the next five minutes."

A few seconds later her son's bedroom door slammed shut, and he stomped down the stairs.

"I haven't had breakfast," he moaned, as if it was her

fault.

"That's what comes of sleeping in so late."

"If you gave me a lift, I wouldn't have to rush."

"I'm busy all day and can't afford the time."

He could be a pain, but she'd been much the same at his age, not that she'd been brave enough to challenge her dad, or at least not more than once. She'd been fourteen when he'd told her she couldn't stay out after 10 pm, and she'd snapped that he was 'a stupid old man'. He'd beaten her for that, beaten her badly, and she'd ended up with a black eye and two broken ribs.

Her father had been a hard man, but you had to be tough to survive in their line of work.

Roma grabbed his bag from the coat rack, walked to the kitchen, and extracted two bags of crisps and a cereal bar from one of the wall cupboards.

"How come you're busy all day?" he asked as he stuffed them into his rucksack.

"It's work."

"Anything interesting?"

"A new venture."

"Can I help?"

She laughed and would have ruffled his hair if he wasn't now two inches taller than her. At five foot ten, she wasn't exactly diminutive herself.

He was broad too, almost indecently so, and it was no wonder he was the powerhouse of the St Paul's Under-16s football team.

"You're only fifteen, Roma, much too young to be involved in my side of the business. Your Uncle Jay's got you running errands for him and you should look upon that as an apprenticeship."

"Yeah, it's all right, I suppose."

"I don't hear you complaining about the money."

He smiled then. She loved it when he smiled.

"So, who are you playing today?"

"Kingswood Wanderers."

"Is that the lot that beat you 3-0?"

"Yeah. Not going to happen this time though."

"How can you be so sure?"

Roma grinned. "Cos I'm gonna flatten their centre-forward in the first five minutes. Put him out of the game."

"Be careful. Make sure the ref's not watching."

"I'm not stupid, Mum."

He turned to leave.

"Hey, aren't you forgetting something?"

His smile returned and he bent down to kiss her on the cheek.

"Love you, Mum."

"Love you, Roma."

Diana shut the front door and reflected on what a wonderful son he was. She'd been careful not to spoil him, conscious that he was fatherless and an only child, and was proud of his development. He could be impulsive, especially when he was angry, but she was confident he'd learn how to control himself as he matured.

Physically, Roma was more than capable of holding his own, but what she most admired was his independent character. He wasn't frightened to speak his mind and would be an excellent addition to the business once he was old enough.

Seventeen, she thought. Once he was seventeen he'd be ready, she was sure of it.

That was less than eighteen months away, which seemed soon, but she'd start him off lightly, perhaps supporting Flynn. If he did that well, she'd give him progressively more challenging roles until she could test him out as a manager and give him his own patch to control.

She returned to her notepad, spent a couple of minutes considering who to call first, then decided to start with Apollo, not because he was her brother, but because this was the first time the two of them had cooperated like this since their dad had died. Apollo was doing well, and delivering decent profits, but what she was asking him to do today was new to him and she had to be sure he was ready.

Plus he lacked a sense of urgency, and she was worried he might mistime things.

He answered after several rings, which was frustrating in itself.

"Hi, Sis."

"How's it going?"

"Fine. Everything's in control."

"The van's ready then?"

"Not quite."

"What do you mean, not quite?"

Apollo laughed. "Stop fretting, Sis. Milo and I are on it now."

"Milo! I can't believe you've involved that pea-brained yokel. A bag of rocks has a higher IQ than Milo."

"He's okay. What he's doing isn't mentally taxing. I don't see the problem."

She sighed. "You're clear on the timing?"

"Don't worry. I'll be there at noon on the dot."

"What do you mean noon?"

Apollo laughed again. "You're too easy to wind up, Di. 11:15, 52 Penrose Avenue. You can count on me."

Diana felt like giving him an earful. This was a big day, and his supposed sense of humour was more than she could cope with.

What was the point though? Apollo wasn't one to take it on the chin, and she didn't have time for an argument. Plus, if she wound him up, he might deliberately do something to skewer the operation.

She hung up without saying anything else and moved to the second person on her list.

Half an hour later, she finished her last call and sat back on the chair, confident that everything was coming together. A part of her wanted to ring Apollo back and emphasise the importance of his role, but she resisted the urge.

She headed upstairs, changed into her black trousers and jumper then retrieved the balaclava from the bottom drawer of her dressing table.

She pulled the balaclava on, looked at herself in the mirror and shivered at the scary reflection that stared back at her.

Come on, Diana. You can do it, and think how proud Dad would be.

Chapter 2

Barbara had a difficult decision to make.

Pilates or yoga?

She'd pre-paid for pilates, and it was at 11:30, but Maureen would probably be there, and she couldn't bear another hour of her bleating about her arthritis. The woman was seventy-eight for heaven's sake. What did she expect? We all have aches and pains at that age. Her own shoulders hurt occasionally, but did she complain all the time?

No, she didn't!

And if Maureen didn't turn up, there was Libby to contend with. Barbara shook her head as she recalled how rude Libby had been the previous week, stopping her halfway through her story like that. She'd said she'd told her before, and then had the cheek to ask why it took ten minutes to get to the point.

What utter nonsense! The birthday card had been marked as £1.99 and had come up as £2.99 on the till. That was a pound, a whole pound! And you couldn't relate the story without describing the journey there, and why she was buying the card in the first place.

Some people!

Yes, yoga was more tempting. She'd put on the DVD her son bought her for Christmas and work her way through the second session. It meant she could stay indoors too, which was a bonus given it was forecast to stay below five degrees all day.

So much for March being the first month of Spring.

She flicked the TV on and had just inserted the DVD when the doorbell went.

To her surprise, it was her next-door neighbour.

"Is everything okay, Jim? Nothing's happened to Gail, has it?"

He smiled. "We're fine, Barbara, but we're going out and I completely forgot I've got a delivery coming. Would you mind taking it in for me?"

"Of course not. Are you going anywhere exciting?"

"We're having lunch in Bristol, and then going to a matinee at the Hippodrome."

"How lovely. I'll be in all day, so pop around when you're back."

"Will do. Thanks."

"I went to Bristol myself last Thursday and you wouldn't believe what happened on the way back."

"Really. Ah…"

"On the way there it was fine. The bus was a couple of minutes late leaving Bath bus station, but that's to be expected, isn't it?" She laughed. "I mean they can't keep exactly to schedule. That would be impossible. And anyway, I wasn't on a deadline. The shops are open late on a Thursday, so I had as long as I needed. I went to John Lewis first because they had a sale in the…"

"Barbara?"

"Yes, Jim."

"I'm going to have to go. Perhaps you can tell me some other time."

"Yes, I'll do that. Although what happened was most peculiar. I should have suspected something when the bus driver looked at me like that, but I didn't dream…"

"Sorry, Barbara. I really must be off. Thanks for saying you'll take the parcel."

He turned and headed back to his house, which was a shame because he'd brought back the memory of the time a delivery driver had dumped a skirt she'd ordered in one of her flower pots. It was doubly interesting because of the tattoo he'd had on his arm, and she was sure Jim would be interested to hear all about it.

Not to worry, she'd tell him when he came to pick his parcel up.

She closed the door, returned to the lounge and watched as the instructor started to describe the first movement of the session.

Barbara sat on the floor ready to copy her lead, and the bell went again.

She paused the DVD, climbed to her feet and returned to the front door, smiling to herself as she did so. It was probably the delivery driver, but might well be Jim wanting to hear the end of her story.

She opened the door wide and immediately put her hand to her mouth. The man in front of her was big, but it wasn't his size that shocked her. He was wearing headgear that left only his eyes and mouth visible.

"What's your name?" he demanded, his voice low and gravelly.

"Why? Who are you? I…"

She started to close the door, but he blocked it with his foot and then stepped through.

Barbara opened her mouth to scream, but he smothered it with a gloved hand, bent down and hissed, "Don't even think of crying out for help. Understand?."

She nodded, and he took his hand away.

"What do you want? I haven't got much money, just some…"

"You're going to make a video."

All sorts of scenarios went through Barbara's head, none of them pleasant.

"A video of what?"

"Your neighbours. They're going out soon, and I want you to film them and give a running commentary."

"What? Why?"

"You didn't answer my question. What's your name?"

"Barbara." She gulped. "Barbara Wadding."

He nodded, retrieved an iPhone from his pocket and

passed it to her.

"Open the camera, Barbara, and put it in video mode."

"I don't know how to."

He shook his head in irritation, took off his gloves, retrieved the phone, clicked a couple of times and then held it so that she could see the screen.

"Press this red button to begin, and press it again to stop. Understand?"

"Yes."

"First, I want you to introduce yourself, and say what's happened today."

"From when I got up?"

He sighed. "No. From when I rang the bell."

"Okay."

She looked down at the phone, clicked on the red button and held the phone out in front of her.

"My name is Barbara Wadding, and I was about to start a yoga session when my doorbell rang. I had considered going to Pilates, but Maureen will probably be there and even if she's not Libby might be. Besides, my son gave me a DVD for…"

"Stop."

She looked over at him. "What?"

"Press the red button."

She pressed it.

"Give it here."

She passed it over.

He clicked play, watched the first few seconds and then deleted the video.

"You took a video of the floor."

"How did that happen? I was looking at the screen."

"You need to switch to the front-facing camera."

"The what?"

"Don't worry. I'll do it." He clicked to change cameras and passed it back. "And this time don't waste time with that shit about Pilates and Maureen and your son. Go straight into me arriving."

Barbara nodded and was about to click the red button again when the phone rang, startling her so much that she almost dropped it.

He held his hand out.

"Give it here."

She passed it back and he accepted the call.

"I'm inside." He paused for a few seconds, his piercing blue eyes fixed on Barbara, before adding, "She's hard work. I'll be there as soon as I can."

He hung up and passed the phone back.

"Right, let's start again."

She swallowed, looked at the screen and pressed the red button.

"Hi. Uh…"

She looked up at him and he gestured for her to get on with it.

"My name is Barbara Wadding, and I answered the door to a man in a balaclava who asked me to make a video of my neighbours. I'm not very good with phones though, and I used the wrong camera. Apparently, it has a front-facing…"

He snatched the phone back and hit the red button.

"Was that okay?"

He replayed it then grunted.

"It'll have to do."

He clicked twice and passed it back.

"I've put it back to the main camera. As soon as we leave the house, I want you to start recording."

"Recording what?"

"Everything that happens next door."

He stood aside and gestured for her to go outside ahead of him.

She shook her head. "It's freezing. I'm not going out there without a coat. I remember one time I didn't wear one when I was going to Mavis's house. It's only in the next street, but I hadn't realised it was so cold outside. After a few yards..."

"Enough."

She noticed him close his eyes for a second, as if frustrated with something, then he held his hand out again and she passed him the phone.

He watched as she retrieved her coat from the rack, put it on and buttoned it down the front.

"Happy now?"

"I wouldn't say I'm happy, well not as..."

"For fuck's sake!"

He gave another sigh, much deeper this time, thrust the phone back into her hand and stood aside.

Barbara walked through the door, lifted the iPhone so that it was focused on the two people standing outside Jim and Gail's front door, and pressed the red button.

Chapter 3

Diana pulled her balaclava on as she approached Penrose Avenue. As anticipated, a police officer stepped off the kerb as soon as she made the turn and held his arm out for her to stop the car.

She lowered the window, and he walked over.

"I'm sorry, madam, but the road's closed." He frowned as he saw the balaclava and then smiled as realisation dawned."Oh. Are you one of the cast?"

She laughed. "How did you guess?"

He returned her laugh. "I assume you're playing one of the baddies."

"That's right. I'm the gang leader. We're starting filming in the next half hour." She paused. "Troy, isn't it?"

He nodded. "Troy Hinchcliffe, but today I'm PC Archer." He pointed at the name badge on his uniform.

"I was told you'd be here. And your friend's positioned at the other end of the street, isn't he?"

"Yes." He grinned. "I know I'm only an extra, but it's exciting being involved. I couldn't believe it when my agent rang. Liam's buzzing too."

"Have you had to turn many people away?"

"Only a few. People are very understanding." He paused. "I was told we'd only be needed for this morning. Do you know if that's correct?"

"Yes. We should be done by noon."

"Will I get a warning when I'm about to be filmed?"

"Possibly, but there's a chance you won't be in the final cut. Our director's up against it today, and it's the interior shots that are key."

"Oh." His face was a picture of disappointment, and she almost felt sorry for him.

"Anyway, Troy, I must get on. Keep up the good work."
"I will. Nice to meet you, Miss, ah…"

She raised the window before he'd finished the question, drove off and watched him in the rearview mirror. He was smiling, doubtless under the impression he'd been talking to a famous Hollywood actress.

Diana was relieved to see the van in position as she turned onto the drive of number 52. Apollo had reversed it in as agreed.

They'd reconnoitred the area twice, and a combination of trees and high hedges shielded his vehicle and hers completely, making it impossible for prying neighbours to see what was going on.

She climbed out and walked towards the front door, then turned when she realised she'd seen movement in the passenger seat of the van. After retracing her steps, she opened the door and Milo looked up from the comic he'd been reading.

"Ugh," he said, which in her experience was as profound as he got. His wide-set eyes and large nose reminded her of one of the trolls in Lord of the Rings, and he had an IQ to match.

On second thoughts, that was unfair to trolls.

"What do you think you're doing?" she demanded.

He looked blankly at her, and she could almost see the cogs turning as he placed her voice.

"Diana?"

"Yes, it's me."

He held his comic up. "Reading."

"I can see you're reading, well, looking at the pictures at least. What about your balaclava?"

He reached into the cubbyhole between the seats, held up his ski mask and grinned, exposing a set of dirty-brown, pointed teeth.

She pointed at his face. "Put it on."

"On?"

"Yes. On." She signalled to show him what she meant. "Over your head."

"Ugh."

He pulled it on, though it was a struggle to squeeze it over his ears.

"Where's Apollo?"

"Inside."

"And why has he brought you?"

"In case."

"In case of what?"

Milo shrugged. "I don't know."

"You don't know?"

"No." He paused. "Yes. Muscle. Apollo said muscle."

"Muscle?"

"Frighteners."

She shook her head. What was her brother thinking? What the couple were facing was scary enough without presenting them with Milo. And besides, the man was a liability.

"Okay. Stay here unless you hear otherwise."

"Yes, Diana."

"And stop calling me Diana. We don't want anyone overhearing our names."

"Okay, Diana."

She sighed. "You can go back to your comic now."

He started to pull his balaclava off.

"Keep it on."

He grunted but left it on and reopened his comic.

Diana turned away. She'd have a word with Apollo later, but right now she needed to join him and check on progress.

Chapter 4

Jim wanted to reach for his wife's hand, but his wrists had been handcuffed together, and he had to content himself with glancing over at her. She looked back at him from the other end of the sofa, her eyes red-rimmed and tears running down her cheeks.

He looked across at the three men in balaclavas standing with their back to the lounge wall. At least they hadn't hurt her, or him for that matter, when they'd forced their way in, but he was worried that might change. Were they terrorists, or activists of some kind? The fact they were making Barbara film everything must mean they wanted to make a statement, perhaps one they would put out on social media, but why pick on them? Or were they a random choice, a means to an end?

"I'm sorry," Barbara said from the armchair opposite.

"Stop apologising and get on with it," the man who'd forced his way into her house said, his accent unmistakeably Bristolian. He pointed at the sheet of paper that she was holding shakily in her hand. "Ask the first question."

She looked down at what was written and as she did so allowed her right hand, the one holding the iPhone, to drop down.

"Keep the camera on those two."

"Right. Yes." She swallowed. "Sorry." She lifted the phone so that Jim and Gail were both in the frame.

"Don't worry," Jim said in an attempt to calm her down. "The sooner we get through this, the better."

A fourth person entered the room, a woman. She too wore a balaclava and whispered in the ear of the man who had been speaking and then stood to one side.

Barbara read out the first question.

Tiger Bait

"What are your names and ages and what is your relationship to Sebastian Thatcher?"

So that's what it's about, Jim thought. *I should have known.*

"We're Jim and Gail Thatcher," he said. "I'm 65 and Gail is 64. Sebastian is our son."

"Question 2," the Bristolian prompted, taking the first sheet from Barbara and handing her a second.

"Is this true?" Barbara said as she read what was written.

"Just ask it."

She looked across at Jim and then read the question out.

"Are you aware that your son's net worth has been estimated at £11 million?"

Jim swallowed. He could see now where this was going.

"That will be based on the value of the company he started. He can't access the funds."

The man took the second sheet and passed Barbara a third.

She looked down at what was written. "I can't ask this."

"Ask it."

She looked across at Jim. "Sorry, Jim."

"Get on with it."

Barbara cleared her throat. "How much would Sebastian be prepared to pay to prevent either of you being harmed?"

"He'd go to the police," Jim replied automatically.

It was the woman who'd entered last who spoke next. She too had a Bristol accent.

"Take his wife into the next room, but leave the doors open so that we can hear her."

"NO!" Jim screamed as two of their captors stepped forward.

The man who'd brought Barbara in held his hand out to stop them.

"We won't harm her if you're sensible, Jim, and if you

say something like that again..." He paused to let this sink in. "Barbara, ask the question again."

Her voice was shaky this time, and Jim could see that she was having trouble coping with the situation.

"How m-m-much would Sebastian..." She swallowed before continuing. "...be prepared to p-p-pay to prevent either of you being hurt?"

"He'd pay whatever it takes."

"Much better, Jim." The man handed Barbara another sheet.

She read the fourth question out, managing to just about hold herself together this time.

"Do you have a message for your son about involving the police?"

Jim looked at Gail and then directly into the camera.

"Don't even think about it, Seb. Pay them whatever it takes."

The tall man nodded.

"Good. That was the last question."

He stepped forward, took the phone from Barbara, stopped the recording and then turned to the other two men.

"You know what to do."

They stepped forward and took hold of Barbara's arms.

"No!" she screamed.

"What are you doing?" Jim said, climbing to his feet. "Leave her alone."

The man shoved Jim in the chest so that he fell back onto the sofa, then leaned over so that their faces were almost touching.

"Your son has to understand the danger you're in, and we need to send a strong message."

He held his hand against Jim's chest as his associates carried a screaming and squirming Barbara out of the room.

Chapter 5

Diana stood to one side and watched as Jim, Gail and Barbara were hustled into the back of the van.

All three had been gagged, which was a relief given the amount of noise the Wadding woman had been making. It wasn't a surprise, given the pain she must be in, and Diana almost felt sorry for her.

Almost, but not quite.

This was business, not personal. That was what her father had always said, and it was her mantra now that he was gone.

All in all, the team had done well, but they needed to get out quickly now that the main part of the plan had been enacted. She was confident they couldn't be seen from neighbouring houses, but it was important not to hang around for too long.

She and Apollo stood side by side as Declan and Flynn climbed into the van to watch over their captives.

"We'll be leaving in a few minutes," Apollo said. "I'll bang on the partition when we're ready to go."

He closed the rear doors of the van and turned to his sister.

"That went well." He lifted the plastic food box he held in his left hand, "and this was a bonus."

She turned and glared at her brother.

"It wasn't necessary. When I said we needed to send a strong message, I meant film of her crying, not…" She gestured to the box, her face a picture of revulsion. "…that."

"It will show we mean business and besides, it was Declan's idea."

"Why on earth did you let him do it? He could have

risked everything. What if the stupid bitch had had a heart attack?"

"She didn't, did she? It's only the end of her finger down to the first knuckle. It's painful, but she'll learn to live with it. Besides..." he chuckled "... the thought of what we did to her once, and might do to her again, will ensure she keeps quiet."

"Yes, but..."

She took a deep breath. This was an added complication which she could well do without.

"How is she going to explain it to her friends?"

"With a mouth like hers, I'd be surprised if she has any."

"For fuck's sake, Apollo. Now is not the time to be flippant."

"It's not like you to swear, Sis."

"First you bring that imbecile Milo along, God knows what for, and then you let Declan do that to the woman. I can't believe it." She shook her head. "Once we've got these three secured, we need to have a family meeting. I'd like Jay's view on what to do next."

"That makes sense." He held the box up again. "I'm sure that between the three of us, we can work out how to exploit this to the max."

"We'd better be off. I'll see you in East Harptree."

She climbed into her Audi, reversed out of the drive and waited for Apollo to exit and head down Penrose Avenue before following.

At the end of the road, she stopped beside the fake police officer and lowered her window.

"How's it been, PC Archer?" she asked and chuckled.

"No problems, Ma'am," Troy said, returning her laugh and giving a salute. "How's filming going?"

"We've finished for the day, so you and Liam can go home."

"Oh," he said, disappointed. "I thought we'd be in the

final cut."

"You will be," she said cheerily, and gestured to one of the nearby houses. "We had a cameraman behind that window, and he reported that he'd taken some great shots."

"I didn't see him."

"It's our director's way of shooting exciting action, the camera behind a window, shaking images, that kind of thing. With any luck, he'll include it in the final film."

"I hope so. I have to admit it would be a first for me to be in a big Hollywood production, even if it is as an extra. Would you believe my last role was in a corporate video for Favershams?"

She wanted to shut him up but needed to tell him about his extra payments.

"Was it?"

She'd never heard of Favershams and was itching for him to get the story out of the way.

"Yes. Mind you, I only got that role because the father of a friend of mine is one of their executives. He runs their cash holding unit or something."

His use of the word 'cash' piqued her interest, but she didn't have time to quiz him further.

"That's fascinating, Troy. Listen, the film's producer is desperate to keep everything under wraps. We're hoping to release it in the summer, but they asked me to emphasise that to you. Can you pass the need for secrecy on to Liam, too?"

"Of course."

"As an incentive, they'll pay you £100 for each of the next four months as long as word doesn't get out."

"Wow! That would be great."

She passed him a pen and a piece of paper.

"Jot your bank details down there and I'll pass it on. He said he'll transfer £200 on the 1st of each month and leave it to you to pass half on to Liam. That way you can avoid your agent's cut."

He did as she asked and passed the sheet of paper back to her.

"Thanks, Miss…"

For the second and final time, she ignored his prompt for her name, raised the window and drove away.

Chapter 6

Luke Sackville tried to stifle his yawn, but it was spotted by James McDonald, Filchers' Head of Human Resources, who, being equally bored, was unable to stop himself from involuntarily copying his colleague.

Unfortunately for James, his yawn was all too visible to their boss.

"Hah!" Edward Filcher said from the end of the table. "Bored, James?"

"Not at all, Mr Filcher. I'm a little under the weather, that's all."

"Excellent. Excellent." Filcher looked down at his printed agenda. "Item seven, cross-departmental affiliations."

Luke sighed. Filcher's Monday morning catch-up with his four department heads was always tedious, and today was no exception. Such meetings could be over-lengthy when he'd been a Detective Chief Inspector at Avon and Somerset Police, but at least they'd been focused on things that mattered.

Not cross-departmental affiliations, whatever they were.

"Co-operation," Filcher said by way of explanation, then waited for comments.

None came.

"Co-operation is critical," Filcher went on. "We in Internal Affairs need to be as one. Sing from the same hymn sheet." He looked at each of his subordinates in turn. "We should look for win-wins and low-hanging fruit. Ideas that help the bottom line."

"Aye," Fred Tanner, the Head of Marketing and a Yorkshireman to his bones, said, "and then we can run them ideas up t' flagpole."

"Exactly, Fred. Look for quick wins, take them off-piste and drill down."

"Make sure they're a strategic fit," Fred added, now enjoying the game.

"Indeed."

As he said this, Filcher noticed that Glen Baxter, who was sitting next to Luke, was struggling to keep his eyes open.

"Glen?" he barked.

There was no response.

Luke nudged the Head of Security, and he sat bolt upright and started blinking his eyes.

"Say what?"

"Glen," Filcher repeated. "Have you got any?"

"Ah…" Glen hesitated as he tried to recall what his boss had been talking about. "Any what, Mr Filcher?"

"Low-hanging fruit. Have you got low-hanging fruit?"

Glen's eyes widened. "Oh. Sorry."

He looked down at his lap and tugged on the zip of his trousers.

Filcher shook his head. "Ideas, man. Not your, ah…" He gestured at Glen's groin.

"Ideas?"

"Yes. Ideas."

"For?"

"For Internal Affairs. So that we work as one."

"Like bees," Fred suggested.

Filcher turned to his Head of Marketing and nodded several times, his hooked nose leading the way. "Excellent, Fred. Good point, well made." He waved his hand at the four men. "You are worker bees under my guidance."

"That makes you the queen," Fred suggested.

"Indeed." Filcher paused, then looked around at the four Heads of Department. "And your ideas are?"

Again, there was silence.

"Mmm. I'll ask Gloria to carry it forward, but we must

circle back to it before the goalposts move." He looked back down at his sheet. "Item eight, Stairway."

"I agree," Glen said, now forcing himself to stay awake.

"Agree with what?"

"Using the stairway. It's good for my quads, and I never use the lift. They need to be on a par with this."

He lifted his right arm and flexed it to demonstrate the size of his bicep.

"Is the other one as big?" Fred asked.

Glen nodded, the sarcasm going straight over his buzz cut.

"Bigger if anything."

"Very impressive."

"Enough," Filcher said. "This is nothing to do with stairs. I am referring to the social media company." He turned to Luke. "Needs ethics. One of your team. The female one."

"Helen?" Luke suggested.

"Perhaps. Or could be one of the others. The one that's good with numbers."

"There are only two women in my team, Mr Filcher. Helen's a legal expert, but I assume you mean Sam. She's an accountant."

Filcher nodded. "That's the filly. Sam. Yes, Sam. Very bright. As smart as many men."

"She'll be pleased to hear that you think that," Luke lied. "So, what's the issue?"

"The issue?"

"You said Sam needs to assist in the Stairway account."

"Indeed. Problem with ethics. Ethical problem."

"And the problem is?"

"Not aware of the details. Below my pay grade. Hah! Speak to the client director."

"Okay. I'll do that. Is it Henry Richardson?"

"Ah…"

"Not any more," James said, coming to Filcher's rescue.

"Henry left Filchers last week to take up a role at Bannermans."

"Have they replaced him yet?" Luke asked.

"They have." James grimaced. "Sorry, Luke, but Stairway's new client director is Cora Evans. I hope that doesn't make it difficult for you."

Glen grinned. "That's interesting," He turned to Luke. "Weren't you and Cora seeing each other's, ah…"

He paused as it dawned on him that he'd got the expression wrong, though he couldn't for the life of him recall the correct phrasing.

"We were seeing each other if that's what you mean," Luke said.

"I thought as much. Yes, you and she were coupling."

"A couple, Glen. We were a couple for a short time."

"Enough," Filcher said. "Leave this with you, Luke. Put, ah… Sam?"

"Yes, Sam."

Filcher smiled, pleased he'd remembered her name correctly.

"Good. Yes. Put Sam on the case. Excellent." He looked back at his printed agenda. "Need to move on. Much to cover. Item nine, Minimising Incremental Overflows."

Chapter 7

Luke was muttering under his breath when he returned to the Ethics Room.

He walked to his desk and dropped heavily into his chair.

"That must be a record," Sam said as she pulled her own chair over to sit opposite.

"It seemed never-ending, and it's an hour and a half of my life I'm never going to get back." He shook his head. "James and I have agreed we've got to do something. The meeting adds zero value, and most agenda items are completely pointless. We spent ten minutes listening to Filcher's opinions on executive car parking spaces for goodness sake."

"What's the point of the meeting anyway?"

"Heaven knows. It's not as if he comes out of it knowing any more about what we're all doing." He sighed. "Filcher likes bigging himself up, and I guess he sees this meeting as an opportunity to demonstrate his authority."

"He's harmless, though."

"Is he?" Luke half-smiled. "Your name came up."

"I'm surprised he remembered it."

"He didn't, but he offered high praise."

"He did?"

Luke nodded. "He said you were as smart as many men."

Sam's eyebrows went up. "He said what?"

"Mind you, he was looking at Glen when he said it."

"He's a misogynistic, old-fashioned, pompous buffoon."

"Filcher or Glen?"

"Both of them." She paused. "Did Fred manage to

dodge out of it again?"

"No. He tried to, but Filcher insisted Lizzie attend the ad agency meeting in his place."

"What about Glen?"

"He was there in body, but slept through most of it."

"Was there anything in the slightest bit useful that came out of the meeting?"

"There *was* one thing. Filcher said your help is needed because of a problem in the Stairway team. How much do you know about the account?"

"I know we took on their finance functions last October but, aside from that, not much. Oh, and I met Henry Richardson, the client director, just before Christmas."

"He's not client director any more. Henry's left Filchers."

"Oh. Who's taken his place?"

Luke hesitated before replying.

"Cora Evans."

He could see that this took Sam aback, though she tried to hide it.

"I see."

"It's not going to be a problem, is it?"

"Of course not!" she blurted out, before immediately adding, "Sorry, I didn't mean to snap. So, what's the issue in the account?"

"True to form, Filcher didn't know. He said it was something to do with numbers, which is about as detailed as he gets, and that's why your name came up, but said I'd need to talk to Cora to find out more. However, rather than be a middleman, I thought it more sensible for you to speak to her directly."

Sam smiled.

"That's not the only reason, is it? You're trying to avoid her." She paused. "Does she still call you 'lover'?"

"Yes," he admitted, returning her smile, "and it gets on

my nerves."

"Okay. Leave it with me."

"Thanks." He looked over at Maj and Helen. "Is Josh around? We could do with a team catch-up."

"He offered to fetch coffees."

There was a click as the door opened, and Josh appeared carrying a tray with five paper cups.

"Hi, guv," he said as he walked over. "I thought you'd be back, so I bought you a double espresso."

Luke took the offered drink. "Thanks, Josh." He called over to the others. "Maj, Helen, can you join us?"

"Sure," Maj replied.

"Be right there," Helen said.

Luke wheeled his chair to the meeting table in the centre of the room and the others joined him.

"Let's keep this brief," he began. "DI Gilmore rang me earlier, and I'm needed in Portishead today. Josh, what are you working on?"

"I've been helping Maj with background research."

Luke turned to Maj. "Can you spare him?"

"Why, guv?" Josh said, suddenly excited. "Is it that Criminology and Ethics course? Am I going on the course? Am I?"

"No, son."

Josh seemed to visibly deflate.

"I'll have time to continue the research myself if you need him," Maj said.

"Good. I'm sure you'll all remember that our contract with Avon and Somerset Police might require one or more of you to work as consultants alongside me. Well, the time has come."

Josh's mouth opened wide and stayed open for several seconds.

"Me, guv?"

"Yes, you, Josh."

"Wowza! What are we doing? Will I be undercover?"

"You'll be assisting in an interview and any follow-up."

"With a perp?"

Helen snorted.

"No, Josh," Luke said. "And we don't call criminals 'perps' in the UK. That's an American term."

"Oh. What do you call them?"

"Criminals."

"Crims?"

"No, criminals. We call criminals 'criminals'."

"Gotcha."

"And you and I won't be interviewing a suspected criminal, we'll be interviewing a witness."

"A witness to what?"

"I'll explain on the drive over."

Luke turned to Maj.

"Have you made any progress with We-Haul, Maj?"

"Early days. I met June Fairbanks late on Friday." He addressed his next words to the others. "She's the one who highlighted the issue."

"The whistleblower," Josh suggested.

Maj nodded. "Yes. Unfortunately, she hasn't got any proof. June overheard two of We-Haul's senior managers talking about reducing the cost of protective clothing and gained the impression they were cutting corners."

"That could be employee exploitation," Helen suggested.

"That's what she thinks, but it's not going to be easy proving she's right."

"Which airports do they work in?" Luke asked.

"Most of the UK ones, though not Heathrow. The company was started up with a focus on commercial cargo but has extended so that they now handle customer luggage as well."

"Are they at Bristol?"

Maj smiled. "Yes. Are you thinking I should pay them a visit?"

"I don't think visiting will do any good. Their work is going to be mainly airside. Is there a way you could join the team in some capacity?"

"June is their Personnel Manager so she might be able to help. I'll give her a call."

"Great."

"Project Douglas," Josh said, apropos of nothing.

They all turned to look at him.

He grinned. "For the crazy wall. Because of the actor." He turned to Helen. "You must remember Douglas Fairbanks, Helen?"

"How old do you think I am?" she demanded angrily.

"Ah… I…"

She grinned, and Josh immediately relaxed.

"Ha, ha. Very funny."

"As yet," Luke said, "I don't think the We-Haul investigation warrants an entry on the whiteboard, but we'll bear your suggestion in mind, Josh."

"Gucci!" He sat back, clearly pleased with himself.

"Helen, how are you getting on with redrafting those clauses for Ambrose?"

"All going well. Should have it finished later today."

"Good. Sam?"

"The Mannings query came to nothing, so I'll concentrate on Stairway."

Josh sat up when he heard this. "The social media company. That's cool. What are we doing there?"

"I don't know yet," Sam said.

"Anything to do with their new AI face-shifter platform? My little brother and his friends are all over it."

She shook her head. "I don't think the issue is going to be with the product side of the business. More likely connected to their accounting."

Luke got to his feet. "Thanks, everyone." He turned to Josh. "Come on, we need to leave."

Josh went to fetch his coat and Luke looked into Sam's

eyes, grabbed her hand and gave it a squeeze.
"Good luck with Cora."
"Thanks. I can't say I'm looking forward to it."

Chapter 8

"How long does it take to get to Portishead?" Josh asked as Luke turned the BMW onto the Lower Bristol Road.

"About an hour."

"Oh, right. Um…"

Luke could sense something was troubling him.

"What's bothering you?"

"I, ah…" Josh hesitated before continuing. "I was wondering if you could give me some advice."

"I can try. Is this to do with work?"

"Oh, no. It's personal. You're…" He paused again. "You're experienced with women, aren't you, guv?"

Luke cast him a sideways glance.

"What's that supposed to mean?"

"Well, you've been around a bit, had multiple relationships."

"Around a bit?"

"Sorry. I didn't mean… It's not…"

"Out with it, Josh."

"You understand women, that's what I meant. You know their ways. How to deal with them."

"To an extent, yes, although I can't profess to be an expert. Are you and Leanne having problems?"

"No. Not at all. We're getting on fine. More than fine. I mean, we have our differences and I know she can find me a tad frustrating. She's accused me of being immature on more than one occasion."

Luke couldn't stop himself from smiling. "I can't understand why."

"Exactimo, guv. I'm a grown-up, a man of the world, a mature adult."

"I wouldn't go that far."

"The thing is, well… I have needs and desires."

"Needs and desires?"

"Yes."

"It sounds like you should see a sexual counsellor."

"No, guv. It's not a physical problem. Well, it could be. My knees anyway."

"Your knees?"

"One of them. I'm wondering if I should use it, and if so, where?"

"Use one of your knees?"

"Uh-huh. I was thinking of a posh restaurant, or should it be at home in our flat with no one else watching?" He swallowed. "I'm worried she'll say no."

It dawned on Luke what he was talking about.

"Have the two of you discussed marriage?"

Josh hesitated for a second before replying.

"Yes."

"Yes?"

"Well… No."

"Make your mind up, son."

"Leanne and I haven't talked about the two of us marrying, but we've discussed *your* marriage."

Luke smiled as the memory came back of him proposing to Jess. He hadn't gone down on one knee though. It had been in the bar after a rugby match that he'd finally summoned the courage to ask her if she'd spend the rest of her life with him. She'd immediately said yes, but Bath's fly-half had overheard, and he'd been faced with an expensive bar bill after his teammates crowded around to congratulate them.

It had been a great day though, and they'd been happily married for more than twenty years before that maniac crashed into her on the zebra crossing…

"Your marriage to Sam, that is," Josh went on, interrupting his thoughts.

Luke was taken aback. "Sam?" He glanced over at the

younger man. "Sam and I aren't getting married, Josh."

"Not yet, but Leanne and I have agreed it's only a matter of time."

"We're not..." He stopped. "Let's get back to the point. You want to propose but you don't know how to. Is that right?"

"Or where to do it." Josh hesitated. "Or exactly what to say."

"Okay. My advice is not to overthink it, but make sure you choose a time when you've got her full attention. Taking her for a meal at a fancy restaurant might work well."

"What about going down on one knee?"

"Do you want to do that? More importantly, would she like it if you did?"

Josh smiled. "I think she'd love it."

"Then do it."

"Gotcha."

There were a few minutes of silence before Josh spoke again.

"You said you'd explain about the witness we'll be interrogating, guv?"

"Interviewing, Josh. We're going to be interviewing her, not interrogating her."

"Is it a woman, then?"

"You're on the ball today, Josh. Yes, it's a woman. Pete rang me on my way to work but didn't have time to give me any details."

"DI Gilmore?"

"Yes. He's been assigned to a cross-force investigation and he's rushed off his feet."

"Wowza. Has his investigation got a codename?"

Luke smiled. "Probably, but he didn't say what it was."

"Right. So... this woman we're seeing. Do you know what she's a witness to?"

"Unfortunately not, so we'll have to play it by ear. I

don't even know her name. All I got from Pete is that she was insistent she be seen as soon as possible."

"Was she distressed on the phone?"

"He didn't say, but we'll need to tread carefully when we talk to her. In my experience, when someone says they've witnessed a crime, or that they're suspicious a crime might be committed, it can be a cry for help. She might well be a victim or a potential victim."

"Right." He paused to consider this for a moment. "This is serious stuff, isn't it, guv?"

"Yes, it is."

"Right." Josh swallowed. "Gotcha... Right."

*

Luke was relieved when he pulled the beemer into Avon and Somerset Police HQ's car park, and they both climbed out.

Josh had spent the final thirty minutes of their journey bombarding him with questions about interview procedures.

Which one of them should sit opposite the 'vic', as he insisted on calling their interviewee? Who would start the recording device? Should they offer the 'vic' refreshments? Was there going to be a one-way window? How should they react if the 'vic' broke down under questioning? Would they be able to find a female police officer available if needed?

It had been endless.

Mind-numbingly tedious too.

"I've got another question," Josh said as they walked to the entrance.

Luke abruptly stopped in his tracks, but Josh carried on for a few more steps before realising that his boss was no longer beside him.

He turned around.

"What's wrong, guv?"

"No more questions. Okay?"

"But…"

Luke sighed.

"Believe me, Josh, you know everything you need to know, and then some. This is your first time in a police interview, so I'll lead on the questioning. Your role is simply to take notes and observe our interviewee closely. It's not rocket science."

"So, I shouldn't speak?"

"You can speak, but only if you think I'm missing something, or you're asked a direct question. Understand?"

Josh mimed zipping his lips.

"Gotcha."

Luke took his police lanyard from his pocket and put it around his neck as they walked through the revolving doors and up to the reception desk. The man behind the counter looked up as they approached.

"Good morning, sir."

"Good morning. I've got my ID," Luke said, holding his lanyard out for inspection, "but my colleague will need a visitor's badge. Could you ring DI Gilmore for me?"

"Of course." He turned to Josh and passed him a clipboard. "Can you complete this, please?"

A couple of minutes later, Pete emerged from the lift and hurried over to them.

"She's here already," he said as he signed Josh's visitor's form, "but I need to speak to you about something else, Luke. The case I'm on has notched up several gears, and I want your opinion on something." He turned to Josh. "You don't mind keeping the interviewee company for a few minutes, do you?"

"Ah…"

"Of course, he doesn't mind," Luke said.

"Good." Pete turned and pointed to a set of double

doors. "The interview rooms are through there, Josh. Sergeant Fowler's on duty, and she'll tell you which room she's in."

"Ah…"

Pete didn't give him time to say anything else.

"I'll take you to our incident room, Luke," he said, "and explain everything."

Chapter 9

Josh walked through the double doors and approached the counter, behind which a middle-aged female officer was bent forward, scribbling away in a notebook.

"Hi," he said. "You must be Sergeant Fowler. I'm Josh Ogden and…"

She didn't look up, but held her hand out to stop him while she continued writing. After a minute or so, she put her pen down, nodded to herself and then lifted her head.

"Have you signed in?" she snapped.

He held up his visitor's badge to show that, yes, he had, and smiled.

She grunted and didn't return his smile.

"It's obvious you've signed in to the building, otherwise you wouldn't have got this far. What I meant was, have you signed into the interview suite?"

"Ah… No."

"Then you need to."

"Gucci."

He tried smiling again, earning a scowl as his reward this time.

She pulled a clipboard from the left of the counter so that it was directly in front of her, lifted the pen and then glared at him.

"Name?"

"I thought I said."

"Name?" she repeated, slightly louder this time.

"Josh Ogden."

She wrote his name down.

"Are you here for a voluntary interview?"

"Ah…"

Luke had said the witness had asked to be seen, so he

guessed this meant it classed as voluntary.

"Probably."

"Probably?"

"Yes."

She sighed. "It's a simple enough question. Did you ask to be in the interview or not?"

"Not... I mean, no. I was asked to attend."

"Then it wasn't voluntary, was it?"

"I suppose not." He raised an eyebrow. "Hang on. You've got this wrong. I'm not the vic, I mean the interviewee. I'm doing the interviewing."

She gave him a look that would have frozen burning coals.

"Then why didn't you say so?"

"I..."

Her hand snapped up to stop him for a second time, and she shook her head in exasperation.

"I take it you're here to see Miss, ah..." She looked down at the clipboard. "Miss T Mitchell? She asked for Detective Inspector Gilmore."

"Then yes, that's me." He paused. "Only it's not me, obviously. I'm Josh Ogden."

She pointed to one of a line of doors along the corridor.

"Room 3."

"Thanks."

He approached the door and immediately thought of a question he should have put to Luke.

Should he knock or walk straight in? What was the correct protocol? He was the interviewer, so he was in control. On the other hand...

"You can go straight in," Sergeant Fowler called over, seeming to read his mind.

"Right. Ah... Thanks."

He hesitated for a second, girded his loins, pressed down on the handle and pushed open the door, half expecting to see a crying wreck of a girl bent low over the table sobbing her heart out.

Instead, what he was faced with was a giant of a woman who spoke in a voice loud enough to wake the dead.

"AND WHO THE FUCKING NORA ARE YOU?"

He took an involuntary step backwards as if she'd struck him across the face.

She grinned, and it was a grin that put him at ease for some reason, but he wouldn't have been able to say why.

"I'm Josh Ogden," he managed to say. "I assume you're Miss Mitchell?"

"TEA!" she said, her voice still strident.

"Oh, right." He gulped. "Ah… Gotcha." His voice went up an octave as he backed towards the door. "Milk and sugar?"

She shook her head. "You're missing the fucking point. You forgot the tea. It's nothing to do with milk and sugar."

"What? Oh… Ah…" His voice went up an octave. "Herbal, then?"

She furrowed her brows. "Are you high on something?"

"Eh?"

"My name's not 'Miss… T… Mitchell.' That stupid bitch outside wasn't paying attention. My first name's Misty. I'm Misty Mitchell. You missed out the 't'."

"Right. I see. 'T' the letter, not 'tea' the drink." He hesitated. "But you *are* the victim?"

"Do I look like a fucking victim?"

"Well, no. Not really."

"Where's DI Gilmore?"

"He can't make it, and asked me to step in."

"You!" she said, a note of incredulity in her voice. "You're the one who's going to interview me?"

"Well, not just me," he admitted. "My boss as well."

"Thank fuck for that. What's his name?"

"Luke Sackville."

"The Colossus? Sam's partner?"

"How did you…" He hesitated. "Hang on. Are you the private investigator that helped Sam with Ollie?"

"That's me." She pulled a business card from her pocket and passed it over. "I'll have that cup of tea now, if you don't mind."

Chapter 10

Luke sat opposite Pete in the incident room.

"The chief initiated Operation Tooting four weeks ago," Pete began, "to bring the leaders of the region's drug trafficking operations to justice. Deaths from misuse were at an all-time high last year, and she believes that an organised crime group may be cornering the market."

"How's it going?"

"We haven't found anything concrete yet. To be honest, progress has been slow."

"But I thought you said it's notched up several gears?"

"The workload has, but that's because a new SIO was assigned last week, and she's stirred things up."

"Who is it?"

"Her name's Nicole Franks. I don't think you'll have come across her. She transferred from Wessex Police a few months ago, having made DCI at the age of thirty-six."

"That's impressively young to make DCI. What's she like?"

"Thorough. Smart too." Pete lowered his voice. "Also extremely ambitious."

"What's she done to stir things up?"

"Her idea is that we bring as many dealers in as possible and pressure them to reveal names."

"It's a good idea, but it'll be like getting blood out of a stone."

"I know, which is why I'd like to bring you in to help, but I wanted to run it by you first before I suggest it to her."

"Suggest what?"

Pete turned at the sound of his DCI's voice.

"Oh. Hello, Ma'am."

Luke looked up to see a woman who if anything appeared to be in her early rather than late-thirties. Of average height and slim build, she had brown shoulder-length hair and vivid green eyes. It struck him that she would be attractive if she smiled, but she gave off the aura of someone who rarely ventured in that direction.

"Hi," he said. "I'm Luke Sackville."

She glared at him. "What are you doing in my incident room, Mr Sackville?"

He smiled. "Please call me Luke."

She didn't return his smile but returned her attention to Pete.

"I take it this is connected to what you want to suggest to me, DI Gilmore?"

"Yes. I think we should ask Luke to help in our interviews, Ma'am."

Her left eyebrow went up. "Really? A civilian?"

"He was in the force until about a year ago."

She turned back to Luke.

"Not dismissed, I hope."

"No. I left for personal reasons."

"Was the job too stressful for you?"

"No. As I said, I left for personal reasons."

"Mmm. And do you have a lot of interviewing experience?"

"Yes, but if you feel you can manage without me, that's fine."

She looked at him for a few seconds, then back at Pete.

"We'll discuss it later."

She turned and walked away.

Pete grimaced. "Sorry, Luke. I thought she was out for the morning. Are you happy to help if I can argue the case?"

"Why not?" He suddenly remembered Josh and stood up. "I'd best be going. Heaven knows what state that poor girl is in after fifteen minutes with Josh."

Pete laughed. "I only met your interviewee briefly when I showed her in, but I can't see her being the type to break down in tears."

"What do you mean?"

"You'll see."

Luke hurried down to the interview suite and approached the counter.

"Hello, Sergeant."

Her head snapped up from her notepad.

"Yes?"

"I'm interviewing alongside Josh Ogden."

"Three." She nodded down the corridor and immediately returned her attention to her writing.

"Thanks," Luke said into the top of her head.

He wasn't graced with a reply.

As he approached the door to the interview room he heard laughing from within. Bemused, he walked in to find Josh chortling.

"…and he was only a fucking grocer," Misty said, to more laughter from Josh.

She spotted Luke and grinned.

"Well, if it isn't Giant Haystacks."

He smiled back.

"Hi, Misty."

"How's Sam?"

"Doing well, thanks. Business going okay? Much work on?"

"Masses. I'm busier than a mosquito at a nudist camp."

Luke sat down beside Josh.

"It's good of you to spare the time to come in."

"I needed to. What I uncovered is too much for me to handle."

"What did you uncover?" Josh asked enthusiastically.

Luke held his hand up. "Not yet, Josh." He looked over at Misty. "We'll record this if that's okay?"

"No skin off my nose."

Luke clicked the button.

"Interview in Portishead room 3 with Misty Mitchell. Also present are Luke Sackville and Josh Ogden. The time is 11:23." He paused. "I'd like to start with some personal details. Please can you state your full name for the record?"

"Misty Maureen Monica Mitchell." She glanced over at Josh. "My parents liked alliteration. Fuck knows why."

"And your address?"

"Apartment 2, Lambert House, Redgrave, Bristol."

"Finally, your date of birth?"

"13th January 1984."

"Thanks. Now, please tell us why you're here."

"It's Flimsy and, before you ask, I'm not talking about a lack of evidence. Flimsy is his name. Flimsy McCoy. Fuck knows how he acquired that nickname, but that's what he calls himself." She hesitated. "Mind you, there's not much more to him than a sheet of toilet paper, so it's an appropriate moniker. Wafer-thin he is, and fucking ugly too. Face acne and puffs on his cheeks. Typical symptoms of coke bloat."

"Drinking too much of it?" Josh suggested.

Misty glanced at Josh and then looked over at Luke. "Is he for real?"

"I'm afraid so."

"Oh, hang on," Josh said. "You're talking about cocaine."

"Give the boy a fucking medal. Anyway, I was on this case for a rich guy, owns a big house in Clifton. His wife's nearly twenty years younger than him and is into running, only he suspects that her outings have more to do with horizontal jogging than getting fit." She paused and looked at Josh. "And by horizontal jogging, I mean sex."

"Uh-huh." Josh swallowed. "Gotcha."

"So, I follow her and ten minutes into the run she rings a doorbell, a bloke answers, and she disappears inside. I snap off a few photos, but they don't kiss or anything, so I park myself in a cafe ready for when she leaves and keep my eye on the windows. That's when I see Flimsy."

"You know him?" Luke asked.

She nodded. "He's always on the streets, sometimes begging, usually dealing. Flimsy's helped me out with information in the past, so I thought I'd see if he knew the man in the house, the one who was with my client's missus at that very moment and in all likelihood banging her brains out." She looked at Josh again. "That also means sex."

Josh smiled weakly. "Right."

"So, I show Flimsy a tenner and ask if he knows the name of the man who lives there. He smiles his wonky fucking smile, and asks if I'm following the blonde that just went in, so I say I am, and he grabs the banknote and gives me the guy's name. I think that's it, but then he says he's got more info I ought to hear that'll cost another forty. 'Course I challenge him, even though I can just throw it on expenses, but he insists it's big news and well worth the money. Fuck, was he right, but it's not something I'm sharing with my client. Don't want to scare him off." She paused and looked at Luke. "Have you heard of Declan O'Brien?"

Luke shook his head.

"Isn't he…" Josh started to say, then stopped. "No. Never mind."

"I hadn't heard of him either," Misty went on, "but Flimsy told me he's a fucking nutter with a violent reputation."

"And that's who this woman's seeing?"

Misty shook her head. "No, his name's Reece Stevens, but Flimsy's seen O'Brien go into his house on three separate occasions. He also overheard the two men talking, but all he caught was the end of it when O'Brien said, *'and kill all three if necessary'*."

"Wowza!" Josh said.

Chapter 11

"Well," Luke said once Misty had left, "what do you make of that?"

"I guess it depends on whether Flimsy McCoy is telling the truth. He could have invented the story to get Misty's money."

"Any suggestions for our next steps?"

Josh considered this for a moment.

"Check if these two are known to the police?"

"Excellent. We should get Flimsy McCoy in for questioning too. I'll ring Pete."

The DI answered straight away.

"How did it go?"

"The woman we interviewed is a private investigator. A drug dealer told her he overheard two men discussing a murder."

"Do you think there's anything in it?"

"There could be. I'd like to see if these men are known to the police, and then get the drug dealer in for questioning."

"What's the dealer's name? He may already be down to be interviewed for Operation Tooting."

"His surname is McCoy, but I haven't got a first name. Everyone calls him Flimsy."

"Just a second."

Pete came back to the phone after a few seconds.

"No, he's not on our list. Look, could you and Josh follow this up? You've got systems access, haven't you?"

"I have, but Josh hasn't. He needs access and also training."

"I'll set that up."

"Great. For the time being, we'll share a screen, and I'll

show him how the systems work."

"When you get this dealer in, Luke, can you probe him on organised crime, see if he knows anything?"

"Will do, Pete."

He hung up and got to his feet.

"Come on. We'll find a hot desk and start work."

Ten minutes later, Luke signed into the PNC and talked Josh through the basics.

It didn't take long to find Flimsy McCoy.

"I'm not surprised he went for a nickname," Josh said. "Anything's better than Torquill." He paused and looked closely at the photo. "Although, I'm not sure I'd have chosen 'Flimsy' if I was that skeletal-looking."

"Concentrate, son."

"Sorry, guv."

Luke scanned the information on the screen. "He's got a record, but nothing major. Fined for shoplifting twice, and last year he received a community order for selling cocaine. Never been in prison though."

Josh wrote this down on his notepad, together with Flimsy's phone number and address.

Luke wheeled his chair back.

"Okay. Over to you. See if you can find Reece Stevens and Declan O'Brien."

"Really, guv?"

"Yes. I'll leave you to it while I go and find Pete."

He made his way upstairs, and was about to knock on the door of the Operation Tooting incident room when DCI Franks pulled it open.

She immediately held her hand out.

"Luke, welcome to my team. I should warn you, we're up against it."

It was said pleasantly enough, but there was still no evidence of a smile.

He smiled anyway as he shook her hand.

"That's not a problem, Nicole."

He saw her baulk slightly at his use of her first name before replying.

"Good. DI Gilmore will instruct you as to what needs doing. Now, if you'll excuse me."

She stepped past him and away.

Pete looked up when he walked over.

"You persuaded her then," Luke said.

Pete grunted. "Only after she'd torn me off a shred for speaking to you before running it past her." He lowered his voice. "She means well, Luke, and she's got some good ideas, but her aggressive attitude is beginning to piss the team off."

It's got to be better than having Edward Filcher as your boss, was what Luke wanted to say, but instead he offered Pete sympathy.

"She's trying to impress, that's all. I'm sure she'll calm down."

"Mmm. I hope so. By the way, she's insisted she sit in on your first interview for Operation Tooting."

Luke's phone rang, and he saw it was Josh.

"Excuse me a second, Pete."

He accepted the call.

Josh's excitement was almost palpable.

"Guv, guv, I found him."

"Reece Stevens?"

"No. He's not there, but Declan Donnelly is."

"Declan Donnelly?"

"Sorry, I meant O'Brien. My mistake. Declan Donnelly's the one on the right, isn't he?"

"What on earth are you talking about?"

"He always stands on the right. Like when they present *'I'm a Celebrity'*."

"Josh, is this at all relevant?"

"No, I guess not. Anyway, I found Declan O'Brien and Misty was right about him. He sounds scary as hell."

"Drugs?"

"No. GBH. Served eight years."

"I see. Note down everything you think might be relevant. I'll be down in a minute."

He ended the call and turned back to Pete.

"Is it okay if I ask one of the team to contact Flimsy McCoy to get him in for interview?"

"Of course. Speak to DC Hammond." He indicated a young man sitting at a desk in the corner. "Robbie."

"Thanks." He grimaced. "And I'll get him to check DCI Franks' availability so that she can check my interviewing skills are up to par."

Chapter 12

Diana was delighted with Ultra Magi-call Plus. Roma had used it to trick his friends, but when he'd shown her its capabilities, she'd realised that it was ideal for her purposes.

The app had several options, and she'd decided to go with '*Deep Man Voice*'. It was lifelike but slightly sinister, which was exactly the effect she wanted.

She opened the app on her phone, clicked on the icon of a bearded man's face, and entered the phone number Jim Thatcher had given her.

It was answered after a few rings.

"Hello."

"Hello. Am I speaking to Sebastian Thatcher?"

"Yes. Who is this?"

"You can call me Zeus."

"Zeus? Is this some kind of prank call, because this is my private line and…"

She interrupted before he could finish.

"This is deadly serious, Sebastian. I require payment for the return of your mother and father and their friend alive."

She let this sink in before continuing.

"Do not consider contacting the police, because I will not hesitate to act if you do. Their lives are in your hands."

"I…" He swallowed. "How much are you asking for?"

"£200,000."

"As a bank transfer?"

She was pleased with this response. It indicated that he wasn't phased by the amount she was demanding.

"Yes. You have 24 hours to set it up. I will ring tomorrow to tell you how the exchange will work." She paused. "After this call, you will receive a video to demonstrate we mean business. Do not show it to anyone.

Do you understand?"

"I understand. How do I know you won't harm them, or that you haven't already?"

"You will have to trust me, Sebastian."

"I won't do this unless I'm sure they're okay. I need to see a photo of them holding today's newspaper."

He was a confident man, and Diana saw that she needed to manage him carefully. He mustn't be allowed to gain the upper hand.

However, his request was reasonable, and there was nothing to be lost by complying.

"Very well."

She hung up.

*

Sebastian's phone beeped, and he was forced to wait while the video downloaded.

It only took thirty seconds, but it felt like an age.

Finally, it completed, and he clicked on play.

An elderly woman started talking, and he recognised her immediately as his mother and father's next-door neighbour. It was clear that she was scared.

"My name is Barbara Wadding, and I answered the door to a man in a balaclava who asked me to make a video of my neighbours. I'm not…"

The video cut off abruptly and switched to a view of two men, also in balaclavas, standing outside his parents' house. They rang the bell and, after a few seconds, the front door opened, and the two men barged their way inside. The camera remained focused on what was now a deserted area until a third man, presumably the man who had ordered her to make the video, instructed Barbara to follow the group in.

The view changed to the hall and then the lounge.

Sebastian watched in horror as his mother and father were pushed back onto the sofa by the two men in balaclavas, who then handcuffed both of them before standing behind the settee so that they were facing the camera.

He shuddered. The image before him was reminiscent of scenes from Belfast in the 1980s.

Barbara asked them questions from sheets handed to her by the third man, who was evidently standing next to or behind her.

She asked for their names and ages, if they were aware that their son's net worth was £11 million, and then whether he'd pay a ransom.

The video jumped, and Sebastian suspected a clip had been edited out.

"He'd pay whatever it takes," his father said.

"Much better, Jim."

This came from the man behind Barbara again, but Sebastian didn't think he was the person who had phoned and sent the video through. That man's voice had been much deeper.

"Do you have a message for your son about involving the police?" Barbara asked.

His father looked briefly at Sebastian's mother, and then turned back to face the camera.

"Don't even think about it, Seb. Pay them whatever it takes."

The man behind Barbara spoke next.

"Good. That…"

Again, the video cut off abruptly.

Sebastian thought that was the end of it, but then it started up again, and the view this time was of his parents' dining room.

Barbara was seated at one of the dining chairs, restrained by one of the men who had an arm across her chest and a gloved hand over her mouth. Her eyes widened as the second man stretched her arm out on the table and then forced her to splay her fingers.

He watched in horror.

Surely they wouldn't, he thought. *No one's that evil.*

"Sebastian?"

He looked up to see his personal assistant standing by the door to his office.

"Are you okay?" she went on. "You look as though you've seen a ghost."

He paused the video and tried to answer normally, but it was difficult when his heart was beating at twice its normal rate.

"I'm fine, Jenny. Can it wait? I'm in the middle of something."

She held out a small parcel about the size of a pack of playing cards.

"I only came in to give you this. It's just been delivered, and it's marked private and confidential, so I didn't like to open it." She smiled. "It's certainly got me intrigued though. I was wondering if it could be a watch."

He tried to keep his hand steady as he took the parcel from her.

She hesitated, and he sensed she was hoping he'd open the package in front of her.

No way was he going to do that.

He had an awful feeling he knew what was inside.

Chapter 13

Sam wasn't looking forward to her meeting with Cora Evans.

It wasn't that she had anything against Cora personally. Indeed, she admired her for her career achievements. Filchers wasn't a great place for women to progress, but she had made it to client director and was tipped to be the next head of sector.

Cora was an independent, forthright woman.

Bully for her.

The fact that she and Luke had dated was irrelevant now that he and Sam were an item. They had split without acrimony, and Cora was always pleasant if they bumped into each other in a corridor or in the canteen.

And yet…

Perhaps it was residual envy, back to when she was keen on Luke but it wasn't reciprocated. She'd felt like she was in a vacuum, and seeing him with another woman had been heartbreaking.

That was why she'd started seeing Ollie, and boy, had that been a disaster from the beginning. He'd been over-possessive and ridiculously jealous and, when she'd finally had enough and ended their relationship, he'd started harassing and then stalking her. The man was a liability.

Not that any of that was Cora's fault.

Right, she thought. *Enough. Let's get this over with.*

She spotted Cora as soon as she entered the Stairway account area. She was sitting next to her secretary as they went through a report together.

Cora looked up and smiled.

"Ah, Sam." She turned to the woman beside her. "We'll finish this later, Candice."

She opened her office door, and Sam followed her in.

"You'll have to excuse the fact that the room is so testosterone-fuelled. Henry only left last week, and I haven't had time to put my stamp on it."

Sam had to admit she was right. The room was reminiscent in many ways of Glen Baxter's office, even down to there being a picture of a large-horned stag deer on one wall, an almost identical copy of the one Glen had.

"Please," Cora went on, gesturing to one of two matt black leather armchairs.

"All I know," Sam said, once they were seated, "is that you have an ethical problem and that it's something to do with numbers."

Cora laughed. "That's Edward Filcher for you. He takes very little in, unfortunately. But before I explain, how's that lovely man of yours?"

"Oh. Ah… Luke's great."

"You're fortunate to have him, you know. He's wonderful in so many ways."

Sam wasn't sure what to say to that and plumped for, "Yes. I'm very lucky."

"If you ever get fed up, I'll be waiting in the aisle, but my advice is to hang on to him. That man's a keeper."

Sam smiled.

"I'm conscious you're very busy, Cora. Perhaps you could explain what the issue is, and then I can get out of your hair?"

Cora returned her smile.

"Of course. How much do you know about Stairway's products?"

"Not a lot. I'm aware there are two. Stairway itself, of course, and also Hugger, though that's fairly new, isn't it?"

Cora nodded. "Hugger's only been around for about a year, but it's proving to be a huge success. It's aimed at teenagers, and incorporates the communication features of Stairway with images generated using artificial intelligence.

It's free to purchase, with the idea being that they start charging when there are over a million users. What that means is that the company is having to fund ongoing research and development." She paused. "There are strong rumours of a software giant, possibly Google, wanting to buy Stairway. The issue I've got is that one of the finance team has told me he believes he's spotted unethical accounting."

"To give the impression that the company is running at a profit?" Sam suggested.

Cora nodded.

"Exactly. I'll ask him to come in."

She left the office and returned a minute or so later, accompanied by a tall, lean man in his late twenties. He wore oversized tortoise-shell glasses, and there was an earnest air about him.

"Sam, this is Damien Fleetwood."

"Hi," Sam said.

They shook hands.

"I'll leave you to it if that's okay," Cora said.

She left, and Damien sat in the vacant armchair.

"I'm not sure if I'm correct," he said, as if to apologise before he'd begun. "Some of the profit entries appear to be overestimated, but I could be wrong."

Sam smiled to try and put him at ease.

"Don't worry. If there's nothing in it, then that's fine, but you were right to flag it up. Where are the anomalies?"

He proceeded to run her through the details.

"I see," she said when he'd finished. "And if you're right, who might be responsible?"

"It could be any of the Finance Team based here, that's six of us."

He gave her the names, and she jotted them down in her notebook.

"And what about people in Stairway itself?"

"There are three Stairway employees with access. The

Chief Executive, Finance Director and Chief Accountant."

Again, she wrote the names down.

"Right," she said. "I think the best bet is for us to sit down at a terminal and go through it all."

They both stood up, and he led her to his cubicle and wheeled a visitor's chair around.

Forty-five minutes later, she had spotted his mistake.

"Those numbers you thought were too high were cash balances. The calculated profits look fine to me."

"That's a relief."

"Yes, it's a good result. However, as I said, you were right to tell Cora what you suspected. It's best to be safe." She hesitated. "One thing I did find odd, though, was in the account used for research and development."

"There are frequent payments out of that one."

"Yes, but did you notice? The payment made today was to a different account from normal."

"Was it? Just a second."

He logged back in, found the account and retrieved the latest transactions.

"You're right." He pointed at the screen. "There's something else. Payments are usually made by the Finance Director, but this one was initiated by Stairway's Chief Executive. It's a larger amount than usual, too."

"And what did you say the CEO's name is?"

"Sebastian Thatcher."

Chapter 14

Luke bent down and stroked Wilkins' ear.

"Be a good boy for Marjorie," he said, then stood up again and passed the cocker's lead over.

"He's always good." She chuckled. "Unless he sees a pheasant, that is. He always thinks he's in with a chance, but he's not caught one yet."

Luke smiled. "And hopefully never will. Thanks again. You're a star. I'll see you this evening."

He walked back to the farmhouse to see Sam emerging through the front door.

"Got everything?" she asked.

He nodded. "My briefcase is already in the car."

They climbed into the BMW and set off, turning left at the end of the drive to head towards the A36. He glanced over at her, a broad smile on his face.

She raised an eyebrow. "What is it?"

"It's the fact we've exchanged keys."

"You find it amusing?"

"No. I think it's fantastic." He hesitated. "That reminds me. I didn't tell you about Josh proposing, did I?"

She was stunned. "He's proposed?"

"Not yet, but he's planning to. He asked for my advice on how to do it."

"What did you suggest?"

"A fancy restaurant and go down on one knee. The old-fashioned traditional way."

"Well done. That's how I'd want it."

He stored this information away in a corner of his brain, not that he and Sam were anywhere near considering marriage. They'd only been going out for three months, for goodness sake.

But still, their relationship was blossoming, so it was worth knowing.

"You've gone very quiet."

"Sorry." He glanced over at her and wondered if she was thinking along the same lines. "I was miles away."

"When do you think they…"

She was interrupted by Luke's phone ringing. He glanced at the screen.

"It's my brother, probably about the weekend."

He clicked to accept the call.

"Hi, Mark. Still on for Saturday?"

"Probably."

Luke could detect something in his tone that suggested there was a problem. He and Sam exchanged a look.

"What's happened?"

"It's Mother."

"Is she ill?"

"No. She's…" Mark paused. "She's becoming more aggressive."

"She's always been aggressive, Mark."

"Verbally, yes, but she's started to hit out."

"Hit out? But she seemed fine when we went to Springdale on Saturday. She wasn't very pleasant, but that's par for the course"

"Danella's just rung me. She said that last Thursday, Mother pushed Alice during an argument and had to be pulled away, but they hoped it was a one-off. Then this morning, she punched Connie, who's ended up with a black eye."

"Poor Connie."

"I haven't told Father. I'm not sure what it would do to him."

"How have you left it?"

"Danella wants me to come in to discuss what to do."

"Do you want me to come too?"

"If you wouldn't mind. I'd like to go in today if

possible."

Luke turned to Sam and mouthed, "Okay?"

"Of course," she mouthed back.

"That'll be fine, Mark. I'm on the way to work now, but I'll try to get away as soon as I can, and hopefully be there early afternoon. I'll give you a call when I leave the office."

"Thanks, Luke."

He ended the call.

"Who were those women Mark was talking about?" Sam asked.

"Danella is the manager at Springdale House, and Connie's one of the senior carers. Poor Alice is a resident. She's a lovely old dear who wouldn't harm a soul." He paused, his mind working overtime. "I'll pop home and grab some clothes on the way to Dorset. Mark and I will need to break the news to Father when we get back, so I'll stay at Borrowham overnight, but hopefully I'll be back at work tomorrow."

The rest of the journey was spent in contemplative silence.

"Are you sure you don't want to head straight off?" Sam asked as they turned into Filchers' car park.

"No. There's no desperate rush. Besides, I said I'd see Glen this morning, and it'd be good to get that over with."

He reversed into a spot, and they climbed out of the BMW and walked towards the entrance door to Filchers' head office.

"Any idea what Glen wants?" Sam asked.

"Not the foggiest, but he was very mysterious about it. He said it was something to do with fads, but that was all."

"Fads? What, like hula hoops and Rubik's cube?"

"Possibly." He opened the door and gestured for Sam to go first. "Perhaps he's going to shun his buzz cut and go for a mullet."

Sam laughed. "Now that would be a sight for sore eyes."

Chapter 15

Luke knocked on the door of Glen's office and walked in without waiting for a reply.

The Head of Security was bent low over his desk, staring at one of his office toys.

"Have you seen this?" he said without looking up.

"It's a Newton's cradle."

"Yes, but have you seen what it can do?"

"Of course, I…"

"Stop." Glen held one finger up. "Watch and learn."

He pulled one of the end balls sideways and released it. It struck the second ball, stopped, and the fifth ball promptly swung away from the other four before returning to begin the process anew.

"Impressive, eh?" Glen said, a broad grin on his face. "It's pre-nuptial motion."

"You mean perpetual motion."

"Yes." His eyes flicked from side to side as each end ball swung away in turn. "Incredible."

"It's not, though."

Glen looked up.

"Not what?"

"Perpetual motion."

"Of course it is." He pointed back at the cradle where the balls were still bouncing back and forth. "This goes on for ages."

"Yes, but not forever."

"It does. If it slows down, all I have to do is lift the end ball again and let go." He was still grinning. "Look." He stopped the balls, lifted the end one high, and repeated the process.

"I bet you can sit here watching this for ages."

"I can, yes."

"Something like that must keep your brain fully active."

"Uh-huh," Glen said, his eyes still watching as the balls swung away from either end.

"You asked to see me." Luke gestured to the Newton's cradle. "I hope this wasn't the fad you wanted to discuss."

"No. This is just a conservation piece."

"Conversation piece."

"Exactly."

Glen dragged his eyes away from his office toy, and seemed to take in what Luke had said.

"Did you say 'fad'?"

"Yes. You told me on the phone you wanted to talk about fads." He laughed. "I suggested to Sam that you might want a mullet."

Glen shook his head. "She's off the mark there. This is nothing to do with fish." He paused and looked into Luke's eyes. "Is any of your team a lesbian?"

Luke furrowed his brows.

"What did you say?"

"I asked if any of your team is a lesbian. On a part-time basis, I mean." He chuckled. "I'm not expecting that any of your staff do it professionally."

Luke was speechless.

"What about Maj?" Glen went on. "When he worked for me, he had a way about him that suggested he might be."

"Maj?" Luke furrowed his brows. "But Maj is a man."

"I know that, Luke. I'm not stupid."

You could have fooled me.

"Men can be actors too," Glen added.

The penny dropped.

"You're asking if any of my staff are thespians?"

"That's what I said."

Luke wished he'd taken Sam's advice and headed straight to Dorset. This conversation could end up being as long-winded as one of Filcher's weekly meetings if Glen didn't get to the point soon.

"Why do you want to know if any of my team are amateur actors?"

"Fads." He paused. "There's a problem, and I wondered if one of your Ethics Team could go undercover. You know, be a sloth."

"Sleuth."

"Yes."

"Which fad are you talking about?"

"There's only one. I've been into it since, well, forever. I'm not just a Chippenmale, you know. I've had small parts in all sorts of productions."

"You've lost me, Glen. What do you mean, there's only one?"

"There's only one FADS. Filchers Amateur Dramatic Society. I'm a member, and we've got a goblin. No, hang on." He scratched his head. "Not a goblin. What do you call someone who trolls you online?"

"A troll."

"That's it. Yes, there's a troll in FADS."

Chapter 16

Sam looked up when Luke walked into the Ethics Room.

"Are you heading off to Dorset now?"

"Shortly. First, I need to update you on what Glen said. Actually, it would be good to get everyone's thoughts." He called over. "Guys, could we have a quick chat, please?"

They all moved to the meeting table.

"I've just been in to see Glen," he began, once everyone was seated.

"Poor wee you," Helen said. "What did he have to say for himself?"

"He talked a lot about sloths, goblins and lesbians but we got to the crux of the matter eventually."

"Lesbians?" Maj said.

"He thought you were one."

"What?"

Luke smiled. "The word he meant to use was 'thespians'. Have any of you heard of Filchers Amateur Dramatic Society, called FADS for short?"

"Aye, I have," Helen said. "I've not been to any of their productions, but I think they did 'Mamma Mia' last year."

"Well, Glen's a member, and it appears there's a major problem with harassment. It started with personal details being shared online, and has progressed to insults and lies."

"Are the only people being harassed members of FADS?" Sam asked.

Luke nodded. "Yes, plus the nature of the attacks, and the confidential nature of some of what's been shared, makes it clear that someone in FADS is the culprit."

"We could call it Project Amdram," Josh suggested.

"That would hardly disguise the fact that it's connected to amateur dramatics," Helen said.

"Oh, yes. I guess you're right. Perhaps Project Mousetrap, or, hang on, what about Project Fidget?"

"Why?" Maj asked.

Josh grinned. "Fidget Spinners are a fad, aren't they? And this is to do with FADS. Get it?" He paused. "Or we could go for 'Douglas', because of that actor from your time, Helen. The one I mentioned yesterday with the same surname as June from We-Haul."

"Aye, that's a bright idea,' she said. "Two projects called 'Douglas' would simplify things no end."

"You're getting ahead of yourself, son," Luke said. "I'm not sure we're going to take this on yet, or how we approach it if we do. Someone joining FADS might work, but we're swamped."

Josh stuck his hand in the air.

"I'll do it, guv. I'll go undercover."

"You're the busiest of everyone, Josh. You've got to be trained in how to use police IT systems, then you'll be helping me with research and interviews."

He looked around the team.

"Any ideas?"

Josh's hand went up again.

Luke sighed. "As I said, you're too busy."

Josh lowered his arm, but his grin returned.

"What about Lily?"

"That's a good idea," Sam said. "Plus, she's an actress, so she'd have no problem blending in."

"You're right," Luke said. "Good thinking, Josh. Would you mind giving her a call to see if she's available? I'd do it myself, but I've got to shoot off."

Josh nodded. "Yes, I can do that, guv. Do you want me to see if she can come in?"

"Yes, please, but make it later this week." He paused. "The other thing, guys, is that my mother's taken a turn for the worse, so I'm going to have to head off to Dorset now. I may be back in tomorrow, but more likely the day after."

"Ach, no," Helen said. "I hope she recovers."

Luke gave a grim smile. "I don't think that's going to happen, Helen, but thanks for the thought." He stood up.

"One thing before you go, Luke," Maj said.

"Yes."

"I spoke to June Fairbanks, and she thinks she can fast-track a temporary employment pass for me so that I can work airside at Bristol Airport. She's hoping I'll have it in time to join the We-Haul team next Monday."

"What job will you have?"

"Baggage handler."

"Good." He looked around the table. "Thanks for the update, everyone. Josh, let me know how you get on with Lily."

"Will do."

"And good luck with your training today. Tell me what you think of DCI Franks if Pete introduces you to her."

"Why, guv?"

"I'm interested, that's all. She's got a reputation for being cold, and I'd be interested to see how she is with you."

Luke grabbed his stuff and headed off to the car park. Once he'd set off, he rang his brother.

"Hi, Luke. Are you on your way?"

"Yes. Just set off. I'll pop home on the way to grab an overnight bag, but I should be with you in a couple of hours."

"Great. See you later."

He hung up and rang Marjorie.

"Hi, Marjorie. My mother's not well, and I'm going to be in Dorset overnight. Is it okay if I leave him with you?"

"Of course."

"Great. Thanks very much."

Logistics sorted, he was about to turn his audiobook on when the phone went.

It was Josh.

"Guv, I've spoken to Lily. She said she'd love to help, and she's between jobs at the moment."

"Has she met Glen?"

"I don't think so."

"She's got that delight to come then. Have you arranged a time for her to come in?"

"Thursday at 10 am."

"Great. Well done, Josh."

"One other thing. DI Gilmore rang and asked if I can go into Portishead for systems training tomorrow and to get my pass. Is that okay?"

"Of course it is."

"Thanks, guv." He paused, and Luke could sense there was something else on his mind.

"What's up, son?"

"I'm going to do it."

"Do what?"

"Propose. I've booked a table at The Olive Tree for Saturday."

"Well done."

"I'm finding it hard to get straight what I should say, though. I don't want to bother you, guv, given what's happening with your mother, and I was wondering if I could ask Sam to help."

"I'm not her keeper, Josh. Why don't you ask her?"

"Thanks. Yes, I'll do that."

Luke was smiling to himself as he ended the call. Josh had initiative, lots of it, but always seemed to be asking permission for the slightest thing.

He was pleased that Lily was available. She had been excellent when she'd worked with them before, and he was confident she'd have no problem coping with Glen.

His thoughts turned to his parents, and he found himself wondering what Danella was going to say. Would his mother be able to stay at Springdale or would she need to move to a different care home?

After a few minutes, Luke realised there was no point in overthinking things, and he resumed his audiobook, keen to find out how the fictional DCI Bone was faring with the challenges he was facing on the appropriately named Isle of the Dead.

Chapter 17

Sam's antennae were twitching.

The payment out of Stairway's R&D account was bugging her on two counts. First, it was paid to a different account from normal, and second, it was the Chief Executive who had initiated the funds transfer.

It was probably nothing, but she wouldn't be doing justice to her role as an ethics consultant if she didn't follow it up.

She checked the destination sort code and found it was a Barclays account. On a hunch, she logged in to her personal Santander account and initiated a transfer, entering Sebastian Thatcher as the payee. She hit enter, and, after a few seconds, the system confirmed that it was his Coutts personal bank account.

After abandoning the transfer, she sat back to consider what to do next.

There could be a simple explanation for what had happened. Perhaps he had used his personal account as a temporary measure because there was a problem with his intended payee. Alternatively, he could be owed the money because he had previously funded Stairway's R&D activities.

But if that was the case, why would he initiate the transfer himself rather than leave it to the finance team?

On reflection, she decided the best thing to do was to speak to Sebastian Thatcher directly and ask him to clarify what had happened.

She googled Stairway, rang the number of their Bristol Head Office and asked to be put through to the Chief Executive.

It was a woman who answered.

"Hello, this is Jenny in Sebastian Thatcher's office. How

may I help?"

"Hi, Jenny. My name's Sam Chambers and I'd like to speak to Mr Thatcher to clarify something."

"Can I ask what this is in connection with?"

"If you tell him it's concerning a payment of £200,000 I'm sure he'll speak to me, and we can get this sorted out."

"Okay. Give me a second."

The phone went silent.

After a minute or so, a man's voice came on the line.

"You'll have to be patient," he hissed. "I'm still sorting the ransom out."

Had she heard correctly?

Did he really say 'ransom'?

Before she could reply he spoke again.

"As I've said, I won't pay a penny until I receive a photo to prove my parents and Barbara are alive and well."

Sam took a deep breath.

"Sebastian, my name's Sam Chambers, and I work in the Ethics Team at Filchers. Did you think I was someone else?"

"You're... Oh, my god!" He gulped. "What have I said?"

"Enough to make me think you should go to the police."

"NO! It's too dangerous."

He hesitated, then started speaking again, his words coming out in a rush.

"You must keep this to yourself. No one can know. Please promise me you won't tell anyone."

It was Sam's turn to hesitate. It was clear from his tone that the man was in dire straits and struggling to cope.

She reached a decision after a few seconds.

"I promise I won't tell anyone, but I'm coming over."

"What! No. There's no need."

"I can tell you're struggling, and I think you'd benefit from having someone to talk things over with. I've worked on cases of abduction in the past, which may help, but at the very least, I can act as a sounding board to help you make what are going to be life and death decisions."

He considered this for a few seconds before replying.

"Where are you?"

"I'm in Bath. I can be there in an hour."

"Thank you, Sam."

She hung up and walked over to Maj's desk.

"Maj, I don't suppose there's any chance I could borrow your car, is there? I need to go to Stairway to discuss that accounting anomaly, and Luke gave me a lift in today."

"No problem."

He passed her his keys.

*

Sam's mind was churning throughout the drive to Bristol.

It was clear that Sebastian Thatcher's parents had been abducted and a ransom demanded.

Other than that, she knew nothing, but it didn't stop her from going over and over different scenarios in her mind. What should Sebastian do if the kidnappers continued demanding money after the first payment? How could he be certain that his mum and dad would be handed over unharmed? Was a single person responsible, or was this a group of individuals?

She'd liked to have talked it through with Luke, but she'd promised Sebastian she wouldn't tell anyone, plus Luke had his mother's deterioration to deal with.

She pulled into a visitor's space at the back of Stairway's office and walked around to the front of what was a smart, ultra-modern building, in keeping with the company's youthful image.

A visitor's badge was waiting for her in reception, and,

after a minute or so, a woman came out of the lift, walked over and offered her hand.

"Hi, Sam. I'm Jenny."

Sam shook her hand.

"Hi, Jenny."

"Please follow me."

She led her to the lift, and they emerged on the fourth floor where Jenny led her to the Chief Executive's office, knocked peremptorily and then popped her head in.

"Sam Chambers is here, Sebastian."

"Show her in, please."

Jenny gestured for Sam to go in.

"Can I get coffee or tea for you both?"

"We're fine," Sebastian said. "Make sure we're not disturbed, please."

"Of course."

She left the room, closing the door behind her, and Sebastian locked it before gesturing to a comfortable-looking pale green armchair.

"Please take a seat."

He remained standing and, while Sam had never seen the man before, she could tell he was under immense pressure. She put him in his mid-thirties, well-built with a short black beard, but what stood out was the pained expression in his eyes.

"Thanks for coming in, Sam. If I'm honest, I could do with someone to talk to. I'm at my wit's end."

He swallowed and took a deep breath before continuing.

"A parcel was delivered to me this morning."

He walked over to his desk, produced a small box from the top drawer and held it out.

"I warn you, what's inside is not very pleasant. It was sent to prove they mean business."

She took the box and opened it, revealing the top third of an index finger nestled in tissue paper.

"It's Barbara's," Sebastian said. "She lives next door to my parents. I'd better explain everything that's happened."

Chapter 18

"You said the man who rang had a tremulous voice," Sam said when Sebastian had finished. "What do you mean exactly?"

"It was very deep, unusually so, but seemed to vibrate as well, and there was an almost tinny sense to it."

"Did you get a sense why? Was it a poor connection? Or could it be because he was nervous?"

"He certainly didn't come across as nervous."

"What then?"

Sebastian paused for a moment and then gave a dry smile. "It's obvious when I think about it. I'm supposed to be a whizz at technology, but it hadn't occurred to me until now."

"What?"

"He was using a voice changer to disguise his voice. But why would he do that?"

"Is it possible it's someone you know? Have you got any enemies?"

"There are people I don't get on with, or that I've had run-ins with, but I can't imagine any of them doing something like this."

Sam reflected for a moment before speaking.

"I haven't got any experience of voice changers. Are they able to turn a woman's voice into a man's?"

"Yes, definitely. Are you saying it might be a woman who's behind this?"

"We can't rule it out. I don't suppose you recorded the call, did you?"

"No, but I've got a call recording app on my iPhone which I can use when he calls again. Just a second." He clicked on his phone a couple of times, then looked up.

"I've turned Otter on so that it will record by default."

His phone pinged, and he looked down at the screen, clicked once and then sighed, shaking his head as he did so.

"It's the photo I asked him to send. At least it proves Mum, Dad and Barbara are alive."

He passed the phone to Sam, and she looked closely at the image on the screen. It showed three people seated on plastic garden chairs. A couple in their 60s, who had to be his parents, were to the left of a woman closer to 80 years old who had a bandaged right hand. All three had grim looks on their faces.

The floor was wooden, while the wall behind them appeared to be metallic and was battered in several places. The man, who was on the left and looked very much like an older version of Sebastian, was holding the Daily Telegraph in front of his chest.

Sam used her fingers to enlarge the image.

"It's today's date on the newspaper," she said, and passed the phone back. "My guess is that they're in a van or a lorry."

Sebastian looked at the photo again.

"Yes, I think you could be right."

His phone started ringing, and he turned it to show her the message '*Unknown Caller ID*' on the screen.

"This must be him again."

He accepted the call.

"Hello."

"This is Zeus. Did you receive the photo?"

"Yes."

"How are you getting on with finding the money?"

"I can transfer it as soon as necessary. I don't want my parents to suffer for any longer than they have to."

There was silence at the other end.

"Well?" Sebastian said. "How soon can we get this over with?"

"The situation has changed."

"In what way?"

"The amount required is now £400,000."

"But you asked for £200,000. Why has it doubled?"

"As I said, the situation has changed. I will send another photo at the same time tomorrow and then call to confirm you have the full amount. We can then arrange the handover."

"But…" Sebastian started to say before it dawned on him that Zeus had ended the call.

*

Diana put her phone down on the kitchen island and smiled to herself.

She'd been anticipating £200,000, but had underestimated Sebastian Thatcher. He had ready access to more money than she'd given him credit for, and she was pleased she had taken the instant decision to push for double the amount. The man was so stupidly rich he wouldn't even miss it.

Should she have gone higher still? Pushed him to half a million or more? No, that was being greedy. The ransom needed to be at a level Thatcher could readily get hold of.

Diana heard the door open behind her and turned to see her son, his school backpack over one shoulder.

"How was your day, Roma?"

"Okay. I'm helping Jay again this evening."

"That's good. Have you heard how Kingswood's centre-forward is?"

"Still in hospital. They're putting a metal rod in his leg."

"At least you managed to put him out of the game without being sent off. That's what matters."

He grinned. "Don't forget we won the game."

Diana laughed. "Yes. That's true. It was a success all

round. I'm very proud of you."

*

"Is it going to be difficult to obtain another £200,000?" Sam asked.

Sebastian shook his head.

"No, but what if he keeps upping the amount?"

Sam considered this for a moment.

"I suspect he acted impulsively when you said you had the ransom money. Perhaps you should ask for extra time when he rings tomorrow, and tell him that finding the same amount again is proving to be a challenge."

"I can see the sense in that, but what about my mum and dad? I want to get them out as soon as possible."

"If you don't ask for a delay, he may well up it to £600,000, so they'll be kept for longer anyway."

"Yes, I guess you're right." He paused. "Sam, I can't thank you enough for helping me like this. I don't suppose you could come again tomorrow, could you?"

"Of course I can. In the meantime, promise me you'll call if there are any further developments."

She gave him her phone number.

"I'll be off now, Sebastian, but I'll see you in the morning. I hope you manage to get some sleep."

He gave a grim smile. "I'll try my best."

Chapter 19

Luke clicked off his audiobook, pleased that it had taken his mind off things during the journey. This fifth outing for DCI Bone was a gruesome tale, but TG Reid had included humour to lighten the load, and although Luke was nearing the end, he still hadn't the faintest idea who the villain was.

As he approached Borrowham Hall, he was struck as always by its combination of Elizabethan grandeur and old-world charm. The decades-old wisteria, bare in winter but covered in clusters of pale violet flowers in late Spring, snaked up one side of the studded oak door before meandering along both wings beneath the first-floor windows. It was going to look stunning come May.

He climbed out of the BMW to see Marion running towards him from around the side of the building. She had a broad smile on her face.

"Oh, geez, Luke," she began, and he noted that there was still no sign of her losing her Californian accent. "You have to see my bug box. It's awesome. I only started on Saturday, but I've already found two ladybugs and a humungous snail that's grey, kind of pale grey with black markings, plus a millipede. Or it could be a centipede. I'm not sure. Perhaps you'll know."

He grabbed the chance to get a word in while she paused for breath.

"I'd love to see it, Marion, but Mark and I have to see your grandmother."

"You're coming back afterwards, aren't you?"

"Yes. I'll be staying the night."

"Awesome. I'm excited about my party on Saturday. Are you excited? Is Sam coming? I hope Sam is coming. I like Sam. I've invited all my best friends, including Lucy and

Sally and Isla and Beatrice and Orla and even a boy, Benny, because he's kind of okay."

"Kind of okay?"

"For a boy. He's not very mature though, even though he's already nine. And we're having a magician. I wonder if he'll make me disappear. I'd like that. Although if he made Isla disappear, that would be better because she's such a snitch."

"A snitch?"

"It's someone who tells tales."

Luke smiled. "Is it?"

"Yes. She told on Beatrice and me and we hadn't done much wrong, just passed notes to each other in class, and they were important messages about the film we went to see. It came out last week, and it's awesome. Have you seen it?"

"Why don't we talk about it later when we get back?"

"And look at my bug box?"

"Yes. Ah, here's Mark."

"Hi," Mark said, then turned his attention to his stepdaughter. "Have you been bothering Luke, Marion?"

"Not at all," Luke said. "Shall we head straight off? We can go in my car."

"Yes. I'm ready."

Mark turned to walk to the passenger side, but, as he did so, his wife appeared at the door, an all-too-typical scowl on her face.

"Mark, you were supposed to put the coat rack up."

He rolled his eyes at Luke before turning round to face her.

"I'll do it later, Erica."

"Mmm." She turned to her daughter. "Come on, Marion. You've got homework to do."

She stood to one side for Marion and gave a final, none-too-pleasant, glance at her husband before following.

"Her and that ruddy coat rack!" Mark said once they'd

set off.

Luke couldn't help laughing.

"If that's the biggest bone of contention between you I wouldn't worry too much."

Mark smiled. "I guess you're right."

Twenty minutes later, they arrived at Springdale House, and Danella, the manager, let them in and showed them into her small office to the left of the reception area.

"How has she been today?" Luke asked once they were seated.

"She hasn't hit anyone, thank goodness, but the staff are on tenterhooks. I'll ask Connie if she can join us."

She rang through, and a couple of minutes later Connie walked in. There were vivid purple bruises below her left eye.

"That looks painful," Mark said. He shook his head. "I'm so sorry."

She put one finger gingerly to the bruising. "It's tender, but it comes with the job."

"That's not true," Danella said. "Or at least it shouldn't be." She turned to Mark and Luke. "I'm sure you'll both appreciate that I can't allow my staff to be at risk of harm. In my experience, once a dementia sufferer like Daphne becomes aggressive, it tends to become worse rather than better."

"What do you suggest?" Mark asked.

"I think you should look at a specialist care home where they can provide one-on-one support. In the meantime, we'll monitor Daphne closely over the next few days. There's always the chance this is a short-term phase." She reached into her desk drawer, retrieved a brochure and passed it to Luke. "Hanover Springs is worth looking at. We had a similar problem with another resident last year, and I believe he settled in well there, and they were even able to calm him down a fair bit."

"Thank you," Luke said.

"Either Connie or I will ring you every day to let you know how she is."

"Do you want to see her?" Connie said. "Daphne was asleep when I left the lounge, but I'm sure she'll be delighted to spend some time with you."

I'm not so sure, was Luke's thought and from the look on Mark's face, his brother seemed to be thinking the same.

"Yes, please," Luke said. "Thanks, Danella."

They followed Connie into the communal lounge area and he immediately spotted his mother on the far side. She was seated next to Bernie, the home's bright green budgerigar, and her head was bent low over her chest.

Connie walked over and tapped her on the shoulder.

"Daphne, your sons are here."

There was no reaction.

"Daphne," she repeated, slightly louder this time. "Wake up."

Daphne slowly raised her head, then her eyes widened and she started flapping her hands wildly. Connie grabbed both her arms to hold them down.

"It's okay. You've had a bad dream, that's all."

After a few seconds, Connie let go, and Daphne looked first at Luke and then at Mark.

Her eyes narrowed. "I know you."

"It's Luke and Mark," Connie said. "Your sons."

"You're the police," Daphne said, a tone of anger in her voice.

"We're not the police," Mark said.

"I'll leave you to it," Connie said, and moved off to the kitchen area.

Luke pulled two chairs over, and he and Mark sat down facing Daphne.

"How are you feeling?" Luke asked.

She glared at him.

"I know you."

"Yes, I'm your son. I'm Luke."

"You're the police."

He decided to try to change the subject and pointed at the budgie.

"Bernie's very pretty."

"Is Bernie in the police?"

"Bernie's a budgie, Mother. He's there, in the cage next to you."

She turned her head to glance at the cage, then turned back again.

"You must be an idiot," she growled.

"Why?"

"They don't have budgies in the police. Why did you say Bernie's in the police?"

Luke sighed.

It was going to be a long afternoon.

Chapter 20

Luke could tell that Mark was feeling as exhausted as he was after an hour spent with their mother.

"Tiring, isn't it?" he asked, once they'd set off from Springdale's car park.

Mark sighed.

"It certainly is. Her repetition, and her fixations on things, are hard enough to cope with, but now there's this fear that she might lash out at any moment."

"It's clear that Danella's keen for Mother to move on, and I can see why. Poor Connie."

Mark pulled out the brochure for Hanover Springs and leafed through it.

"I'll give this place a ring when we get back, and see if I can arrange for us to visit them in the morning before you head back to Bath."

"Good idea. We've also got to tell Father. I'll take the lead if you like."

"Thanks."

Luke's phone rang, and he saw that it was Pete.

"Do you mind if I take this?"

"Not at all," Mark said.

Luke accepted the call.

"Hi, Pete."

"Robbie's arranged the interview with Flimsy McCoy. He's coming into HQ tomorrow, and Nicole wants it to be you and her conducting the interview. Are you okay with that?"

"I am if it's the afternoon."

"1:30 okay?"

"Should be. I'll come to the Tooting incident room."

"Great. I'll see you then."

"Tooting?" Mark asked when Luke had hung up.

"It's a project name. Teams at Avon and Somerset Police use a similar system to the one used for storms, but instead of people's names, they use locations in England."

He smiled.

"Why are you smiling?"

"My team uses a different system. Have I mentioned Josh to you?"

"He's the grad, isn't he?"

"That's the one. He loves coming up with project names, but his approach is to give them a very tenuous link to the topic."

The phone rang again.

"Talk of the devil."

He accepted the call.

"Hi, Josh."

"Hi, guv." He was whispering. "You know my proposal?"

"Project Fidget or Project Douglas?"

"Eh?" He paused. "No, the one with…" Josh lowered his voice still further. "…one knee. You know, where I ask Leanne if she'll, you know."

"I'm following you, son. What of it?"

"I was wondering if I should ask Nathan first."

"Nathan?"

"I'm worried he might say no, then what would I do? I'll need to phrase it carefully."

Luke was trying to make sense of what Josh was jabbering on about, then it dawned on him what he might mean.

"Is Nathan Leanne's dad?"

"Uh-huh. What do you think? Should I ask his permission?"

"Yes, it would be a nice courtesy."

"All I want is to tell him I love Leanne and ask if it's okay with him if I ask her for her hand in marriage. How do you think I should phrase it?"

"What about 'I love Leanne. Is it okay with you if I ask her for her hand in marriage.'?"

"Gotcha. Thanks, guv. You're great with words." Josh's voice went back up to normal volume. "Coming, Leanne."

The line went dead.

Luke glanced over to see Mark was smiling.

"What is it?"

Mark's smile broadened.

"Are you Josh's boss or his father?"

"What do you mean?"

"It doesn't matter."

Ten minutes later, they parked outside Borrowham Hall, received the customary welcome from Marion, who revealed she'd solved the centipede mystery and had acquired several more bugs for her collection, and then headed inside.

Erica was standing at the bottom of the stairs with her arms folded and a frown on her face.

Mark sighed. "Erica, we have to talk to Father now, but I promise I'll put the coat rack up as soon as we've finished."

"There's always an excuse, isn't there?"

She turned and stomped upstairs.

"Mark is in the poopie," Marion sang, apparently taking great pleasure from this exchange between her mother and stepfather. "Mark is in the poopie."

"Do you want to go up and speak to her?" Luke asked.

Mark shook his head. "No. Let her stew on it. Come on, let's find Father."

Hugo was in the library, seated in an armchair and staring out of the window.

"Hello, Father," Luke said. "We need to talk about Mother."

"Mark's told you about her behaviour, has he?"

"Yes. We've just been in to talk to Danella about next

steps, but obviously it's your decision."

"Next steps?"

Mark produced the brochure for Hanover Springs from his pocket and passed it over.

"Mother's going to need one-on-one supervision," Luke said, "and Danella recommended we consider that care home."

"What?" Hugo looked briefly down at the brochure, then back up again. "We can't move her. Daphne's settled at Springdale. She's used to the place."

"I don't think there's any option. Did you know she gave Connie a black eye?"

Luke could see the distress in his father's eyes as he took this in.

"No," he said, almost under his breath. "I didn't know that."

Mark's phone started ringing. He looked down at the screen.

"It's Danella."

He accepted the call.

"Hi, Danella." He listened. "Oh, no," he said after a few seconds. "Is she okay?" He looked Luke in the eyes as Danella spoke again, and it was clear that something serious had happened. "I see. Yes, of course. I'll ring you back as soon as I've done that."

"Has she punched someone else?" Hugo asked.

"No." Mark swallowed. "Mother collapsed. They think it was a heart attack."

"Is she okay?"

Mark shook his head. "I'm sorry, Father. I'm so very, very sorry."

Chapter 21

It was almost 11 pm, and Sam was becoming more and more concerned. Luke would normally have rung her long before this, and she'd tried to call him herself, but each time it had gone straight to voicemail.

She'd tried phoning his brother, but the same thing had happened, though for all she knew that might be standard practice for Mark.

It wasn't standard practice for Luke, though.

She'd WhatsApp'ed him as well, trying to keep the tone of her texts measured, hiding her increasing sense of panic.

What if he'd been involved in a car accident? Or fallen over and banged his head?

It was nonsense thinking like that. In all likelihood, there was a simple explanation. Perhaps he'd dropped his phone and broken it. Or the battery had run out, and he'd forgotten to pack his charger.

But if that had happened, surely he'd borrow someone else's mobile.

She glared at her phone as if it was to blame and, as if by magic, a name appeared on the screen.

It was a four-letter name, but it wasn't 'Luke'.

Sam closed her eyes for a second.

Why, oh why, was the fool ringing her now of all times?

She thought about declining the call, but she knew what her ex was like. He'd keep trying and trying, not stopping until she answered.

With a deep sigh, she clicked the green button.

"Tony, what do you want?"

"Hello…" There was a short pause, then a hiccup, then, "…Sammy."

The two words were drawn out in a way that told her he

was at least two sheets to the wind, more likely three or four.

"Why are you ringing?"

Tony belched before managing to get a word out.

"Ransom."

She involuntarily drew her head back from the phone, finding it hard to believe what she'd heard.

"What did you say?"

"Ransom. Iss…" Tony paused, and seemed to suck in a deep breath as if the next word was too complex for his addled brain. "…aduction."

Abduction!

Did he say 'abduction'?

This was hard to take in. First 'ransom' and then 'abduction'.

But how on earth could Tony have anything to do with what had happened to Jim and Gail Thatcher? They were worlds apart. Besides, her ex-boyfriend might be a full-on village idiot, but there was no way he'd be involved in a crime of any sort, let alone a kidnapping.

Would he?

She heard a woman's voice on the phone.

"Tony, is Jazelle there?"

He paused as if trying to take this in, before saying, "Iss for you."

After a couple of seconds, Jazelle came on the line, her gravelly imitation of a sexy Marilyn Monroe voice more reminiscent of cheap, smoke-filled nightclubs than '*Some Like It Hot*'.

"He's rat-assed, Sammy. Pissed as a newt."

"What about you?"

"Fine, ta. On the rag, but shouldn't complain. You keepin' okay?"

Sam took a deep breath.

"No. I meant, are you sober?"

"Oh. Yeah, 'course. Why?"

"Tony said 'ransom' and then 'abduction'. What was he talking about?"

Jazelle giggled, a high-pitched cackle that might have come from the love-cross of a hyena and an angry chicken.

"Tone couldn't get his words out proper, but wanted to show off to you. Wasn't content with me saying I was proud of him."

Sam could feel her heart thumping in her chest.

"Show off about what, Jazelle?"

"The woman in the pub. She said he was handsome, didn't she?"

"Handsome?"

"Yeah, and he thinks she was trying to seduce him. Very proud of it, he is. Mind you, she had to be fifty, but he's got his beer goggles on, ain't he?"

"So, he was saying 'handsome' and 'seduction'?"

"Yeah, but he's so sloshed that one syllable's a challenge. Two or three ain't got bugger-all chance." She paused. "You coming to our wedding?"

This change of subject threw Sam completely off guard.

"Your wedding?"

"Yeah, we're getting married in the summer. Told you, didn't I, when we ran into each other a couple of months ago? Still ain't told Tone though."

"I've got to go now, Jazelle."

"You can bring someone if you like. Tone and me is into exchanges."

"Exchanges?"

"Yeah. Where we do swapsies. Keys on the table. Know what I mean?"

Sam knew full well what she meant, but chose to ignore the question.

"You'd best see how Tony's doing."

"Yeah, probs. He's just been sick, and he's lying in it. Byesies, Sammy."

"Goodnight, Jazelle."

Sam ended the call.

A split-second later it started to ring, and she was relieved to see that this time it was Luke's name on the screen.

"Luke. Thank goodness. I was getting worried."

"Sorry," he said. "I've had my phone switched off, and time got away from me."

She could sense the tiredness in his voice. Something else, too. Was it tension?

"What's happened?"

"My mother's passed away. They think it was a heart attack."

"Oh, no! How's Hugo?"

"In pieces."

"Do you think you'll need the rest of the week off?"

"I honestly don't know at the moment."

"Where's your father?"

"He's in the library with Mark." He paused. "He hasn't shed a tear, and I wish he would, but he's too proud and stubborn. When I left them he was in reminiscence mode, running through all the happy times he and my mother had together. He's even smiling on occasions, but I can see it's not genuine. He's trying to mask his real emotions."

"I understand if you need to get back to them."

"I do, but it would be good to talk to you for a few minutes. How was your day?"

Sam had already thought through what she was going to say, having promised Sebastian she'd keep the abductions a secret, but now it was doubly important that she keep Luke from the truth. She didn't want to heap more pressure on him.

"I met Stairway's CEO to straighten up an anomaly I found in their accounts."

"How did it go?"

"As I suspected, there was nothing in it, but he'd

spotted some oddities himself, and asked if I'd go back in tomorrow to help him unearth what's going on."

"What kind of oddities?"

The last thing Sam wanted was to continue talking about this. Lying to Luke didn't sit comfortably, even though she had no choice.

"Company assets that may have been intentionally undervalued. I'm sure it won't take me long to sort it out."

"Are you sure this is an ethics issue? If not, it might be better to pass it back to Stairway's finance team to deal with."

"It might be," she said, hating the fact that she was having to continue telling falsehoods to the man she loved. "In any case, I promised Sebastian I'd help him out, so I owe it to him to return tomorrow."

"Fair enough." He paused. "I'd better go now. Good luck tomorrow."

"Thanks. Take care, Luke. I love you."

"I love you too, Sam."

Chapter 22

"Have you got ants in your pants?" Leanne asked, as she watched her boyfriend trying for the third time to make a neat knot in his tie.

Josh grinned. "I'm excited, that's all."

He looked in the mirror and frowned at the lumpen mass near the top button of his shirt.

"This tie's broken."

"What do you mean it's broken? Ties don't break. Here, let me."

He sat on the end of the bed, and she stretched his tie around his neck, tied a neat Windsor knot and tightened it under his collar.

Josh stood up, walked back to the mirror and nodded in approval.

"Thanks, Leanne. Now, where are my shoes?"

He bent down to look under the bed.

Leanne walked to the shoe rack, retrieved his black loafers and passed them over.

"What's with you today? You went to police HQ with Luke on Monday, so it's not as if it's your first visit, but you're practically bouncing off the walls. You hardly touched your breakfast, and that's never happened before."

"It's a big day. I pick up my police badge."

"It's not a police badge, it's a temporary visitor's badge."

"And I'm having training. Special police training."

"You're learning how to use their IT systems, not how to conduct a drugs raid or carry firearms."

"It's a first step. I'm going to be a police consultant." He puffed his chest out. "I'll be fighting for truth, justice and a better tomorrow."

"Wasn't it Superman who said that?"

Josh's cheeks went slightly pink.

"Might have been."

Leanne shook her head and walked over to kiss him.

"You're very sweet, Joshy, and I love you."

"Good... Ah, me too. Looking forward to our meal on Saturday?"

"That was a sudden change of topic."

"Well, it's a nice place, The Olive Tree. Very special. For, ah... Us... You and me... To go... Together." He swallowed. "Very special."

"You said that."

"So? Are you excited?"

"Not as excited as you, clearly. Come on, or you'll miss your bus."

*

Just over an hour later, Josh approached the entrance to Avon and Somerset Police's Headquarters.

He was momentarily tempted to take a selfie of himself in front of the sign, but that would be childish, and he was a proper person.

A police consultant!

"Gucci!"

"What did you say?"

He turned to see a woman standing beside him, one eyebrow raised.

"Did I hear you right?" she went on. "Did you say 'Gucci'?"

"Ah... Yes. It kind of means 'cool', which is what this place is."

"I take it this is your first time to Avon and Somerset's HQ?"

"Second, but today I pick up my visitor's badge and I'm learning how to use the IT systems. I'm joining DCI

Franks' team."

"Are you indeed?"

He grinned and nodded.

"Uh-huh. I'm going to be a police consultant. Are you on the course too?"

She shook her head, a vague smile playing across her lips.

"No. I already know how to use the force's systems."

"Are you a police officer then?"

"I've been a serving officer for well over a decade."

"Coolio." He lowered his voice. "Have you met DCI Franks? I'm going to be in her team. Do you know if she's easy to get on with?"

"Easy to get on with?"

"Yes. I'm worried she might be cold and distant."

Her eyebrow went back up, but she didn't say anything. Josh shrugged.

"I guess I'll find out for myself."

"You certainly will, but I'd be careful not to cross her if I were you. You don't want to get on a senior officer's bad side."

He fired a finger gun at her.

"Gotcha. I'll bear that in mind"

He spotted Pete over her shoulder. "Ah, here's DI Gilmore. He set up my training for me."

She turned around. "Good morning, Pete."

"Good morning, Ma'am. Morning, Josh."

"Hi."

Josh hesitated as he replayed this briefest of conversations in his mind.

'Ma'am' was like 'guv', wasn't it? Used when speaking to a more senior officer.

Which meant…

Pissedy-piss-piss.

She couldn't be, could she?

He swallowed.

"I'm glad you two have met," Pete said. "Come on, Josh. Let's get your pass and I'll show you where the training suite is."

"Right, yes. Nice to meet you, ah… Ma'am."

"You're a civilian, Josh," she said, and there was no longer any trace of a smile. "DCI Franks is fine. And if we get to know each other better, perhaps we can move to Nicole. Of course, that depends on whether you warm to me or not."

"Ah…"

She turned and walked to the entrance.

Chapter 23

Sam smiled as Sebastian's PA approached reception, but all she received in response was a slight narrowing of the eyebrows and a movement of her mouth that almost reached sneer level.

Sam was confused, but continued smiling.

"Good morning, Jenny."

"Mmm."

This was said with disdain and followed by a slight shaking of the head. There was evident disapproval, but Sam couldn't fathom why.

Jenny turned away without saying another word and walked to the lift.

Sam followed, conscious that you could cut the atmosphere between them with a knife. She decided to confront the issue head-on.

"You seem annoyed with me, Jenny. I'm sorry if I've done something to upset you."

"Upset me!" She looked around to check no one was listening, lowered her voice and shook her head again. "I can't believe women like you."

"What?"

"Sssh. We'll talk upstairs."

The lift arrived and, once they were inside, Jenny pressed the button for the 6th floor rather than the 4th.

"What do we need to talk about?" Sam asked once the doors had closed.

"You know full well."

A hundred thoughts flashed through Sam's brain.

Was Jenny aware of the kidnapping and ransom demand? If so, did she think she was one of the abductors? Or, had she seen what was in the parcel delivered to her boss the day before?

The lift doors opened, and they emerged onto what appeared to be a maintenance floor.

Jenny led the way out, waited for the lift doors to close, and then turned and rounded on Sam.

"Sebastian is a good man. I don't know how you can take advantage of him like this."

"What do you mean 'take advantage of him'? I'm helping to sort out a few accounting anomalies, that's all."

"You can't kid me, Sam." She gave a dry laugh. "I bet Sam isn't even your real name. How much is he paying?"

Sam's heart sank.

Somehow, Jenny had indeed found out about the ransom, perhaps by listening in to the phone call he'd received from Zeus.

But if she'd listened in, she'd know Sam wasn't involved.

No, there had to have been another way she'd found out.

"Has he told you what's going on, Jenny?"

"He doesn't need to tell me."

"Did you overhear something?"

"Why? Did you think you were making a lot of noise?"

"A lot of noise?"

"He told me he doesn't want any visitors except you today. I've had to turn two directors away already. My god, you've got your talons into him, haven't you?"

Sam was beginning to connect the dots.

"Are you and Sebastian more than work colleagues, Jenny?"

"Why do you ask? If we were, would that make you stop?"

"Are you?"

"No, we're not, as it happens." She swallowed. "Not that it's any of your business. Why would I tell someone like you anything about my private life?"

The tears were flowing freely now, and Jenny dabbed below her eyes before continuing.

"He could at least have hired you to come to his home. Bringing you to the office is… is…" She gulped. "…so hurtful."

It would have been laughable if it wasn't so tragic. Jenny had gotten completely the wrong end of the stick, perhaps understandably, given she and Sebastian had gone from not knowing each other to locking themselves in his office for two mornings running.

The situation was compounded by the fact that Jenny was clearly in love with her boss.

It wasn't as if telling the truth was an option. It was essential that as few people as possible knew about the kidnapping, and besides Sam had promised Sebastian she wouldn't tell anyone.

She decided to build on the lie about 'accounting anomalies'.

"You've got this all wrong, Jenny. I'm not a call girl."

Jenny sighed again, even more deeply this time, and it was clear that she saw this as bad news.

"So, how did you two meet?"

"No, you don't understand. Sebastian and I aren't in any kind of relationship, sexual or otherwise. We met for the first time yesterday, and I am, as I said, here to help with financial issues."

"Why would I believe that?"

"I'm an accountant at Filchers, the company that Stairway outsourced its finance team to."

She pulled her phone out and called Helen's number.

"Hi, Sam," Helen said.

"Helen, I'm with Jenny, Sebastian Thatcher's PA. Could you explain why I'm here, please?"

"Ach, can you nae tell her yourself?"

"It's for security reasons. I'll put you on speaker."

She clicked the button.

"Hi, Helen," Jenny said. "Sam says she's an accountant."

"Aye, that's right. She works alongside me in the Ethics Team at Filchers, and our boss asked her to look into some payments queries at Stairway. Sebastian is the CEO, isn't he?"

"Yes."

"That'll be why she's there then."

"Thanks, Helen," Sam said.

"Nae problem."

Sam hung up.

"If it's simply payment queries," Jenny asked, "why the locked door and secrecy?"

"Sebastian suspects that one of the company directors may be siphoning off money to pay for gambling debts."

"My god! Which one?"

"It would be wrong of me to say, and at the moment it's only a suspicion."

"I see." She hesitated. "I'm sorry I thought you were a, you know…"

"Not to worry. I've been called worse."

"Really?"

Sam laughed. "Well no, probably not, actually."

Chapter 24

"I take it you haven't heard anything?" Sam asked, once Jenny had left Sebastian's office.

She was sitting on the sofa, watching as he paced backwards and forwards.

He stopped walking and turned to face her.

"Nothing." He tried to smile, but it was a poor effort. "I'm sorry if I look rough."

"I'm not surprised. I don't suppose you managed to get any sleep?"

"Not a wink." He sighed. "I only hope Mum and Dad are okay. Barbara, too." He shook his head. "I can't believe anyone could do something like this."

"Have you been able to obtain the extra £200,000?"

"Yes. I called in a favour from a friend, and it's already in my account. He'd be good for more too if we need it."

"Have you thought about asking for a delay?"

"I'm not sure I could bear to."

"In that case, perhaps you should emphasise the difficulty in obtaining the extra money when Zeus calls."

He nodded. "Yes, I'll do that."

Sebastian resumed his pacing, pulling out his phone every now and then to check he hadn't missed a text.

"Sebastian," Sam asked after a couple of minutes, "would you have confided in anyone else if I wasn't here?"

"I wouldn't have dared. Zeus warned me not to tell anyone else."

"What about Jenny?"

"Jenny?"

"You must have to share secrets with her, and the two of you seem to get on well."

"We do, yes, and she's a good listener, but I wouldn't

want to burden her with…"

His phone pinged, and he stopped talking abruptly, pulled it from his pocket and clicked on the message that had come through

"It's another photo. God, they look in a bad way."

He passed the phone to Sam. As on the day before, it showed Jim and Gail Thatcher and Barbara on white plastic chairs. His father again held the day's Daily Telegraph.

The phone started ringing, and she passed it back.

Sebastian answered and put it on speaker.

"Hello."

"This is Zeus. Have you got the funds?"

"It wasn't easy. That kind of amount…"

"I don't want the details. Have you got the funds?"

"Yes."

There was a slight hesitation at the other end, and Sam mentally crossed her fingers that Zeus didn't ask for still more money.

"Have you got a pen and paper?" Zeus asked.

"Just a second." Sebastian pointed to his desk, and Sam grabbed the Post-its and a pen and passed them over. "Okay. I'm ready."

"The money needs to be transferred to Zeus Holdings, sort code 17-44-43, account number 23467948."

"Okay. I've got that. How is this going to work?"

"Do you know East Harptree Wood?"

"It's south of Bristol, isn't it?"

"Yes. Be there at 2 pm today, park in the car park, and take the path signed to Switham Chimney. After a few hundred yards, you'll see a sign on your left saying '*No Public Access - Forest Operations*'. Follow that track and one of my colleagues will find you and lead you to your parents and their neighbour. You will then transfer the money and, once we have checked it is in our account, you will be allowed to take them away."

"Okay."

"You must come alone. We will have eyes on that car park, so don't even think of bringing anyone with you. Also, none of the four of you must ever mention any of what has happened to anyone. This episode has to go with you to your graves." There was a pause to let this sink in. "We know where your parents live, Sebastian, and you saw what happened to Barbara."

"I understand."

There was a click, and the line went dead.

Sebastian shook his head.

"Zeus has planned this down to the last detail, the ruthless bastard."

He looked over at Sam.

"Thanks for your help, but you heard what he said. I'm going to have to do this on my own."

"I agree, but…" She looked at her watch. "It's just gone eleven. I should have time."

"Time for what?"

"Let me check something a minute."

She googled East Harptree Wood and scrolled through to check she was correct.

"What are you doing?"

She looked up and smiled.

"I was right. The woods are popular with dog walkers."

"And?"

"I'm going to take my partner's dog for a walk. If I leave now, I should be able to pick him up and get to the woods by 1:30, long before you get there."

"That'll be dangerous. What if they see you?"

"They probably will, but I'm just an unconnected woman walking my cocker spaniel. I'll stick to the tracks but keep my eyes open in case I spot them arriving or leaving."

"It's not necessary. I'm going to pay the ransom."

"But success will egg them on to do it again to another poor family. If there's a chance, any chance at all, that they can be caught and put in prison, we ought to take it."

Chapter 25

Luke looked across at his brother, who had bags under his eyes and a drawn look, not that he was feeling the brightest himself having had little more than an hour's sleep.

"Are you sure it's okay for me to leave, Mark?"

"Yes, you go. Now that we've made the funeral arrangements, I can handle things here. Father needs someone to talk to, but I can manage that on my own."

"Thanks. Have you thought about Marion's birthday party?"

"Erica and I have discussed it, and we're going to go ahead."

"I think it's a good idea. Apart from anything else, it will help distract Father, if only for a couple of hours. Do you need help setting up?"

"No. We'll be fine."

Luke stood up just as his father returned from the toilet.

"Father, I'm going to leave now but I'll be back on Saturday."

"Okay, son," Hugo said as he gently lowered himself into his armchair before turning his attention to the window and the terraced gardens at the back of Borrowham Hall.

Luke turned back to his brother.

"If you'd like me to come back before the weekend, please say, won't you?"

"I will, I assure you."

Luke grabbed his coat and bag, put them in the back of the BMW and climbed into the driver's seat, taking a moment to compose himself before setting off.

He glanced back at the front of the house, trying to

Tiger Bait

recall happy moments spent there with his mother, but they had been few and far between. He'd been closer to his nanny than his parents when he was young, regarded as a necessity to carry on the line but of little use to the Duke and Duchess of Dorset otherwise.

Was he being unfair?

He didn't believe so. She'd made her feelings about him clear enough.

His father had at least mellowed in his later years, and they now had a companionable, if not warm, relationship.

Sighing, he turned the engine on and turned onto the drive.

Once he was on the main road towards Bath, he rang Robbie in the Operation Tooting incident room.

"DC Hammond."

"Hi, Robbie, it's Luke. Thanks for arranging the interview with Mr McCoy."

"No problem. It's been brought forward and is all set for 1:30. DCI Franks would like to meet you fifteen minutes beforehand to prepare."

Luke looked at the clock on the dashboard and then at the console.

"I'm travelling up from Dorset, and my SatNav is telling me I'll be there at 1:20. Can you warn her I may be a few minutes late?"

"Will do. Your pre-meeting will be in interview room 3, and you'll see McCoy in room 5."

"Thanks."

He hung up and called Marjorie.

"Hi, Marjorie. Thanks for looking after Wilkins overnight."

"No problem, Luke. He was as good as gold."

"Great. I'll be back to fetch him at around 6 pm."

"Oh. Didn't Sam tell you?"

"Tell me what?"

"She picked him up about ten minutes ago. Said she

fancied taking him for a long walk."

That was certainly odd. Nice for Wilkins though.

He ended the call and rang Sam.

"Hi, Luke. How are things down there?"

"Father's struggling, as you'd expect, but Mark's happy to hold the fort, so I'm on the way to Portishead." He paused. "I've just rung Marjorie, and she told me you've picked Wilkins up."

There was a slight hesitation before Sam answered.

"You remember I told you I was back in with the CEO of Stairway this morning?"

"Yes, I remember."

"Well, we resolved those accounting issues, but it was a heavy session. I decided to have a long lunch break and take Wilkins for a walk. That's okay, isn't it?"

"Of course it is. Why was the session heavy?"

There was another pause, and Luke was beginning to think that she was hiding something from him.

"Sam, what aren't you telling me?"

More hesitation.

He was concerned now.

"Was this man aggressive? Or did he try it on with you?"

"No. Nothing like that."

"What was it then?"

Another pause.

"We resolved those apparent accounting anomalies. It was all a misunderstanding, but his secretary, Jenny. She…"

Sam gave what she hoped was a reasonable simulation of a laugh.

"She accused me of being a call girl."

Luke sucked his jaw in.

"She what?"

"Jenny's in love with him and reached the wrong conclusion when Sebastian and I were shut in his office for two mornings running."

"I trust you convinced her you weren't?"

"In the end, yes, but it was stressful."

"You deserve a relaxing walk after that. Where are you taking him?"

"I'm not sure yet."

"I can tell you're driving, though."

"Yes. I, ah… I thought I'd head west and see if I come to any woods."

"Okay. I'll see you later. Have a good time."

"Take care, Luke. I love you."

"I love you too, Sam."

Chapter 26

It was 1:25 when Luke walked into room 3 in Avon and Somerset's interview suite.

DCI Franks looked up from the report she was reading and made a point of looking at her watch.

"Sorry I'm late, Nicole. I had to drive up from Dorset."

"Aren't you based in Bath?"

"I am, but I stayed at my parents' house last night."

"Mmm. Well, you should have set out earlier. One of the things you'll learn about me is that I like to be punctual, and that extends to my team."

Luke's instinct was to let her have six barrels, but he knew he was overtired, and the last thing he wanted was to ruin what was already a strained relationship.

He contented himself with a sigh, pulled out the chair opposite her and sat down.

"Let's get on with it, shall we?"

She looked at her watch again.

"We haven't got long. We're seeing Mr McCoy in five minutes."

"It won't do any harm if we keep him waiting."

She glared at him. "As I said, Luke, I like to be punctual. Now..." She opened the folder on her desk. "I see he's a known dealer, but very low in the organisation. Why have you suggested we bring him in for questioning?"

"A private detective reported that McCoy overheard a man say, *'and kill all three if necessary'*."

"And? Evidence that is three times removed is practically worthless. Besides, he could well have misheard, or simply have been spinning a tale to impress. Even if he is telling the truth, are those six words really sufficient to pull someone in for questioning?"

"I believe so. The man McCoy overheard is a known criminal who spent eight years inside for armed robbery."

"Mmm. Well, now he's in, we may as well see him. I'll let you take the lead."

She stood up and looked over at Luke.

"I must say, you look very tired. Are you sure you're up to this? Did you have a late night?"

"Worse than that. I didn't manage more than an hour's sleep."

"Were you celebrating something?"

He shook his head. "No. Far from it."

"Good, because it's the middle of the week, and I expect my team…"

Luke had had enough.

"Stop being so bloody difficult!"

She was visibly affronted. "What do you mean? Luke, this is out of order."

"If you must know, the reason I had a bad night is because my mother died yesterday evening."

Her mouth opened, but no words came out.

"My brother and I were up all night consoling our father."

Her mouth closed.

"Oh. I see." She hesitated. "I, ah… I don't know what to say."

He stood up.

"Let's get on with it, shall we?"

He opened the door for her, and they walked to the next but one room. Again, he opened the door and followed her in.

Flimsy McCoy was sitting on the opposite side of the table nursing a mug of tea. Misty had been right, the man was all skin and bones. He had large brown eyes set in a pock-marked face and could have played Tolkien's Gollum without need for a make-up artist.

A uniformed constable stood in the corner of the

room.

"Thank you, officer," Nicole said. "You can leave now."

"Very well, Ma'am."

He left, and Luke sat down opposite McCoy, while Nicole took the seat next to him.

McCoy looked up at Luke, then at the DCI, then back at Luke and kept his eyes there as he took another sip of his tea.

"You're the one in charge I assume, and not the wee lassie."

Luke was surprised at the strength of his Scottish accent, though his name should have been a giveaway.

"I'm Luke Sackville, and this is DCI Franks."

"Oh, right." He glanced at Nicole. "DCI, are you? You're young. Pretty too. I guess that must have helped."

He grinned, revealing a mouth containing more gaps than anything else. The five teeth remaining were nicotine-brown and at bizarre angles to each other.

Nicole glared back, but didn't say anything.

After a few seconds, his grin disappeared, and he returned his attention to Luke.

"Why am I here, big man? I'm an honest person, always have been."

"I'm going to record this interview, Mr McCoy." Luke clicked the button. "Interview with Torquill McCoy in Room 5, Avon and Somerset HQ. Present are Luke Sackville and DCI Nicole Franks. The time is 13:37."

McCoy grinned again.

"Almost forgot my real name. I haven't been called Torquill since I was sucking me wee mammy's titty." He turned his less-than-charming smile back in Nicole's direction. "Pardon my French, DCI Franks."

"Thank you for coming in, Mr McCoy," Luke said.

"Flimsy, please. No one calls me Torquill and certainly not Mister. I've been Flimsy for years."

Luke smiled disarmingly. "You said you're an honest

man, but that's not true, is it?"

"Of course it is. Very honest."

"Would you agree that peddling class-A drugs is dishonest?"

"Of course, that's why I didnae do it." He shook his head. "Bad for you, drugs."

He put his hand to his face, as if subconsciously recognising the damage inflicted by his addictions.

"You received a community order last year, Flimsy. What was that for?"

"That was for selling smack, but I dinnae do it nae more. That's what I meant. Part of my past, it is."

"The thing is, Flimsy…" Luke bent forward over the desk as if confiding in the other man. "…I don't believe you." He paused to let this sink in. "Redland's where you do your deals, isn't it, on the edge of the Downs around the Westbury Road area?"

"No. I go for walks there sometimes, that's all."

"That's not true. If we wanted to we could put surveillance on that area, and it wouldn't be long before we caught you red-handed."

Flimsy started rocking from side to side on his seat, visibly uncomfortable with the route the conversation was taking.

"Who's your supplier, Flimsy?"

"I told you…"

Luke held his hand up. "For a second offence, you'd be looking at a spell inside. You don't want that, do you?"

Flimsy didn't reply, but looked sullenly across at Luke.

"Do you get your drugs from Declan O'Brien, Flimsy? Is he your supplier?"

"Declan? No, I don't have anything to do with that violent bastard."

"You know him, though?"

"Yes, but he's nothing to do with Jay."

"Jay?"

"What?"

"You said 'Jay'. Who's Jay?"

"I didn't say 'Jay'. I don't know anyone called Jay."

"He did say 'Jay', didn't he DCI Franks?"

"That's what I heard," Nicole said.

"I didn't. Never." He looked nervously at Luke, then Nicole, then back again.

Luke reached over to the recording device.

"Shall I play the recording back so that we can check?"

Flimsy glared at the machine as if by doing so he could melt it. After a few seconds, he muttered something under his breath.

"Sorry," Luke said. "I didn't catch that."

"Jay's the main man. I haven't met him, and I don't know his surname, but I've heard him mentioned."

"Who by?"

"People."

"The people who provide you with drugs to sell?"

"No. Just people." He sniffed. "Friends."

"Friends who know the head of the local drug cartel?"

Flimsy didn't bother answering this question.

"What are their names, Flimsy?"

"I'm not a grass."

"Why would you be grassing if they're friends and not middlemen in a drugs racket?"

"I'm not giving you their names."

Luke could see he wasn't going to get any more out of the man. McCoy might not have met Jay, nor even know his full name, but he knew enough to be frightened of him.

"Okay. Going back to Declan O'Brien, I believe you overheard him talking about killing three people. Is that correct?"

"I knew it was a bad idea telling Misty that," Flimsy muttered under his breath.

"What exactly did O'Brien say?"

"Nothing."

"Nothing?"

Flimsy swallowed. "I was desperate for, ah… for food and needed money, so I made it up. She gave me forty quid."

"You made it up?"

Flimsy looked sheepishly at Luke, and they both knew he was lying.

"Yes. I made it up."

"Okay. I think we're finished." He turned to Nicole. "Unless you've got any questions, DCI Franks?"

"No, I'm fine."

"Interview ended at 13:56."

He pressed stop on the recording device.

Chapter 27

Jim was worried about Barbara.

She was extremely pale and becoming less and less communicative. At present, she was asleep, her head flopped down over her chest, but he was concerned that if their ordeal went on for much longer, her body would give up on her.

At least her finger didn't seem to be causing too much pain. Their captors had provided antiseptic and bandages, and Gail was checking it regularly. It looked hideous, but there was no sign of infection, which had to be a good thing.

He looked over at their guard, the tallest of the men taking shifts supervising them. All three had been careful to keep their faces hidden, and not to use names when talking to each other, but he would never forget the sound of their voices.

This one had a strong northern Irish accent, possibly Belfast, and had been the one who mercilessly hacked off Barbara's fingertip. He stared back at Jim through the slits in his black balaclava.

At least the van was heated, and their captors had provided thin mattresses and sheets, not that Jim had managed more than a few hours sleep since they'd been incarcerated. Food had been Tesco sandwiches three times a day which, while boring, had been adequate. Toilet arrangements had been another thing altogether, only possible when there were two guards present and necessitating squatting among the trees surrounding the vehicle.

There was a knock on the van door, and the tall man opened it.

"What is it?"

"It's happening now."

This was the guard with a West Country accent. Somerset, Jim thought. He and the third guard, an Australian, were about the same height, but the local man was stockier and spoke slowly as if his brain was struggling with the challenge of delivering words in the right order.

He pulled the door open, and he and the Australian clambered in. Once inside, the Australian closed the door behind them.

"What now?" the Irishman asked.

"Orders are to gag them, tie their hands behind their backs and take them to the handover point," the Australian said.

He handed the other two men cloths and rope, and as one they walked towards Jim, Gail and Barbara.

It was the local man who approached Barbara. He looked down at her.

"The old woman is asleep."

"No shit, Sherlock," the Australian said as he tied the cloth around Gail's mouth, pushing some of it in her mouth and tightening the gag behind her head until she squealed.

"What do I do?"

The Australian sighed. "Here. You finish this one. I'll wake her."

They exchanged places, and the Australian pushed Barbara hard on the side of her arm.

She immediately came to, lifted her head and opened her mouth. Before she had the chance to scream, he covered her lower face with his hand and bent so that their eyes were only inches apart.

"Do you want to keep your remaining fingers?"

Barbara nodded, her eyes wide and staring.

"Then don't make a fucking sound, dearie."

She nodded again, and he tied her gag.

Jim allowed the Irishman to tie his gag, then stood up to enable his hands to be fastened together behind his back.

Once all three were secured, they were led to the back of the van, then down onto the forestry track.

The Irishman and Jim went first, the Australian and Gail behind, while the local man and Barbara brought up the rear.

There were tall conifers to either side, thickly planted so that Jim could see no more than ten or fifteen paces into them.

They continued for eighty yards or so before turning left. Thirty paces after that, they took a right and almost immediately came to a halt.

"Don't move, any of you," the Irishman said.

After a few seconds, three people stepped out of a track ahead of them.

Jim was relieved to see Sebastian. The other two, one male and one female, wore all black and balaclavas.

The woman held a laptop open. She said something to Sebastian, who looked over at his parents, then back at her, nodded and bent forward to key something in.

He stepped back.

The woman typed on the keyboard several times, then folded the screen down and nodded to the man by her side.

"Bring them here," he called to the three guards.

Jim recognised his voice. This was the man who had forced Barbara to video the abduction.

The guards walked their captives to within a few yards.

"That's close enough."

The woman with the computer was about to say something, but hesitated as they all became aware of rustling in the forest. Suddenly, there was a flash of brown, and a cocker spaniel appeared as if out of nowhere.

The dog looked over at the group for a second, then ran to the nearest tree and cocked its leg.

"What was that?" the balaclava'd woman said.

"The dog is having a piss," the man with the Somerset accent said.

"Not that, idiot. Listen."

Jim heard it too this time. It was a woman's voice, and she was calling.

"Wilkins! Come here, boy."

The Irishman drew something out of his pocket, and Jim watched in horror as he pressed a button and a six-inch blade slid out of its sheath.

"Keep them here. I'll deal with the woman."

The call came again, and it was clear the woman was drawing nearer.

"Wilkins! Wilkins!"

The Irishman advanced towards the trees, but as he approached the spaniel, the dog lifted his front lip, revealing a full set of incisors bounded by vicious-looking canines, and let out a low, menacing growl.

The Irishman stopped in his tracks.

The dog looked up at him for a second, as if about to pounce, then seemed to think better of it, turned and ran back into the woods. Within seconds, he had disappeared from view.

The balaclava'd woman returned her attention to Sebastian.

"Set your timer. When five minutes have passed, remove the gags and rope and take these three to your car. Not before. Understand?"

"Yes."

Sebastian set his timer.

The woman nodded to the others, and the five kidnappers jogged back in the direction of the van.

Sebastian turned to his mother and father, tears in his eyes. He reached for his mother's gag, but she shook her head violently.

He pulled his hand back.

"I'm sorry, Mum. I'm so sorry."

Chapter 28

Sam hadn't seen any trace of the kidnappers, which was disappointing.

She'd arrived at East Harptree Wood at twenty past one and had speed-walked to cover as much ground as possible, Wilkins as ever diving in and out of the trees and never seeming to tire. Despite walking down most of the approved trails, and even some of the tracks marked '*No Public Access*', there had been no sign of any people acting mysteriously, let alone men in balaclavas or a hidden van. However, the woods were extensive, so that didn't necessarily mean they weren't there.

For a moment, she'd thought she was onto something when Wilkins chased a rabbit into the forest. She'd followed him into the trees and heard him growl but, after calling him several times, he'd lolloped back, and she assumed he'd come across something larger that had startled him, perhaps a deer or even a wild boar.

She looked at her watch. It was now two-thirty. If Sebastian had been successful, and the abductors hadn't pulled some kind of trick on him, he should now be on the way back to Bristol with his mother, father and Barbara.

Which meant he would be calling her at any moment.

Her phone rang as if on cue.

She accepted the call without looking at the screen.

"Hi, Sebastian. Are they okay?"

"Sam?"

Shit, shit, shit.

"Oh. Hi, Luke."

"You sound disappointed."

She was going to have to lie again. God, she hated having to lie to him.

"Not at all. I'm out of breath, that's all. Wilkins and I have had a brisk walk, and we're on our way back to the car."

"I see." He paused. "Who's Sebastian?"

"Sebastian?"

"Yes. You thought I was Sebastian."

"Oh. He's the CEO of Stairway."

Luke laughed. "The man whose secretary thought you were a prostitute?"

"Yes, but I didn't find what she said very amusing. I'm surprised you do."

"I'm trying to make light of it, that's all."

"Well, I'd rather you didn't."

"Look, I'm sorry, Sam. I didn't realise it had upset you so much."

She realised she'd snapped because she was so tense, and wished she could tell him why. She took a deep breath in an attempt to control herself, but she was wound as tight as a drum and felt on the edge of tears.

After a few seconds, she drew in a deep breath and spoke.

"It's me who should apologise, Luke. It wound me up and… and I shouldn't have had a go at you."

"Don't be silly. All couples have tiffs. The important thing is that we have complete trust in each other. No secrets ever."

She didn't reply, and there was another silence before Luke spoke again.

"I take it you didn't get to the bottom of all of Stairway's financial issues?"

"What do you mean?"

"When you thought I was Sebastian, you asked, 'Are they okay?'. I assume that means you weren't able to resolve everything."

"Are you cross-examining me?"

"Not at all."

"Yes, there are a couple of issues outstanding, but I assure you I'm able to handle them on my own."

"I don't have any doubt of that."

"Good. The last thing I need right now is to be micromanaged."

There was another awkward silence.

Sam sighed. She was only on the periphery of the tragic events that had embroiled Sebastian and his family, and yet she felt like she had the world on her shoulders.

"Are you still there, Sam?"

"Sorry, Luke. I..." She swallowed. "It's been a rough day."

"You can tell me all about it when we get home."

I wish I could. I really wish I could.

She tried to pull herself together.

"I'll drop Wilkins off and head straight to the office. It'll probably be getting on five by the time I get there."

"I'll be there about the same time." He paused. "I love you, Sam."

Her voice was trembling as she replied.

"I love you too, Luke."

And I wish you were with me right now.

She ended the call, and her phone immediately started ringing again. This time she looked down before answering.

"Hi, Sebastian. Did everything go okay?"

"As well as could be expected. My mum and dad are shattered, but otherwise seem fine. Barbara's not faring too well, though. We're going to go straight to my parents' house where we can check on her. Mum being a nurse helps."

"Was the exchange smooth?"

"It was very slick. They're an organised outfit, and had it planned down to the last detail. They were also careful not to reveal their faces or call each other by name." He hesitated. "The only scary moment was when your partner's dog appeared, and we heard you shouting for him. I recognised your voice immediately."

"Wilkins appeared?"

"Yes. One of the kidnappers pulled a knife and was ready to attack. It was lucky the dog decided to leave because it was the man who severed Barbara's finger. If you'd appeared out of the trees, I think he'd have gone for you."

Sam shivered at the thought.

"Is there anything at all that would enable you to identify any of them?"

"No. I'd know their voices if I heard them again, but apart from that there's nothing. Look, thanks for your help, Sam. Talking to you has helped no end, but my parents and I have to try to move on. It's going to be impossible to forget what's happened, but we've got no choice other than to keep this whole episode a secret and look forward. They made it clear what they would do if we involved the police. You won't tell anyone, will you?"

"Of course not." She paused. "Promise you'll let me know how they are though, especially Barbara."

"I will, Sam. Bye for now."

"Goodbye, Sebastian."

Chapter 29

Luke rang Mark as soon as he left Portishead. It went to voicemail and he left a brief message.

Five minutes later, his brother rang back.

"Sorry, Luke. Father was telling me all about the day he and Mother met." He paused. "For the fourth time."

"How's he faring?"

"He's coping well, I'd say, given it's been less than 24 hours. Marion's fantastic. She's just this minute got home from school, and has dragged him off to help her make a birthday cake."

"Father making a cake? I'd be surprised if he knows where the kitchen is, let alone how to use the oven."

Mark laughed. "Heaven knows what it'll turn out like, but you could see his spirits lift when she appeared."

"Do you want a hand with the funeral arrangements?"

"No, it's okay. Erica's on the case. It might be a wake to us, but to her it's a party, and organising parties is very much her thing. Plus, she's loving the fact that she'll have to invite all those Lords and Ladies."

"Well, if you do need help with anything, please let me know. I can drive down anytime if you need me to. Failing that, Sam and I will be there on Saturday, probably mid-morning."

"Great. I'll see you then."

He hung up, and his mind turned to Sam.

That business with the secretary at Stairway had upset her a lot, more than he would have expected. Normally, she'd laugh something like that off, but it seemed to have really got to her. Could it be that there was more to it than met the eye? Had this PA been rude? Or worse?

What he was sure of was that there was nothing in what

she had thought. He trusted Sam completely.

The question bugging him now was how to deal with the issue when they were next alone together. Would she prefer him to talk about it to her, to listen while she ran through what had happened and how she felt, or was it a no-go area that he should avoid mentioning?

It was a minefield, that's what it was.

Churchill had once described the Soviet Union as '*a riddle wrapped in a mystery inside an enigma*', but he could as well have been talking about women. Did they like to vent their feelings, listen to suggestions, avoid the subject or something else completely?

It was laughable to think that Josh had asked him for advice on how to talk to Leanne, convinced that he understood their ways and how to deal with them.

The lad was a long way off the mark.

After a few minutes of making no decision whatsoever, Luke decided to play it by ear. He'd let Sam raise the subject and take it from there.

He clicked on his audiobook, but had only been listening for five minutes when his phone rang.

It was DCI Franks.

"Hello, Nicole."

There was a slight hesitation before she spoke, and he sensed she was still uncomfortable with him using her first name.

"We didn't have the chance to discuss the interview with McCoy," she said. "What did you think?"

"I'm convinced he was lying."

"Me too. That story about Declan O'Brien saying he might kill three people was clearly fabricated to earn him £40."

"No. I meant he was lying to us about O'Brien not saying that."

"Come on, Luke. You're using what he said to fit a theory. A low-life like him would say anything for the price of his next fix."

"He might do, but it's not just my opinion. Misty is also convinced he's telling the truth."

"Misty?"

"Misty Mitchell. She's the PI that I interviewed with one of my team. Have you met Josh?"

"Josh? Yes, I have. He works for you, does he? That explains a lot."

"What do you mean?"

She hesitated and chose to ignore the question.

"It seems to me that you value the opinion of this private investigator over that of your DCI, Luke."

Luke took an instant decision not to rise to the use of the term 'your DCI'. However, what he would do was find an opportunity to have a face-to-face with DCI Nicole Franks. She was a high-flyer, with undoubted skills as a police officer, but would alienate her team if she didn't improve her people skills.

He changed the subject.

"What about this man called Jay? Did you believe Flimsy when he said he was the main man?"

"I'm not sure. It could be another story made to impress, or because Flimsy was uncomfortable with the line of questioning."

"But you're following up on it?"

"Yes, Luke. I've got one of my team researching it right now. I don't need you to tell me how to do my job."

Luke bit his tongue for the second time.

"How's the investigation going overall?"

"It's going well. DI Gilmore will be in touch when your services are next required."

The line went dead.

Charming.

He called Misty, who answered immediately.

"Well, if it ain't my favourite gigantosaurus. How's things, Luke? You had Flimsy in yet?"

"That's why I'm ringing. He claimed he'd lied to you about Declan O'Brien."

"He what? The scrawny little tosser. Lied to me, my arse."

"Do you think you could have another word with him?"

"Nothing would give me greater fucking pleasure."

"He also mentioned someone called Jay. Flimsy called him 'the main man' but backed down when I pressed him. You don't know who this Jay is, do you?"

"No, but I can ask a few questions."

"Are you sure? This is a police investigation, but I'm only a consultant. I'm not authorised to pay you for your services."

"No problem. You can owe me one."

"Thanks, Misty."

Chapter 30

Diana couldn't keep the smile from her face.

It had gone like clockwork. The only glitch had been Declan cutting the end of the old woman's finger off, but even that had worked in their favour. The rich son had been so frightened of what might happen to his parents, he'd happily paid double the amount she'd been expecting.

Her only regret was not pushing him higher, perhaps to half a million, but that would have required another day of keeping their captives hidden away and would have added extra risk. No, she'd played it just right.

As far as she was concerned, it was a victimless crime too. No one had been hurt, well practically no one, and the wealthy founder of Stairway wouldn't miss a few hundred thousand off his bank balance.

Her dad would have been proud of her. She wasn't just keeping the family business going, she was growing and extending their operations. What's more, this abduction was only the start of what promised to be a highly successful new venture. Running protection brought in regular money, but this was a step up.

Plus, she had the germ of an idea for how to make the rewards considerably higher. Toby, the actor they'd employed to keep the road clear, had inadvertently planted the seed. She'd start planning tomorrow, look Favershams up, and take it from there. With luck, she'd be in a position to put a proposition to her brothers at the weekend.

But right now, she owed it to herself to relax and have a mini celebration. She grabbed a glass, poured herself a decent measure of vodka, then added some diet coke from the fridge.

She was about to add a couple of cubes of ice, when

Tiger Bait

she heard the door open behind her.

"Are you celebrating, Mum?"

She turned to see her son and noticed for the first time that he had the beginnings of a moustache on his upper lip. Her little boy was becoming a man.

"I am, actually."

"Was this the new venture you were talking about?"

She nodded, then dropped the ice cubes in her glass, and took a sip of her drink before replying.

"We finished today, and it all went smoothly."

"Can I have a beer to help you celebrate?"

"You most certainly cannot. You're not even sixteen, Roma."

"At least tell me what you were up to."

"I'll tell you on Sunday when the family come around for lunch."

"Uncle Jay's keen to know as well."

"What do you mean?"

"He heard a rumour you were up to something, and was grilling me yesterday evening."

"Well, you and he will have to be patient for a couple of days." She hesitated and took in his tracksuit bottoms and dark grey hoodie. "You working for him again today?"

He nodded. "Running some gear around the Clifton dealers."

"You be careful. The police are always sniffing around, and you need to watch your back. Some of those dealers are untrustworthy, too."

"Don't worry, Mum. I know what I'm doing." He pulled a switchblade from his pocket and grinned. "I've got this if I need it."

"Good boy."

He bent down to kiss her on the cheek.

"I'll see you later, Mum."

"See you later, Roma."

Chapter 31

Josh swallowed his mouthful. and looked longingly at the remainder of the quiche Lorraine that sat invitingly in the middle of the table.

"Do you mind if I finish it off, Mum?" He turned to his girlfriend. "Unless you want it, Leanne?"

"No, I'm fine. You have it."

He turned back in time to see his younger brother sliding the last slice onto his plate.

"Eh! What are you doing? I wanted that."

"I'm a growing boy," Noah said with a grin. "I need my nourishment."

"You could at least share it, half-pint."

Noah picked his plate up, licked the top of the quiche, and stared across at his brother.

"Do you want some now, Joshy-baby?"

Why was it that when Leanne called him Joshy he felt warm and loved, but when his brother did it all he wanted to do was swipe out at the little twerp?

"That's not very nice, Noah," their mum said.

"It is," he said, as he put a forkful of her creation into his mouth. "It's delicious."

"That's not what I meant, and you know it."

Noah was still looking at Josh, and the grin hadn't left his face.

"It's a case of losers, weepers, finders, keepers." He paused. "And you, big brother, are the loser."

"You're being childish."

"No, I'm not."

"Yes, you are."

"No, I'm not."

"Yes, you are. You're fourteen and acting like you're

seven."

"And you're the real man, are you?"

"I am indeed. Do you know where I was today?"

"Flinchers?"

"It's Filchers, and no, I was at Avon and Somerset Police's head office."

"Did they arrest you for impersonating a grown-up?"

Josh puffed his chest out. "I was receiving police training, as it happens."

For once, Noah looked genuinely impressed.

"You were? What, in how to arrest people and the like?"

"Ah… Kind of, yes."

"Joshy, you're exaggerating," Leanne said, and addressed her next comment to Noah. "He was learning how to log onto their computers."

"It was more than that," Josh squealed. "I can access the Police National Database now, look perps up, that sort of thing. I'm going to be interviewing suspects, too."

"That *is* impressive," his mum said. She looked at her other son. "You've got to admit that's impressive, Noah."

"I suppose."

She turned back to Josh.

"Who will you be working for?"

"Still the guv, but also the DCI in charge of Operation Tooting." He tapped his nose. "It's a top-secret investigation, and I can't reveal what we're looking into."

"Drug dealers," Leanne said. "It's common knowledge."

"Leanne!"

"So what's this DCI like?" his mum asked.

"Very young to be a DCI. Attractive too."

Leanne turned in her chair so that she was facing her boyfriend and looked him straight in the eyes.

"Really?"

He nodded, completely oblivious to the message she was sending him.

"Attractive?" she went on.

"Yes… Oh."

He swallowed as it dawned on him that he'd done it again.

Open mouth, insert foot.

That was him.

Every time.

Would he never learn?

"Ah…"

"Is this DCI a man or a woman?" Noah asked.

He turned to face his brother.

"A woman, numbnuts. I wouldn't have said I found her attractive otherwise.

"Oh," Leanne said. "It isn't just that she's generally attractive. *You* find her attractive. My boyfriend finds her attractive."

"No, definitely not."

"But you just said you did," Noah said.

"Yes, you did," his mum added.

Now he had all three against him.

"I, ah… She's attractive for her age. Yes, that's what I meant. Not my type, but attractive for an old woman."

"How old is she, Josh?" his mum asked.

He shrugged. "Early thirties, perhaps."

"And that makes her an old woman?"

"Ah…"

He now had his girlfriend and mother staring daggers at him, while his brother was grinning through the last mouthful of the quiche that should rightfully have been his.

He was not having the best of evenings.

Then, he heard a snort from his left, followed by another from his right.

Within seconds, his girlfriend and mother were laughing fit to burst.

"You're nasty to me," he said.

His mum wiped her eyes and stood up.

"Anyone for dessert? I've made apple crumble."

"Yes, please," Josh and Noah said in unison.

"A small piece for me please," Leanne said.

"Any other news?" his mother asked, once they'd all finished their puddings.

"We're going to The Olive Tree for a meal on Saturday," Josh said.

"That's an expensive place. Are you celebrating something special?"

"No, nothing like that," Josh said hastily. "Fancied a special meal, that's all. Didn't we, Leanne?"

"It was your idea."

"Ah… Yes. Changing the subject completely, how's Nathan?"

Leanne raised one eyebrow. "My dad's fine. Why do you ask?"

"Just a polite enquiry. And he's at home all week, is he?"

"Yes. Mum is too. That's where they generally are. It's where they live."

"Good. Right. Gotcha. Is there any more crumble, Mum?"

Chapter 32

Luke and Sam were halfway to the office, and neither had said much since they'd left Norton St Philip. Normally, their silence was companionable, but he sensed a chill in the air, and he was sure it had to be his fault.

But what had he done wrong?

They'd had a pleasant enough evening: a decent cottage pie, which he'd prepared, followed by a binge-watch of three episodes of 'Shetland'.

Then, this morning, they'd had a couple of boiled eggs each, and briefly discussed the fact that Lily was rejoining the team.

He hadn't mentioned her confrontation with the woman at Stairway, deciding it would be better to leave Sam to raise it if she wanted a shoulder to cry on or simply to talk it through.

She hadn't.

Was that his mistake?

He glanced over and saw that she was staring fixedly out of the side window.

This was no good. He couldn't let her stew on things like this. She was obviously upset.

"Do you want to talk about it?"

She didn't ask 'about what', but that was understandable. It was clear what was troubling her.

She sighed.

"I wish I could."

"Look, this woman clearly upset you a lot. If you need to get things off your chest, I'm here for you."

"It's not…"

She hesitated.

"It's not what?"

Sam shook her head.

"It's not… It wasn't Jenny that upset me. I mean, I wasn't exactly pleased that she thought that of me, but something else happened."

"What, Sam? You can tell me."

"I can't, that's the thing." She paused. "Can you pull over?"

"Sure."

There was a parking area a few hundred yards further on, and Luke turned in, stopping the car behind an open-sided café-on-wheels carrying a large sign above the serving hatch reading 'A Dish called Wanda'.

He turned to face her, grabbed her hand and gave it a squeeze.

"What happened, Sam?"

She looked into his eyes.

"You're going to have to trust me on this, Luke."

"Of course. I trust you completely."

She sighed again, even deeper this time.

"The reason I've been distant is nothing to do with Jenny. Sebastian, Stairway's CEO, asked me to help with a personal issue. I did, and everything has turned out okay, but he made me promise not to tell anyone."

"Why you, though? He only met you for the first time the day before yesterday."

"When I first rang him, I said something which he wrongly interpreted as me knowing his secret. He then blurted it all out to me, and I offered to help."

"Is this something to do with his sexuality?"

Sam gave a half-laugh.

"You couldn't be further from the truth."

"But if it's all been resolved, why is it still upsetting you?"

"Because what happened wasn't very nice." She hesitated. "That's an understatement. It was bloody awful."

"And you're sure there's nothing I can do to help?"

"No… Well, yes. Listening to me now is helping no end. All I ask beyond that is that you bear with me while my mind processes what happened, and forgive me for not telling you anything."

He smiled.

"There's nothing to forgive, Sam. You promised him you wouldn't share his secret, so you have no choice other than to keep it to yourself."

"Thanks for being so understanding."

"No problem."

He gestured to the dirty van they were parked behind.

"Fancy a greasy burger?"

She laughed. "No."

"Good. Neither do I."

He took his hand from hers and put the car into drive.

"Right, let's get into work and see what joys Filchers has in store for us."

Fifteen minutes later, they entered the Ethics Room to see that the three other members of the team were already in and hard at work.

Maj and Josh were sitting side by side, while Helen was standing at the whiteboard. She'd stuck three colours of Post-its to it and was staring at them and occasionally moving them around.

"Hi, you two," she said. "You couldn't give me a wee hand, could you, Luke?"

"Of course. Just let me dump my coat and bag."

A couple of minutes later, he joined her.

"What's all this, then?"

"A woman by the name of Peggy Livingstone left a voicemail overnight. She raised a concern about misleading advertising."

"In one of our accounts?"

"No, by Filchers itself."

Luke was surprised.

"I didn't even know we ran adverts."

"We don't. What she said was that we're making false claims online about the savings we make for our clients."

"Did she give any details?"

"No, and she didn't leave a number either. There's no Peggy Livingstone in our directory, so she's not an employee." She pointed to the Post-its. "I've been trawling through our website seeing where we mention savings, and as you can see it's just about everywhere, multiple times for each of our seven sectors. Without speaking to her further, it's like looking for a needle in a haystack."

"Is there anything that strikes you as out of line?"

"This government sector claim seems odd," she said, pointing to a yellow Post-it on which she had written '*Border Force*' at the top, and underneath '*Overheads down 60%?*'.

"And also, these two in the Telecomms sector…"

She indicated two orange Post-its, one headed '*Cablecom*' and the other '*Hills plc*'.

"The trouble is," she went on, "all this is, is me guessing what's out of line. Do you think I should carry on, or leave it for now unless and until she rings back in again?"

Luke scratched his chin.

"I suggest you spend today on it, to see if you unearth anything that's truly out of kilter, although judging by the number of Post-its, it's not going to be an easy job. Why not ask Sam if she can give you a hand?"

"Good idea. I'll do that."

"Once you've done as much as you can, take your thoughts to Fred Tanner and see what he thinks. As Head of Marketing, he ought to be able to confirm what's genuine and what's not."

Chapter 33

It was almost eleven when Leanne rang from reception to say that Lily had arrived.

Luke went downstairs to find the two women deep in conversation. Lily turned when she saw him and smiled.

"Hi, Luke."

He returned her smile.

"Hi, Lily." They shook hands. "Thanks for saying you'll help us out."

"It's a pleasure. I was delighted when Josh rang." She turned back to Leanne. "I'll catch you later, Leanne, and give you more details."

They walked to the lift.

"I was telling her all about the proposal," she said, as they waited for it to arrive.

Luke raised one eyebrow, looked briefly back towards reception and lowered his voice. "Why would you do that?"

"Why wouldn't I? It's a once-in-a-lifetime opportunity."

The lift doors opened, and Luke gestured for Lily to enter, but before she could do so there was a loud harrumph behind them. It was a sound Luke recognised only too well.

Lily turned around.

"Are you okay, sir?"

Filcher was dabbing the end of his not-inconsiderable nose with a silk handkerchief.

"I'm fine, young lady."

"Are you sure, because that cough sounded chesty?"

"Mmm."

He refolded his handkerchief, inserted it back into the top pocket of his pin-striped jacket, and then pushed between them and walked into the lift.

Lily and Luke followed him in.

"New team member?" Filcher said, indicating Lily with a nod of his head.

"This is Lily," Luke said, as he pressed the buttons for the third and fourth floors. "I've told you about her before. She helps us out occasionally. Lily, this is Edward Filcher. He's my boss."

"Director of Internal Affairs," Filcher said, puffing his chest out as he said it. "Senior position. Report to the Board." He looked Lily up and down. "This is good, Luke. Get them young, before they, you know…"

Luke shook his head. "No, I don't know."

"Ah… Settle."

"Like snow?" Lily asked.

Filcher ignored her.

"Assets," he said. "Valuable assets. Until…" he held his hand palm-down above his waist and swung it out in an arc before returning it to the top of his trousers.

"Until we have babies?" Lily suggested.

"Indeed."

The lift stopped at the third floor and the doors opened.

"After you," Luke said.

They stepped out and Lily turned around to look back at Filcher.

"Nice to meet you, Mr Filcher," she said. "I'll try not to get pregnant during this assignment."

Filcher nodded his approval.

"Good girl, Tilly. Good girl."

The lift doors closed.

Lily turned back to Luke.

"Wow!"

"If you think he's a challenge, wait until you meet Glen."

"Glen?"

"Glen Baxter. I'll explain later, but first, tell me why you told Leanne about Josh's plan."

"Josh's plan?"

"Yes. You said you told her all about the proposal."

"The..." Lily's smile returned, and it was even broader this time. "Is Josh going to propose?"

"You said you knew?"

Lily laughed.

"I was telling Leanne about the part I've got in a regional tour of *'The Proposal'*. It's a theatrical version of the film that starred Sandra Bullock and Ryan Reynolds." She paused. "So Josh is going to propose, is he? Do you know when?"

"Saturday evening. He's taking her to a posh restaurant in Bath."

"Good for him."

They entered the Ethics Room and the other three team members walked over to greet her.

"It's great you're working with us again," Josh said. He tapped the side of his nose. "And when you've got a moment, I'd like to ask your advice on something."

"Work-related or engagement-related?"

"Engagement-re... Hey! How did you know?"

"We all know," Helen said. "The only person in the dark is Leanne."

Josh smiled at Lily. "You're an actor."

"Aye. I think she knows that," Helen said.

"What I mean is, if Lily can pretend to be Leanne, I can try the whole one-knee business and practice my words."

"You definitely need to practice them," Lily said with a laugh, "if your idea of romance is to describe your proposal as 'the whole one-knee business'."

"Would you mind, though?"

"Of course I don't mind."

"Thanks."

"Right, Lily," Luke said. "I suggest we pop to the canteen, and I can explain what I need you to do."

Tiger Bait

Five minutes later, they were seated by one of the canteen windows, Luke with a black coffee and Lily with a glass of sparkling water.

"Congratulations on getting a part in '*The Proposal*' by the way."

"Thanks. I'm not the lead, but I'm in a few scenes so it's a real breakthrough."

"That's great news." He took a sip of his drink. "How much did Josh tell you?"

"Not much. He said it was something to do with amateur dramatics, but that's about it."

"Yes, it's Filchers Amateur Dramatics Society, called FADS for short. Someone is harassing members, and we need to find out who it is and put a stop to it."

"What sort of harassment?"

"It's all electronic, a mixture of emails and social media posts. Some of it includes information that only a member of FADS would know."

"You mentioned someone called Glen?"

"He's the one who highlighted the issue."

"You suggested he can be challenging."

Luke smiled. "He can be, but I don't think you'll have much difficulty dealing with him, not going by the way you handled Filcher."

"Is Glen a chauvinist as well?"

"Most definitely, but he's also…" He stopped talking.

"Also what?"

He lowered his voice.

"…not the brightest."

"Change the bulb."

Luke turned in his seat to see Glen Baxter standing behind them.

Chapter 34

"What did you say, Glen?" Luke asked.

"If a bulb's not the brightest, then change it. You need more lumens."

This was said almost absent-mindedly as Glen took in the attractive young woman on the opposite side of the table.

"Or is it watts?" he went on. "It's one or the other."

He held out his hand.

"I don't think we've been privileged."

Glen was gazing directly into her eyes, although Luke had the distinct impression he was finding it hard to resist looking a foot or so lower.

She smiled.

"No, we haven't met. I'm Lily."

"How perfidious."

"Perfidious?"

He nodded and grinned, displaying a full set of brilliant white teeth.

"Perfect and delicious. Your name sounds like the flower." He hesitated. "Now, what's its name?"

"Lily."

"That's it. There are other flowers used as people's names, but they're not as perfidious as yours." He paused, and Luke could almost see the cogs going around. "Rose is one. Daisy too. Not forgetting McDougalls."

"I believe we're going to be working together, Glen."

"How delightful. It's lovely to think you and I will be under covers together."

He slid into the chair next to Luke and opposite Lily, his teeth still on display.

"I believe you're a professional actor, Lily."

"Yes, and I love it. It's a real thrill performing in front of a live audience."

Glen nodded. "I agree. I'm semi-professional myself."

"Are you?"

"Yes. And the production FADS is currently putting together suits me down to the ceiling."

"The ground."

Glen dived off his chair to look for whatever it was that she'd dropped.

"No, I meant it suits you down to the ground."

"Oh!"

There was a bang as part of Glen collided with the underneath of the table, and he emerged with his hand to the top of his head. After looking at his fingers, to check he wasn't bleeding, he grinned again, his sparkly whites back on show.

"As I was saying, this production is ideal for me. Taking clothes off is a speciality of mine."

Lily raised one eyebrow.

"He's in an outfit called the Chippenmales," Luke explained.

"I see." She turned back to Glen. "'*Privates on Parade*'?"

He looked down at his trouser zip to check it was done up.

"No," Lily went on. "I meant, is the play FADS is working on '*Privates on Parade*'?"

He shook his head.

"It's '*The Full Monty*'. I'm playing Guy. The part could almost have been written for me."

"Guy?" Lily asked incredulously. "I didn't realise you were…"

"…muscular and well built? Oh, yes." He raised his right arm and flexed his bicep. "I work out, you know."

"Do you? I'd never have guessed."

"I have a high-protein diet which is handy because in the play I have to eat a lot."

Lily looked confused.

"Eat a lot?"

"Yes. There's one scene where a character remarks on how big Guy's lunchbox is."

Luke decided to move the conversation on before it got completely out of hand.

"Glen, would you mind running through your concerns?"

"Of course not. Top of my list is growing my team to sixty."

Luke sighed.

"I meant your concerns regarding the online trolling."

"Oh. Right. Yes. I first became aware of the issue when a photo of me was posted on a members-only Facebook group."

Lily pulled a notepad and pen out of her handbag.

"Do you mind if I take notes?"

"Not at all."

"When was this?"

"About four months ago."

"And what's the name of the Facebook group?"

"Posers UK. The thing is, it wasn't me at all, or at least not entirely. Someone had put Donald Trump's head onto my body."

"I see."

"I knew it was my body because it said 'My name is Glen' just below the belly button."

"They'd added it in Photoshop?" Lily suggested.

"No. It's a tattoo." He reached for his shirt buttons. "Do you want to see it?"

Lily shook her head.

"Definitely not."

"They also made insulting and rude comments in the post, saying that I took steroids to bulk myself up."

"Did they tell lies as well?" Luke asked.

The sarcasm went straight over Glen's head.

"Yes. They accused me of being a convicted burglar, which is absolute nonsense. I've never taken anything in my life."

"Aside from the steroids," Lily suggested.

"Exactly. They also said things about my mother which were untrue. Hurtful too."

"And you had no idea who had posted this?" Luke asked.

Glen shook his head. "Absolutely none. I asked Meta to take the post down, but they refused. Something to do with the first amendment to their contribution." He hesitated. "Or was it constipation?"

"Could it have been constitution?" Lily suggested.

"That was it. They said it would be denying free speech."

"And were there more posts after that first one?"

"Yes. Every week there are one or two more. Not just on Posers UK either. There are nude photos of me posted on other Facebook groups as well, including Bodies-R-Us, Special-Ceps and 8-Pack."

"Always with Donald Trump's head on your body?"

"No. Sometimes it's women. Mother Theresa was one. And the comments have become worse and worse. Whoever's doing this should be done for their libido." He hesitated. "Or is it slander?"

"The word you're searching for is libel," Luke said. "When we talked the other day, you mentioned that other people in FADS had been targeted."

"That's right. After the first three weeks, I confided in Anthony, and he told me the same thing had happened to him."

"Anthony?" Lily asked.

"Anthony Baddington. And he told me that Mary Hesketh and Inigo Daniels had the same problem."

Lily noted the three names down.

"And these are all in FADS?"

Glen nodded. "Anthony and Mary are actors, and Inigo's the director. The four of us got together last week and realised it had to be someone in FADS. That was when I decided to ask Luke if one of his team could look into it."

"Do they know you've come to me?" Luke asked.

"No."

"Good. Let's keep it that way. There's nothing to say one of those three isn't the guilty party and faking attacks on themselves to put the scent off." He paused. "Glen, I think the best way forward is for you to introduce Lily as someone who wants to join FADS. Would Inigo be the best person for her to meet? You said he's the director."

"Yes, that makes sense." He turned to Lily. "What shall I tell him your name is?"

"Lily Newport."

"I meant your stage name. I'm Glen Gloss when I'm with the Chippenmales." He smiled, clearly proud of himself. "It's because I shave my chest and apply olive oil before every performance to make me look silky."

"I think you mean 'silly'," Luke suggested.

Glen shook his head.

"No. Silky. Definitely silky."

"I think it's best if Lily uses her real name. And you can tell Inigo she works for the Ethics Team. There's no point in lying where we don't need to."

"Shall I tell him she's a professional actor as well?"

"No, Glen. Please don't tell him that."

Chapter 35

Luke noticed that Lily couldn't stop herself from smiling as they walked back from the canteen.

"You look amused. I take it you didn't find Glen as much of a challenge as I feared you would."

She laughed.

"He's hilarious. And when he said the part of Guy could have been written for him." She shook her head. "He clearly doesn't realise Guy is gay, and that he's going to have a kissing scene with whoever's playing Lomper."

"I'd like to be a fly on the wall when that happens."

Luke paused as he reflected on what he'd just said.

"Actually, no I wouldn't. In fact, the very thought makes me feel nauseous."

"What would you like me to do while I'm waiting for this meeting with Inigo, the director at FADS?"

"Please can you help Helen? She's struggling with an investigation into potentially misleading advertising."

"Okay, I'll do that."

When they reached the Ethics Room, Lily walked over to Helen who was standing beside the whiteboard, the entire surface of which was now covered in orange, yellow and green Post-its.

"Luke said you could do with a hand."

"Oh, you're a wee darling. That would be fantastic. You see this group here." Helen indicated six yellow Post-its to the right of the board. "If you could look each of these up…"

Luke left them to it.

He smiled across at Sam who had a faraway look in her eyes. She was still fretting, he could see that, and he wandered over.

"Are you okay?"

She looked up and tried to smile.

"Not quite, but I'm getting there."

"If you need to talk…"

She leaned forward and squeezed his hand.

"Thanks, Luke."

He returned to his desk and called Pete to see if there had been any developments. He answered straight away.

"Good timing, Luke. We've got two mid-level dealers in this afternoon and could do with you co-interviewing one of them."

"Alongside Nicole?"

Pete laughed. "No. I think she saw enough to let you off without a minder."

"That's something, I suppose."

"The plan is that you and I interview one, while DCI Franks and DS Morris interview the second."

"Are the people we're interviewing known to each other?"

"We believe they are, and that's her reason for getting them in at the same time."

"To see if they give something away. That's a good idea. What are their names?"

"Tyrone Goodwin and Reece Stevens."

"That's interesting. Reece Stevens is the man who was with Declan O'Brien when Flimsy McCoy overheard him talking about a possible murder."

"In that case, do you want me to see if I can swing it so that you and I interview Stevens?"

"Yes, please. What time do I need to be there?"

"One to one-thirty. They're due in for 2 pm and you know how DCI Franks likes prep time."

"And punctuality."

"Tell me about it."

Luke hung up and called Misty.

"Fucking hell," she said by way of a greeting, "It's only

been twenty-four hours. What do you think I am, Superwoman?"

"The reason I'm ringing, Misty, is because I'm interviewing Reece Stevens this afternoon."

"The geezer the blonde was banging?"

"The very same. Aside from the fact Flimsy told you he'd seen Declan O'Brien go into Stevens' house several times, is there anything else you know about him?"

"I know the snively weasel's scared of him."

"The snively weasel being Flimsy?"

"Right first time."

"Any idea why he's scared of Stevens?"

"Well, I'm guessing you're not interviewing him because he's a fucking philanthropist."

"No, we believe he's a mid-level drug dealer."

"Well, there's your answer, then. Flimsy's the turd at the bottom of the shitheap, and he'll be scared of all the bigger turds higher up. Stevens is probably his supplier."

"What about O'Brien? Do you believe he's in the same operation?"

There was a pause while Misty considered this.

"No. He's a thug pure and simple, I reckon."

"He's been in prison for armed robbery."

"There you go, then. From what I've heard he doesn't strike me as the sort who'd involve himself in drugs. Violence is more his style." She hesitated. "I'll wander down this evening and see if I can grab another word with the weasel, ask the slimy fucker why he lied to you."

"Do you mind ringing me afterwards?"

"No problem. I'll ask Flimsy about this guy Jay too, see if I can squeeze any more out of him."

"Thanks, Misty."

He hung up and walked back over to Sam.

"I'm needed in Portishead this afternoon. Are you okay to hold the fort?"

"Sure." She smiled, but it was strained. "So long as I'm

not having to sit in for you at one of Filcher's meetings."

"It sounds like you're feeling a bit better."

"A little, yes."

"Good. I'll see you later."

Luke was putting his coat on ready to leave when his phone rang. He looked at the screen before answering and was surprised to see it was Pete.

"Has something happened, Pete?"

"We've got a third dealer in this afternoon. Name's Mickey Wright."

"Same time?"

"Yes. DS Morris is going to interview him with Robbie, and DCI Franks asked if Josh could sit in with her to interview Goodwin."

Luke was shocked.

"She specifically asked for Josh?"

"Yes, she met him yesterday and something about him must have impressed her."

"That's good. It should be okay. Just a second."

He called over to Josh.

"Josh, can you come to Avon and Somerset HQ with me to sit in on an interview?"

"Wowza! Gucci!"

"I heard that," Pete said and chuckled. "I take it that's a 'yes'?"

"It is indeed. We'll see you in an hour or so."

Chapter 36

DCI Franks was already seated at the table in the centre of Operation Tooting's incident room when Luke and Josh arrived.

She glanced at the clock on the wall.

"Are we early?" Luke asked.

"Five minutes, but that's fine. The others will be here soon."

"Thanks for asking for me, ah… DCI Franks," Josh said.

She looked over at him for a second.

"Is this your first interview, Josh?"

"Yes… Ah… No."

"Which is it?"

"No. I interviewed Misty Mitchell, a Private Investigator."

"On your own?"

"Partly. Before the guv joined me."

"The guv?"

"It's what he likes to call me," Luke said.

"Because he was a DCI," Josh said.

Nicole raised one eyebrow. "You were a DCI, Luke?"

"I thought you knew."

"No. Pete said he worked with you, but not for you. Ah, here are the others."

Pete, DC Robbie Hammond and DS Morris sat at the table. The latter had salt and pepper hair and looked to Luke to be in his early fifties. He introduced himself as Cliff.

"Thanks, everyone," Nicole began. "As you know, we're seeing three men we are confident are dealers. Cliff, can you position yourself in the waiting area after we've finished here so that you can see how they react to each other?"

"Will do, Ma'am."

"Good." She looked around at the others. "It's highly likely these men will 'No Comment' their way through the interviews. However, I want us all to press hard, mention the other two and see if we can force something out of them. Pete, what do we know about these individuals?"

"Not a lot, Ma'am. They're known to the force, and Goodwin and Wright have both got records, but we've got nothing concrete on them."

"In that case, it's all the more important that we squeeze something out of at least one of them."

"What about throwing the name 'Jay' out there?" Luke suggested. "See if that provokes a reaction."

"Who's Jay?" DS Morris asked.

"He may be someone high up in the gang, possibly even at the top."

"The name was mentioned by a low-level dealer that Luke interviewed," Nicole said. "It may have been said as a deflection but yes, okay, let's throw the name at them to see if we get a bite." She paused. "Any questions?"

No one spoke.

"Good. We'll talk again after the interviews." She turned to Josh. "Come with me, Josh."

"Gotcha."

He stood up and followed her meekly out of the room.

Pete's phone rang.

"Hello. This is DI Gilmore." He paused for a few seconds. "Okay, I'll be down in a few minutes."

He ended the call and turned to the others.

"Stevens and Wright are already here. It seems that they arrived together."

"That's brazen of them," Luke said. "No sign of Goodwin then?"

"Not yet. I suggest we give it at least fifteen minutes to give the three of them a chance to see each other."

Chapter 37

"Let's go into room 4 and I'll explain your role, Josh," Nicole said as they entered the interview suite.

"Gotcha."

"And stop saying 'gotcha'."

"Gotcha... I mean, right. I won't say it, boss, ah... Ma'am... ah... DCI Franks."

She stopped walking and turned to face him.

"For heaven's sake, call me Nicole."

"Gotcha."

She sighed, closed her eyes for a split-second, and then pushed the door to interview room 4 open and marched in, Josh following behind.

"I'll sit over there." She indicated the seat on the far side of the table. "You sit next to me, and we'll put Goodwin opposite."

"Got..."

She glared at him.

"Right, ah..." He swallowed. "...Nicole."

"Good. But in front of the interviewee you refer to me as DCI Franks. Understand?"

He nodded, then bent his head to one side.

"Tell me, Nicole, are you a bad cop?"

"I beg your pardon."

"Not as in crooked. I'm sure you're not crooked."

"That's a blessing."

"I meant, as in good cop, bad cop. I was thinking that I could be all nice, offer him a drink, that sort of thing, while you have a real go. Give him that look you're so good at."

"What look?"

"The one where your eyebrows almost touch, like this." He frowned and looked her in the eyes. "It's very intimidating."

"I do that?"

"All the time. I can see DC Hammond's right scared of you."

"Is he?"

Josh nodded.

"DS Morris too, despite being about fifty years your senior." He smiled. "So, are you going to be a bad cop to my good cop?"

"Can I remind you that you are not a police officer?"

"No, right, but still…"

She considered what he'd said for a few seconds.

"Actually, why not give it a go?"

Josh grinned.

"And don't say 'gotcha'."

His grin grew wider.

There was a knock at the door, and a uniformed constable walked in.

"Tyrone Goodwin's here, Ma'am."

"Can you show him in, please?"

"Will do."

She left the room.

"You kick off by offering him a drink, Josh, and we'll take it from there. Okay?"

"Gotcha."

The PC returned a minute or so later and held the door open for a man who Josh judged to be in his mid-twenties. He was black, with a completely shaved head, a full beard and the word 'Mum' tattooed on his neck. He also wore his swagger as if it was a uniform.

Josh stood up, smiled and offered his hand.

"Hi. Tyrone, isn't it? I'm Josh. Nice to meet you."

Tyrone looked briefly back and sniffed, but didn't take the offered hand.

"Please…" Josh gestured to the seat opposite Nicole. "…take a seat. Can I get you a cup of tea or coffee?"

"Nah."

Tyrone pulled the seat out from under the table, and descended into it so that his buttocks were on the very front edge while his body was reclined back at 45 degrees. He looked decidedly uncomfortable, but it was clear that he was making a statement.

And the statement was along the lines of, *'I'm relaxed and haven't got anything to hide, and I'm not frightened of anyone, least of all you'*.

Tyrone shifted his feet, and for a moment it appeared that he would go a step further and put them on top of the table, but he contented himself with another sniff before appearing to spot DCI Franks for the first time.

He looked her up and down and then looked back at Josh.

"Who's ya bitch?"

Nicole slammed her fist onto the table, causing Josh to jump and Tyrone to almost slide off his chair.

"I don't care to be called a bitch, Mr Goodwin!"

Josh was pleased to see that she accompanied this with one of her 'looks', and it seemed to have the desired effect.

"Nah," Tyrone said. "I was meaning you is fit, that's all, innit?"

She continued glaring at him and pressed the record button beside her.

"Interview with Tyrone Goodwin at 13:55 on Thursday, 6th March," she said, her eyes never leaving his. "Also present are DCI Nicole Franks and Josh Ogden."

She paused for a second before continuing.

"What's your full name?"

"Tyrone Power Goodwin."

"Date of birth?"

"25th June 2001."

"And how long have you dealt drugs?"

"I don't."

"That was harsh, DCI Franks," Josh said, looking at

Nicole and shaking his head.

He turned back to the interviewee.

"I'm sure you don't deal drugs, Tyrone. You look like a law-abiding person to me." He pointed to the other man's neck. "And you obviously love your mother."

Tyrone sniffed.

"All we want is to ask you a few questions," Josh went on, "and then you can get back to work. What do you do for a living, by the way?"

"This and that."

"This and that?"

"Yeah. Bits and bobs."

"Don't give us that shit," DCI Franks spat out. "You work for Jay, don't you?"

Tyrone's eyes widened for a second, enough for Josh to see that he recognised the name.

Josh turned to Nicole again.

"Just because he works for Jay, doesn't mean he deals drugs for him."

"Exactly," Tyrone said. "I do odd jobs. Don't deal. I'm a handyman, ain't I?"

"So Jay won't mind you being in here?" Nicole demanded. "He won't worry about his empire coming crashing down because we're onto you?"

"Why should he? I do DIY, I told you. Mend things. If things ain't right, I fix 'em."

"That's exactly what you do," she snapped. "You provide fixes. Class A fixes. Heroin, cocaine, crystal meth. The list goes on."

"Also harsh, DCI Franks," Josh said. "I'm sorry, Tyrone. My colleague's picking on your words and deliberately misinterpreting them."

"Yeah. Exactly."

"And I'm sure Jay really appreciates you being around, given the size of his house. There must be a lot of fixes needed."

Tyrone sniffed again.

"Yeah."

"And I imagine you're a lot cheaper than handymen around where he lives. Expensive area, that."

"Yeah." Tyrone had half an eye on Nicole, wary that she might bang her fist again. "Clifton's right pricey, innit?"

"Especially that part of Clifton."

"Yeah. Royal York Crescent's proper lah-di-dah. Must have cost him a mill or two."

Josh shook his head. "Alright for some, isn't it? What about you, Tyrone? Do you make much from being a handyman?"

"A what?"

"You said you're a handyman."

"Oh, yeah."

"So do you earn a good living from it?"

"Enough."

"Does Reece also work for Jay?" Nicole asked.

"Who?"

"Reece Stevens. Don't pretend you don't know him. Does he also run drugs for Jay?"

Tyrone glanced over at Josh, who was still smiling, then back at Nicole.

"Well?" she asked again, her voice raised. "Does he?"

"I want a solicitor. I ain't saying nothing else without a solicitor."

"Do you know Mickey Wright?"

"No comment."

"What about Flimsy McCoy?"

"No comment."

Nicole sat back and smiled.

"Interview ended at…" She looked at her watch. "…14:15."

Chapter 38

Luke and Pete decided to keep Reece Stevens waiting, in the hope it would put him on edge, and it was a quarter past two before he was brought into room 2.

He was a tall man, perhaps 6ft 2 or 6ft 3, and had an arrogant air, his good looks and height serving to boost his sense of self-importance. It was also clear that the wait to be summoned hadn't lessened his opinion of himself.

Luke stood up as Stevens approached the table, so that the other man could see that he had the better of him by three or four inches. It was a small gesture, but he had found in the past that it helped put suspects in their place.

"Please sit down, Mr Stevens," Pete said. "May I call you Reece?"

"You can call me King Charles if you like," he said with a sneer. "No skin off my nose."

He and Luke took their seats, and Pete clicked the record button.

"Interview with Reece Stevens in Interview Room 2 at Avon and Somerset Police HQ. Also present are Luke Sackville and DI Pete Gilmore. The time is 14:19."

"You're quite the womaniser, Reece," Luke said, once they'd captured his personal details.

Stevens smiled as if to say, *'I'm successful at it as well'*.

"And you don't mind if they're married, I believe. Tell me, have you got a special thing for blondes? Or is it only blondes who are married to much older men?"

The interviewee's smile broadened.

"Have you two brought me in for advice? Is that what this is?" He looked from Luke to Pete, and then back to Luke. "Not getting any at home, boys?"

"Funnily enough," Luke said, "We haven't brought you

Tiger Bait

in as a sexual counsellor, have we, DI Gilmore?"

"Indeed not," Pete said. "We've got much more serious matters to ask you about."

Luke leaned forward over the table and glared at the other man.

"Listen, Reece. Your petty meddling with drugs doesn't interest us in the slightest. You're right down at the bottom of the heap. We're after the big boys."

"I'm a…"

Stevens stopped himself just in time.

"You're a what?"

"Nothing."

"No, the reason we've brought you in is for something much more serious than low-level drug distribution."

"Oh, yes? What's that then?"

"Murder."

"Don't be fucking stupid." He nodded his head towards the door. "I saw Mickey out there. I know why you've pulled me in."

"How well do you know Declan O'Brien?"

Luke saw that this had come as a shot out of the dark, and that while Stevens had prepared himself for questions about drug dealing, he hadn't expected O'Brien to be mentioned.

"Who?" he managed to say, trying but failing to maintain his composure.

It was Luke's turn to smile.

"You can't fool us, Reece. He told you there might be three killings in the offing, didn't he?"

Stevens shook his head.

"I don't know what you're talking about."

"And I don't believe you, Reece. If O'Brien's done something bad, and believe me, we know how evil he can be, you're there with him, supporting him, aren't you? We know you and Declan are like brothers."

"What do you mean, we're like brothers?" Stevens

shook his head. "You're not pinning anything he's done on me."

"You admit you know him, then?" Pete asked.

"We've met, yes. Once or twice. But I don't work with him. He's one crazy bastard."

"But," Luke said, "you both work for Jay, don't you?"

Stevens' eyes widened. It was a clear tell.

"No comment."

"You deal drugs for him, don't you? Farming it out to others, and taking a healthy cut for your efforts?"

"No comment."

"But you're not at the bottom of the heap. That was my mistake. You're more of a middleman. Am I right?"

"No comment."

"Is your patch Brislington?" Pete asked.

"No comment."

"What's your main earner?" Luke asked. "Heroin or crack, or is it something else entirely? I heard MDMA's big at the moment."

"No comment."

Luke and Pete exchanged a look.

"Interview ended at 14:37," Pete said, and clicked the button to stop recording.

*

DCI Franks, DS Morris, DC Hammond and Josh were already seated around the incident room table when Luke and Pete returned.

"How did it go?" Nicole asked as they sat down.

"Very well," Pete said.

"Ours too." She turned to her Sergeant. "Cliff, could you summarise your interview with Mickey Wright?"

"It won't take long, Ma'am. Unfortunately, we didn't get much out if him. He's a cocky little sod and went straight into no comment-ing."

"He reacted to the mention of Jay though, Sarge," DC Hammond said.

"Yes, he did, Robbie. Still no-commented, but it was clear he knew who he was."

"It was the same with Tyrone Goodwin," Nicole said. "Pete, did your man do the same?"

Pete nodded. "Yes, Stevens knows Jay alright."

"He also admitted he knows Mickey Wright," Luke added, "and Declan O'Brien as well."

"O'Brien? You're still ploughing that furrow are you?"

Luke smiled. "Yes, Nicole. I am."

"The real breakthrough we made," she went on, "and this is down to Josh…" She glanced at Josh whose cheeks immediately started to go pink. "…is that Goodwin told us where Jay lives."

"That was a major slip-up," Pete said. "I can't imagine his boss being pleased if he finds out." He looked at Josh. "How did you manage to get that out of him?"

"I asked him, that's all."

"You're being modest," Nicole said, then turned back to Pete. "Josh established a relationship with him, and they started chatting as if they were best buddies. He laid a trap and Goodwin dropped straight into it."

"So where does he live, Josh?" DS Morris asked.

"Royal York Cresent in Clifton. He didn't say what number though."

"It shouldn't take long to find out," Nicole said. "Robbie, see if you can find him on the electoral register."

"Will do, Ma'am."

She stood up, the meeting clearly over.

"Nicole," Luke said, "can I have a word?"

She looked at her watch before answering.

"What is it?"

"Is there somewhere we can talk privately?"

"If this is about Declan O'Brien again…"

"It isn't."

She sighed.

"Okay. We'll return to the interview suite. But you'll need to keep it brief."

Five minutes later they were back in interview room 2.

Nicole walked in ahead of him, turned and stood ramrod straight with her back to the wall.

"What do you want, Luke?"

"Why don't we sit down?"

"I told you, I haven't got long."

"And that's part of the problem."

"Problem? What do you mean, problem? I'm the SIO on this investigation and I can't afford to waste time with, with…" She gestured to him.

"Being nice to your team?" Luke suggested.

She glared at him.

"What's that supposed to mean?"

"Nicole, can I speak frankly?"

"I think you already are."

He sighed. This was going to be even harder than he'd anticipated.

"Well, I'm going to sit down, even if you're not."

He sat at the table and, after a shrug of her shoulders, she walked across and took the chair opposite.

He smiled.

It wasn't returned.

"That's another problem," he said. "You never smile."

"What on earth is this about?"

"Don't get me wrong. You're an excellent detective, Nicole."

"Am I supposed to be flattered?"

"Hear me out. The first thing Pete told me when he said you were running Operation Tooting was how smart you are. I've heard it from others, too, and it's clear the chief constable of Wessex Police rated you, otherwise you wouldn't have made DCI at such a young age."

He paused.

"However, I think you may be missing a trick."

She didn't respond.

"Please don't be offended, because all I'm trying to do is help, but I'm going to be blunt."

She sat back and crossed her arms.

"Nicole, you need to focus effort on spending time with the members of your team, and on being less abrasive and more friendly. You're their boss, but that doesn't mean you have to put them in their place all the time. The odd 'please' or 'thank you' wouldn't go amiss either. Try to relax. That's why I mentioned smiling. Believe me, the team will perform a lot better if they like you than if they're intimidated by you."

Her arms were still crossed, but she was at least listening.

"Is there anything else?"

"Yes. Try to avoid looking at them the way you do when they've made the slightest slip-up. I can see from their faces that it rubs them up the wrong way."

She swallowed, and he saw from her face that this last comment had hit the mark.

"Josh told me about that," she said, her voice slightly quieter. "He called it 'my look'. I'm not even aware I do it, but he said it's intimidating." She sighed. "He also said that Robbie's scared of me."

"As I said, Nicole, and I meant it, you're an excellent detective. All you need to do to be even better is behave more naturally. What we do is a serious business, but that doesn't mean you have to walk around as if you've got a broom handle up your bum."

She laughed at this, the first sign he'd seen of her lightening up, then looked him in the eyes.

"You might have a point."

He smiled again, and this time she smiled in return.

"I guess my first thank you should be to you, Luke.

What you've said makes sense. I'm sorry if…"

He held his hand up.

"Don't apologise." He stood up. "I was in the force for more than twenty years, Nicole. The least I can do is to help a colleague out. I hope you weren't offended by me approaching you like this."

"Not at all, Luke. Thanks again."

"Don't mention it."

Chapter 39

Tyrone was already under the bridge when Reece arrived, leaning nonchalantly against the stone archway, a cigarette between his lips.

He dropped the cigarette to the ground when he saw him, stubbed it out with the toe of his Nike sneakers, grinned, and held out his fist.

"Okay, bro'?"

They fist-pumped.

"Cool as," Reece said. "Seen Mickey?"

"Not yet. What's occurin', man?"

"Wanted to talk about this afto."

"No harm, but the pigs ain't got nothing on us. Not a fucking thing. No needs to worry."

"Still."

He paused as he saw Mickey Wright jogging towards them, the ever-present Bristol Rovers baseball cap perched back to front on top of his head.

Tyrone turned when he saw where Reece was looking, and held his fist out again.

"How's it hanging, Mickey?"

"Good, man. Good."

They fist-pumped.

"How'd it go for you, Mickey?" Reece asked.

"In Portishead?"

"Well, not on the fucking moon."

Mickey grinned, revealing a single gold incisor at the centre of his upper row of teeth.

"Fucking breeze. They got a big fat nothing on us, and they know it. All I did was 'no comment' my way through it. Didn't even bother with a solicitor." He shook his head. "Dunno what they dragged us in for anyways."

"All three of us at once is odd," Reece said. "Could be they're having a clampdown."

Tyrone nodded. "Could be. Next thing might be raids."

"Yeah," Mickey said. "Won't do 'em no fucking good though, not now we've got Annie's place."

"Did they ask either of you about Jay?" Reece asked.

"They said his name, yeah," Mickey said. "I didn't say nothing mind." He laughed. "Well, I did. I said 'no comment'."

"You, Ty?"

"Nah."

"What do you mean? They asked you, or that it didn't come up?"

"They asked, but I didn't say nothing. Same as Mickey."

There was a hesitancy in his response that made Reece think it hadn't been as straightforward as he was suggesting. However, he decided to let it pass.

He shook his head. "Not good that they know Jay's the main man."

"Yeah," Mickey said. "Likes to keep a low profile, don't he?"

Reece hesitated. "You two know Declan O'Brien?"

Tyrone shook his head.

"Nah. Who's he?"

"I know Declan," Mickey said. "Works for Lady Di, don't he? Your height, Reece, but broad with it. Hard bastard too. Don't take no prisoners." He gave a dry chuckle. "If he came round my pad and demanded money I'd pay it, no fucking hesitation. He'd have your knackers off in the blink of an eye."

"Why you askin'?" Tyrone asked.

"They asked me about him, too."

"What'd they say?"

"That he might have killed three people."

"Has he?" Mickey said, in an almost gleeful way that suggested he'd love it if the answer was 'yes'.

"Not that I know of, but he was boasting to me about a big money scam he's part of. Said it might mean taking out three people."

Tyrone raised an eyebrow. "And the pigs were specific about three? How the fuck would they know that?"

"Beats me."

"If he mouthed off to you," Mickey said, "Maybe he told others."

Reece shook his head. "No, he wouldn't do that. Me and Declan go way back. There's no one else he'd confide in."

"Could someone have been earwigging?"

"Nah. No way… Hang on, that crackhead Flimsy was there."

"Flimsy McCoy?" Tyrone said.

"Yeah. He was sat in the gutter. Both of us thought he was doped up and out of it, but maybe…"

"Fucking snitch," Mickey said, and then laughed. "Wouldn't like to be in his shoes if Declan finds out."

"Could he have heard anything else?" Tyrone asked.

Reece considered this for a moment. "It's possible."

"You should tell Declan," Mickey said. "Then he can sort Flimsy out once and for all."

"He'd probably kill the bastard."

"Wouldn't be a great loss," Tyrone said. "Especially if he's grassing on everyone."

Reece nodded. "You're right. I'll give Declan a bell."

"Good idea, man," Mickey said and grinned again. "Fuck, I'm glad I'm not in Flimsy's shoes."

"We done?" Tyrone asked. "I need to go to Annie's, pick up some gear."

"Me too," Mickey said. "Laters, Reece."

They all fist-pumped again and Reece watched as the other two walked away in the direction of Kingswood.

He pulled out his phone, then hesitated. The call he was about to make could well lead to the early demise of one

Flimsy McCoy.

But then the snivelly so-and-so had snitched to the police, so he deserved anything coming his way, and it wasn't as if he was going to be sorely missed by anyone.

He made the call.

"Good evening, Reece me boy," Declan said when he answered, his voice wavering slightly and a buzz of chatter in the background.

"How did it go?"

"Like clockwork." He lowered his voice. "Twenty grand I made, fucking twenty grand. I'm having a wee drink to celebrate."

"That's good, Declan. Did you have to, you know…"

Declan laughed. "No. A good craic it was. Smooth as silk."

"You remember telling me you might have to take three people out?"

"Yes, but as I said, there was no need."

"The thing is, the police know you said that."

"They what? I haven't said that to anyone else, Reece. Did you tell them?"

"Of course not. Do you know Flimsy McCoy?"

"No. Who the fuck's he?"

"He's a waste of space, that's what he is."

"And?"

"He was there when you told me, and he must have overheard and told the police."

"Do you know where I can find him?"

Reece gave him the details.

"Leave it with me," Declan said when he'd finished. "I'll have a wee word and make it clear I'm not very happy with him."

Chapter 40

Lily's phone rang.

She looked across at Helen.

"Hopefully, this is it."

"Aye, fingers crossed."

She accepted the call.

"Hello."

"Lily, it's Glen. Are you ready for intercourse?"

She couldn't help smiling. Despite having only met Glen the day before, she knew exactly what he meant.

"You've arranged for me to talk to Inigo?"

"I have. He's coming to Filchers for a meeting this afternoon, and suggested we meet for lunch. I thought we could go to Costa Coffee over the road."

"That would be great."

"Good. Shall we say 12:30?"

"That would be great. Ah, what's Inigo like?"

"I think you'll like him. He's flammable though."

This was a new one.

"He's flammable?"

"Yes. Theatrical. Extravagant."

"Ah, you mean flamboyant?"

"That's what I said."

"Thanks for arranging it, Glen."

"No problem. I'll see everything of yours at 12:30."

He hung up and Lily turned to Helen.

"I'm seeing the director at 12:30."

"That's grand news."

"In the meantime, I think we're making progress."

She walked over to the whiteboard.

"I think we can rule these out," she went on, pointing to two of the entries on green Post-its on the whiteboard.

Helen nodded. "I think you're right. What we need to do now is…"

She stopped speaking when she realised that Josh was standing to one side of them with his hand in the air.

Helen turned to face him.

"Do you need the toilet, Josh?"

"Ha, ha." He pulled his arm down. "Ah… I was wondering if… Could I, ah… borrow Lily?"

"Is this to practice what you referred to yesterday as 'the whole one-knee business'?" Lily asked.

Josh fired a finger-gun at her.

"Got it in one."

"Go on, away with you, you two," Helen said with a wave of her hand. "And you be honest with your feedback, Lily."

"Don't worry. I will be."

"Thanks, Helen," Josh said. He turned to Lily. "I booked the Royal Crescent Room on the ground floor. It's a massive meeting room, but it was the only one available and we can pretend it's The Olive Tree."

He led the way downstairs and was pleased to see Carys on reception, which meant Leanne had to be on a break.

They approached the door, and he held out his hand to stop her.

"You go in and sit in the middle along one side. I'll come in as if I've just come back from the loo, and we'll take it from there."

"Okay."

She went inside to find it was indeed a large room, with seating for sixteen around a rectangular glass-topped table.

She sat at one side next to two doors marked 'AV Equipment' and waited for Josh to enter.

*

Leanne was trying to concentrate on the problem at hand, but her mind kept returning to what Josh had said to her that morning.

His cheeks had been pink, always a sign that he was either embarrassed or being economical with the truth, and he'd revealed that he had something momentous to tell her. She'd pressed him, but he'd insisted that he wouldn't tell her until they were at The Olive Tree at the weekend. All he would say was that it would change their lives forever.

And then Lily had appeared.

Supermodel-attractive Lily, the person her boyfriend had once lied to her about, saying she had plain looks and heavily overweight.

He'd lied because he was worried she'd be jealous.

Or so he'd said.

Was it possible that he'd done so to put her off the scent?

She shook her head. Thinking like this was nonsense, absolute nonsense. He loved her, she knew he did.

And yet...

Josh had been acting so strangely. He was keeping something from her, she was sure of it.

She swallowed.

Was he going to dump her? Was that what Saturday was all about? She didn't think she could bear it if he did.

But what else could it be?

No, this was stupid. She needed to confront him, force him to tell her what he was hiding. Whatever it was, it had to be big, so big that he was only prepared to reveal it when they were out for a posh meal.

She tried to force her attention back to the audio-visual equipment. The client director who used The Royal Crescent Room the day before had reported a fault with the sound, but she couldn't for the life of her see what was wrong. There had to be a lead plugged in incorrectly, but which one? It needed to be fixed before the afternoon when Ambrose Filcher was presenting to potential investors.

It was no good. There had to be at least twenty different cables, and her mind was too befuddled with thoughts of Josh for her to think straight. Perhaps she'd be better asking Carys to take a look.

She was about to open the doors to return to the meeting room when she heard a voice.

And not just any voice, it was Josh.

He cleared his throat, then started speaking, his voice slightly deeper than normal.

"You're beautiful."

Leanne gasped and put her hand to her mouth.

"I knew from the moment we met," he went on, "that we should be together. I don't want this to end."

There was a clunk.

"I'm alright," he said, his voice back to its normal pitch. "I banged my knee on the table, that's all."

"No problem," a woman said. "What you're saying is lovely, Josh."

Leanne gasped again.

She recognised the voice immediately.

It was Lily.

"Shall I continue, or start again?" Josh said.

"Continue."

"Okay. Ah…" His voice deepened again. "I don't want this to end."

"You said that."

"Right… Ah… What we've got between us is wonderful. When I look into your eyes I know that you love me as much as I love you."

"Oh, Josh, that's so moving."

Leanne could have throttled Lily right there and then.

"Thanks," Josh said. He cleared his throat. "Will you do me the honour of being my bride?"

Leanne briefly considered storming through the doors

and laying into both of them, but she decided to wait until she'd heard Lily's response.

Though it was obvious from the way she'd been talking that she was going to say yes.

The bitch.

"Well?" Josh asked, again his voice oddly higher in pitch. "What do you think?"

Leanne put one hand back to her mouth as she waited on tenterhooks for Lily's response, her other hand on the door handle, ready to storm in as soon as she'd said 'yes'.

"I thought it was marvellous, Josh. Heartfelt and sincere. It almost brought tears to my eyes."

Cow.

"Leanne is going to say yes, of course she is."

Leanne was poised to pounce, to let them hear exactly what she thought, when Lily's words replayed in her mind.

"FUCK!" she said.

"Leanne?" Josh said.

She took a deep breath, opened the door and plastered a smile across her face.

"Hi."

"Are you alright?" Lily said. "Your cheeks are pink."

"I'm fine. I was, ah..." She turned to indicate the equipment in the room. "...trying to fix the AV kit. Are you two having a meeting?"

"Yes," Josh said. He looked at Lily and then back at Leanne. "Did you hear any of what we said?"

"No." She shook her head violently from side to side. "No. Definitely not. Can't hear a word from in there. Not a thing."

"That's a relief. Ah... I mean, not that it would have mattered. We were only talking about work matters, weren't we, Lily? About, ah..."

"Ethics," Lily suggested.

"Yes, that was it. I was explaining about it, about them. About ethics."

"Great," Leanne said. She indicated the meeting room door with her thumb. "I'd better be getting back to Carys."

She dashed past them and made her escape.

Chapter 41

"I'm off to see Inigo now," Lily said. "Wish me luck."

"Ach, you'll be fine," Helen said.

"I'm sure it'll go well," Josh said, "and thanks for earlier. I feel a lot more confident about the, ah…" He grinned. "…whole one-knee business."

"I'm pleased I could help."

Glen was at the reception desk talking to Leanne when she arrived downstairs. Josh's girlfriend looked across at her, and for some reason seemed slightly embarrassed.

"Are you okay, Leanne?"

It was Glen who answered.

"She's fine." He lowered his voice. "Leanne was just telling me that she's into it."

"Into it?"

He nodded.

"In a big way."

"He means I know about your pretence," Leanne said.

For a split second, Lily thought she meant Josh's practice session, but then it dawned on her what she meant.

"Josh told you about FADS?"

"Yes."

"Do you know Inigo?"

"Reasonably well, yes. He's in here every week or so, always talks about acting. The two of you will have a lot in common, except, well…"

"What?"

"He's very… How can I put it?"

"Flamboyant," Glen suggested. All his pearly whites were exposed, and he was clearly proud to have mastered a new word.

"Exactly. Over the top. Nice, mind, but very in your

face."

"I only hope he lets me join."

Lily turned to Glen.

"We'd better be heading over. It's almost 12:30. See you later, Leanne."

"He inhales your personal space," Glen confided as they made their way to Costa Coffee.

Lily was still trying to translate this little gem when Glen said, "There he is."

She followed his gaze to see a small, rotund man seated at a table next to the window. He was bald on top, with grey hair on either side, but what most set him apart was his pair of pince-nez spectacles.

He looked up from the book he was reading and shouted across the room, causing most people to look up at the sudden noise.

"Glen, Glen! Good to see you, old boy!"

Inigo stood up, removed his glasses, placed them on the book he'd been reading, and waddled over.

She was wrong about him being small.

He was tiny, not much more than 5 ft, and she was instantly reminded of Danny de Vito.

Rather than stay a yard or so away, and perhaps offer his hand in greeting, Inigo continued until his forehead was almost touching Lily's chin and then craned his head back and looked up at her.

"And you, gorgeous girl, must be Lily?"

She instinctively wanted to back away, but didn't want to appear rude.

"That's me."

"And you'd like to join FADS, I understand. Excellent, excellent."

He was no more than a few inches away, but was speaking loudly enough for the entire room to hear every word.

"I'll get lunch," Glen said. "What will you have, Lily?"

"A sandwich, please. Chicken and sweetcorn if they've got it."

"And you, Inigo?"

Inigo moved to one side, his face now inches from Glen's chest, and was forced to bend his neck back almost at right angles to catch the bigger man's eyes.

"Empanada."

Glen pulled a sad face.

"That's unfortunate. Is it painful?"

"He means he wants one of those," Lily said, pointing to a stack of empanadas beneath one of the counters.

"Oh, I see. So, that's a chicken and sweetcorn sandwich for you, Lily, and an I'm-a... Ah... an impala-da-da for you, Inigo."

He grinned, pleased with himself.

"I'll bring them over."

Lily followed Inigo back to his table, relieved that it would keep him a reasonable distance away. Initial impressions were that he was nice but, as both Glen and Leanne had suggested, very over the top.

She gestured to the book lying beneath his pince-nez spectacles.

"What's that you're reading?"

"The script, dear girl, the script."

"Of *'The Full Monty'*?"

"The very same. Wonderful production, and Glen will make an excellent Guy. Him being gay helps, of course."

He was still practically shouting every word, and this last sentence brought more looks from people at other tables.

"Is it the play, or the musical?"

"My, my. I'm impressed you know there are two versions. We will be performing the play."

"I'd love to have a part in it, Inigo, if that's possible."

"Of course it is. If it's not an impertinent question, how old are you, Lily?"

"Twenty-two."

"I see."

He opened the book and turned to the front where the characters were listed.

"You'll be aware that the majority of the characters are male, but... Ah, there is Mandy, of course."

"Gaz's ex-wife?"

"The very same. The challenge there is that you would be playing someone with an 11-year-old son."

He leaned over the table, squeezed Lily's cheek between his index finger and thumb, and then peered into her eyes from a distance of no more than five or six inches.

"A touch of make-up here and there, and I'm sure you'll be fine."

He called over to Glen, who was paying for their food some ten yards away.

"Lily will be Mandy."

This attracted more stares and a few mutters from other diners.

"Don't I need to audition?"

"No need, my dear."

He lowered his voice so that it was slightly below megaphone level.

"To be honest, finding actors is fiendishly difficult in Filchers."

"Sandwich," Glen said, passing Lily's plate to her, "and, Inigo, here's your, ah..."

He passed him his empanada without completing the sentence, then took a seat, putting his own plate on the table in front of him and the tray to one side.

"Are those all for you?" Lily asked, indicating the eight boiled eggs on Glen's plate.

He nodded.

"High protein. Low fat. Builds muscles."

He put a whole egg in his mouth and started chewing, all the while managing to maintain his grin, though fortunately his teeth were no longer on show.

She turned back to Inigo.

"How many in FADS?"

"Only ten of us, my dear. I'm continually looking for additions to our merry band but, as I said, it's difficult."

She watched as Glen popped a second egg in his mouth before continuing.

"Will you be acting as well as directing?"

"Oh, yes. I will be taking on the role of Gerald."

"The one with the gnomes," Glen said as he reached for his third.

"And does everyone in FADS get on well with each other?"

Inigo hesitated.

Glen swallowed audibly then said, as he picked up egg number four, "I told Lily what's been happening on social media."

Inigo shook his head.

"It's awful, and I can't understand the reasoning behind it. They had a real go at me on Facebook, called me all sorts of names. Very hurtful. But I'm sure you'll be okay, my dear."

"Who do you think is behind it?"

"Well, it has to be one of the ten, because of what's been said. Not Anthony or Mary though, I'm sure of that."

He looked over at Glen, who was deciding which of the remaining eggs should be next, though to Lily they all looked identical.

"Do you think it might be Ian, Glen?" Inigo asked. "Or even Sylvia? She and I often have our differences."

Glen shrugged.

"Could be either."

He inserted egg number five into his mouth.

"Ian's a definite possibility," Inigo went on. "He's playing Lomper, and was very annoyed when I told him he and Glen have a scene where they have to kiss.

There was a loud splutter as egg number five was spat back out onto the plate.

Chapter 42

Luke was compiling his monthly progress report for February. It was a total waste of time and energy, and he knew it would be filed but never read. However, Filcher insisted it was completed close to the end of each month, which meant he was already several days late.

He looked up when Lily returned from lunch.

"How did it go?"

"It went well. Inigo's nice, if a trifle eccentric, and I'm now a fully signed-up member of FADS."

"That's great. Any clues as to who the troll might be?"

She shook her head.

"There are ten in FADS, eleven now I've joined, but it's not going to be easy finding the culprit."

"Would it help if you ran through the options with the whole team?"

"Definitely."

"Good, because we've got a myriad of separate investigations on the go, and I think it would be useful if we all put our heads together."

And it means I can put that blessed report aside for the day.

He called to the others.

"Can you all join Lily and me at the table, please?"

They agreed, and a minute or so later everyone was seated.

"New project, guv?" Josh asked.

"No, but I'm conscious we've got several cases on the go, and ought to be working as a team rather than individually. I think it would be a good idea if we shared what we're up to."

He turned to Helen.

"I see you've cleared the whiteboard, Helen. What

happened?"

"I gave up on the approach I've been taking because it didn't seem to be getting me anywhere. Until I started looking into this, I didnae realise how much advertising Filchers does. It's everywhere."

"Okay. Well, it's handy you cleared it, because I'd like to use the board for the different projects we're working on."

"Including Tooting?" Josh asked.

Luke nodded.

"Yes, including Tooting."

He looked over at Helen again.

"Would you mind?"

"Not one bit."

She stood up, grabbed some marker pens, and walked to the whiteboard.

"Can you begin by separating the board into five sections please, Helen? One for each of the projects we've got on the go."

She drew four vertical lines in black.

"Thanks. Now can you write the project names at the top of each section? We'll start with Stairway."

She wrote Stairway at the top of the left-hand column.

"Shouldn't it have a project name?" Josh said.

"There's no need," Luke said, "and besides, it's almost finished. That's right, isn't it, Sam?"

She had been rolling her pen back and forward on her notepad, and it was only hearing her name that made her look up.

"What?"

"I said, you've almost finished the Stairway case."

"Oh… Ah, yes, that's right. Just a few loose ends to tie up."

He looked back at Josh.

"So, we'll stick with Stairway. Okay, son?"

"Sure," Josh said, but he slumped in his seat, clearly disappointed.

"Good. Helen, let's add your investigation into advertising. Josh, any ideas for a name for it?"

Josh immediately sat upright again.

"Loads." He turned to Helen. "It's about exaggerations in advertising, isn't it?"

She nodded.

"What about Project Hyperbole, then?"

"It's a mouthful," Maj said. "And a bit obvious."

"Baloney, then or… I know. Big Whopper?"

"People will think we're investigating Burger King," Helen said.

Josh tapped his nose.

"That's the point, isn't it? A project name needs to be unrelated to the subject matter so no one can guess. Like Operation Tooting."

"Okay," Luke said. "Let's go with 'Big Whopper'. And add Tooting as the third."

Helen wrote 'Big Whopper' and 'Tooting' at the top of columns 2 and 3.

"Next, we'll add Maj's We-Haul investigation."

"Project Douglas," Josh said. He turned to Lily. "I suggested it because the whistleblower's name is Fairbanks. See what I did there?"

She smiled but didn't say anything.

Helen added 'Douglas' at the top of column 4.

"And last, but not least," Luke went on, "there's your investigation, Lily. Josh, what bright ideas do you have for that one?"

Josh sat forward in his seat, thought for a moment, and then said, "Project Rainbow."

"Project Rainbow? Why Rainbow?"

"There you go. Unrelated, so no one can guess, but obvious too, if you're in the know. Richard of York gave battle in vain."

He looked around at the other members of the Ethics Team and was faced with blank looks all around.

After a few seconds, it was Lily who broke the silence.

"Hang on. Isn't that a way of remembering the colours of the rainbow?"

Josh grinned and fired a finger-gun at her.

"Exactimo. And I is for Indigo, which is like Inigo."

"Wow, that is lateral thinking," Maj said.

"Thanks," Josh said, taking this as a compliment.

"Rainbow it is," Luke said, and Helen added it at the top of the final column.

"Good." He read from left to right. "There we have it. Stairway, Big Whopper, Tooting, Douglas and Rainbow."

He looked over at Sam, who subtly shook her head, indicating that she didn't want to start with her project.

"I suggest we start with Project Rainbow. Lily, what are the names of the people who may have been trolling other members of FADS?"

Chapter 43

It took nearly two hours for the team to work through four of the projects on the whiteboard.

"I think that's all we can do on Big Whopper," Luke said when they'd finished, earning a double thumbs-up from Josh, a regular occurrence when one of his project names was mentioned.

Luke turned to Sam.

"Do you want to discuss Stairway, Sam?"

"There's no need. I'm sure everyone's had enough, and anyway, the case is finished now. Everything's resolved."

"Was there anything unethical going on?" Maj asked. "Any nasty business?"

Sam looked back at him for a moment and swallowed before answering.

"No. It was a false alarm."

"It took a lot of effort for a false alarm," Helen said. "Two trips to Bristol, and when you got back you looked like you'd been through the wringer."

Sam tried to smile, but it was a poor attempt.

"Yes. I thought I was onto something, but it was nothing."

"What did it turn out to be?" Josh asked. "Didn't you say money had been paid into someone's personal account?"

"It had, but it was done accidentally. As I said, it turned out to be a wild goose chase."

"Right, guys," Luke said, recognising that Sam was desperate for the subject to be closed down, "I think we're done. Thanks for your time. It's getting on for half-past five now. Why don't you all head home, so that you can get on with your weekends and return refreshed on Monday."

"Aye, I'm up for that," Helen said. She turned to Josh. "I hope all goes well tomorrow, Josh."

"Thanks." He stood up, grabbed his coat and followed Helen out, Lily and Maj close behind.

Sam remained seated and Luke looked across at her.

"Are you okay?" he whispered.

She sighed.

"Not really," she whispered back. "I think I'll ring Sebastian and check everything's okay."

He watched as she picked up her phone and left the Ethics Room.

She was down, very down, and he wished he could help, but he also understood that she had told Sebastian she wouldn't reveal his secret, and he wasn't going to press her into breaking that promise.

He sat back and looked up at the whiteboard. It had been a very productive session, and his team had once again proved their worth. Sam, who was usually full of ideas, had been the least participative, but even she had thrown in some real nuggets.

They'd spent longest on Big Whopper. Helen had summarised the potential cases of misleading advertising that she'd uncovered, and there had been over twenty of them. She and Lily had eliminated eight, Fred Tanner had helped her remove six more, and as a team they managed to rule out another four.

The problem was that there were still seven left, and they appeared to be borderline unethical, but no more than that, with the claims made by Filchers statistically accurate if questionable. As Josh had pointed out, what the company had said was similar to a toothpaste manufacturer claiming that 9 out of 10 customers preferred their product, while failing to mention that those 10 customers were all employees.

In the end, they'd decided that Helen should stop working on Big Whopper for the time being. She would pick it up again if Peggy Livingstone, the person who'd left the original voicemail, phoned back.

However, the bonus was that this meant Helen was free to help Lily with Project Rainbow, and no one doubted that the harassment in FADS was genuine. What's more, it was nasty and vindictive. Lily had been shown material by Glen and Inigo that included extremely distasteful doctored images accompanied by baseless accusations.

Finding the culprit wasn't going to be easy though. FADS had ten members and the only one they could readily rule out was Glen.

Minimal time had been spent on We-Haul, or Project Douglas as Josh had christened it, other than to brainstorm ways in which the organisation could be exploiting their employees. Maj had done some background research, but couldn't join the team at Bristol Airport until he received his airside pass, so it was still early days.

They'd agreed to revisit it once he'd been onsite for a day or two.

Operation Tooting was a different matter altogether. Luke was pleased with the input the team had given when he and Josh had described the outcome of the interviews with Misty, Flimsy McCoy and the three drugs middlemen.

What was more, he had told them what Josh had achieved in his interview alongside DCI Franks, and how she had praised him for it afterwards. The lad had received a round of applause from the others, and well-deserved it was too.

After much discussion, they had concluded that there were two key questions that needed answering. First, this Jay character was clearly key. Was he indeed the gang leader running drugs operations in Bristol? And second, what exactly was the role of Declan O'Brien, and how did he factor into everything? It was clear he was violent, and he was known to be an associate of Reece Stevens, but was he another drugs middleman, or was he something else entirely?

It was important to find out more about both men and, in Luke's opinion, O'Brien in particular. Unlike Nicole, he believed Flimsy had been telling the truth when he'd told Misty about the potential killings.

He decided to ring Misty and make sure she was on the case.

"Don't tell me you're calling to nag?" was her greeting when she answered.

He laughed.

"I am actually."

"Well, your timing is, as ever, fucking impeccable. I'm on my way to see Flimsy now. Tell you what, I'll put this on speaker when I find him, and we can cross-examine the little scrote together."

"No need for that, just ring me as soon as you've finished."

"Ah, there he is. I thought he might be down this alley." She hesitated. "Oh, fuck!"

He heard her running.

"What is it, Misty?"

She didn't respond, but he heard her say, "That's unbelievable," followed a few seconds later by, "Thank Christ!"

She came back on the line.

"It's Flimsy. There's a pulse, but it's faint. I'm going to have to hang up, Luke, and call for an ambulance."

"Overdose?"

"No. He's been attacked. Got to be one sick bastard too, judging by the state of his face."

The line went dead.

Chapter 44

Helen climbed onto the number 5 bus, pleased that she had a couple of days of relaxation ahead. She and Bob had decided to head up the Kennet and Avon canal on Saturday, the plan being that they would moor up at the George in Bathampton, have a meal, stay on his narrowboat '*Smoke and Mirrors*' overnight, and then cruise back to Saltford Marina after breakfast on Sunday.

She took a window seat halfway down, and gazed blankly out as the vehicle wound its way towards the centre of Bath, her mind on Project Big Whopper.

If she was honest, the investigation into unethical advertising had been boring and she was relieved it had been shelved, even if only temporarily. There had been times in her career when she'd have relished nothing more than a complex case such as that one, with lots of desk work and analysis of reports. However, being in the Ethics Team had made her realise that she gained more satisfaction from being up and active and, yes, occasionally at risk.

Not that she'd ever tell Bob that. He'd worry too much.

Joining FADS to try to find the online troll had the promise of being more exciting. From what Lily had said, it was unlikely the director would turn down her request to join, though whether she'd have to act or not was another thing. Was there a role for a Scottish woman in her late fifties in '*The Full Monty*'? Probably not, but she could always offer to help behind the scenes or to be a prompt.

She descended from the bus at the bus station and was pleased that the 172 for Paulton was about to depart. Time was tight. She needed to pick up her bag and groceries from home, drive back to Saltford and prepare a meal for four ahead of Ronnie and Becky arriving.

*

Helen had only just put the quiche in the oven when she heard a noise from the front of the boat.

She looked over at Bob. "It sounds like they're here."

He put his book aside and stood up as Ronnie and Becky walked into the galley.

"Hi Mum. Hi Bob," Ronnie said.

Helen embraced her son then his girlfriend, pleased to see they both looked well. Becky was an attractive young woman, her large brown eyes complementing her long brown hair and heart-shaped face, but tonight she was particularly radiant.

"Grab a seat," Bob said. "Drinks?"

"Beer for me," Ronnie said.

"Becky?'

"Sparkling water, please."

"I'll have a Prosecco, Bob," Helen said. "Aren't you joining me, Becky?"

Becky hesitated for a second and glanced at her boyfriend before returning her attention to Helen.

"No. I'll stick with water, thanks."

"Are you certain? It's Friday tonight, so no work tomorrow. Surely one glass won't hurt you."

As Helen said this, she suddenly put two and two together.

The glow on the wee girl's face, the declining of a glass of bubbly.

It all added up.

She nodded in understanding, smiled and held her arms out.

"Come here, my wee darling."

Becky walked up to Helen, and they hugged again.

"Congratulations," Helen said as Becky stepped back.
"Thanks."

Bob handed Becky her glass of water.

"Have you got a new job?"

Ronnie laughed. "More life-changing than that, Bob." He grabbed his girlfriend's hand. "Life will never be the same for us again."

"Ah, I see." Bob grinned. "My mistake. Where is it?"

Ronnie looked down at Becky's tummy, then back at Bob.

"You won't be able to see it yet, probably not for a few months."

Bob took a sip of his drink and grunted.

"I guess that's solicitors for you."

Ronnie raised one eyebrow.

"Solicitors?"

"Get away with you, Bob," Helen said. "You can be a right eejit sometimes."

"What do you mean?"

"They're not moving house, they're having a bairn." She turned to Becky. "Have you told your parents?"

"Not yet. Dad's presenting at a banking symposium in Paris this week. He's not back until tomorrow, so I thought I'd wait until then."

"And when is the wee one due?"

"The first of November."

"How wonderful. You'll need to think about moving, won't you? Find somewhere with two bedrooms."

"We will, but there's no rush. The baby will sleep in our bedroom for the first few months."

"What about sex?" Bob asked.

Becky's face immediately went pink, and Helen decided, again, to drag him out of the hole he was digging.

"What Bob means is, are you going to find out if it's a boy or a girl?"

It was Ronnie who answered. "We haven't decided yet.

I'd like a surprise, but Becky wants to be able to decide on a name."

"And what about work?"

"I'll probably take a year off," Becky said. "I want to spend as much time as possible with the baby." She gave a dry laugh. "I wouldn't mind a break if I'm honest. It's been a tough week."

"She was nearly attacked yesterday," Ronnie said.

"Attacked?" Helen said.

"Ronnie's exaggerating," Becky said. "All the man did was push me on his way out of the shop. I was more worried for Abdul."

"He shoved her to the ground," Ronnie said, "and he had a knife."

"A knife!" Helen said.

"Who was this man?" Bob asked. "And who's Abdul?"

"Abdul's a butcher. I don't know him very well, but his father is one of my clients. Mr Khan broke his hip, and I'm trying to find him affordable ground floor accommodation, but at the moment he's living at the back of his son's shop in Bristol." She paused. "Mr Khan was asleep when I arrived, and rather than wake him up I decided I'd return to see him next week. When I emerged from the back of the shop Abdul and this man were arguing. My instant thought was that he was a customer, but I heard him say something that suggested it was him asking for money rather than the other way around."

"What did he say?" Helen asked.

"I only caught the end of it. It sounded like '*a hundred pounds to prevent it*', but he had a thick Irish accent so I could have misheard."

"What happened then?"

"I walked past them and towards the chicken, as if I was a customer, and the man turned, glared at me and told me to get out, only he put it more forcefully than that. I stood my ground, said '*Why should I?*', and he said, '*because of this*' and showed me his knife."

"That was taking a big risk."

"That's what I said," Ronnie said.

"I think Abdul was worried what might happen next because he immediately said, '*Okay. I'll pay*', and the man replied with, '*You've got three days*', then barged into me and left."

"What was this man like?" Helen asked.

"He was big. Well-built too. Early thirties I'd say, and very rough. Not the kind of person you'd want to run across in a dark alley."

"Did you go to the police?"

Becky shook her head.

"Abdul made me promise not to. He said it was a gambling debt and he didn't want his family to know about it."

Chapter 45

Sam was sitting in one of the rear seats of the BMW and had a strong grip on Wilkins' collar.

"Is your belt done up?" Luke asked.

"Nearly. Just a second… Sit, Wilkins… No, sit… Not on me, over there… Sit…" There was a click. "Done."

Luke put the car into drive and glanced at the console.

"The satnav's saying an hour."

Sam sighed.

"That's an hour too long. He'd rather be in the front with you… No, boy."

"What happened?"

"He tried to lick my nose."

Luke laughed.

"I'll have a word with HR on Monday and see if I can change this for an estate or a hatchback."

"Please do." She paused. "Thanks for not pushing me regarding Sebastian."

"A promise is a promise."

"I appreciate it though. If the…"

The phone started ringing and she stopped speaking.

Luke saw who it was and clicked to accept the call.

"Hi, Maj."

"Hi, Luke. On your way to Marion's birthday party?"

"Yes."

"Good luck. I hope she has a great time."

"Thanks. Hopefully, it'll be good for my father as well, take his mind off things for an hour or two."

"June Fairbanks has just rung."

"The woman from We-Haul?"

"Yes. My airside pass has been approved. and she asked if I can go in tomorrow. Is that okay with you?"

"Of course. Any idea what you'll be doing?"

"Not a clue. All I know is that I've got to be there for 9 am."

"Okay. Good luck with it. I'll speak to you on Monday."

He hung up and looked at Sam in the rear-view mirror. "I was hoping that was an update on Flimsy McCoy." The phone rang again. "Ah, this must be her."

He accepted the call without looking at the display.

"Hi, Misty."

"This is DCI Franks, Luke."

"Oh. Good morning, Nicole."

"Did you think I was that private investigator you've been working with?"

He decided to ignore the thinly veiled accusation embedded in her question. He wasn't 'working' with Misty Mitchell but, even if he was, it was none of her business.

"That's right. Misty promised to give me an update on Flimsy McCoy's condition. I take it Pete told you that McCoy was badly beaten and left for dead yesterday."

"He did, yes, and that's the reason I'm ringing."

"Is he on the mend?"

"I am not calling to give you an update on the man's condition, Luke. I'm ringing to instruct you to keep that woman out of police business. As you're aware, it was against my better judgement to allow you and Josh to join my team. However, involving civilians in Operation Tooting is one thing, but I absolutely draw the line at using the services of a private investigator with a dubious reputation."

Luke wasn't going to let this one pass.

"What do you mean by 'dubious reputation'?"

He caught Sam in the rear-view mirror giving him a thumbs-up.

"Okay, maybe I over-stepped there but, whatever her past, she has no business being part of a major investigation into organised crime."

Luke didn't respond.

"Well? What do you have to say?"

"Two days. That's what I have to say."

"What are you talking about?"

"That's all it took. Two days."

"All it took to do what?"

"I can't see you, but if I could, would you be giving me one of your looks?"

"One of my... Oh!"

"We talked about this on Thursday, Nicole. You have to trust your team more and stop rushing to hasty conclusions."

"And keep that broom handle from reinserting itself?"

"Exactly."

There was silence at the other end.

"I'll see you next week, Luke," she said after a few seconds. There was another pause. "Thanks."

The line went dead.

"That was full on," Sam said. "What are you, her personal counsellor?"

Luke laughed.

"She's a great copper, but way too intense. She needs to lighten up and, as you heard me say, trust her team. If she does that she'll do well, I'm sure of it."

*

Marion was upstairs when Luke and Sam arrived at Borrowham Hall, and the first person they saw was Amy, the young housekeeper, who was walking through the hall with two large silver salvers under one arm.

"Oh, you've brought Wilkins," she said, and bent down to pet him. "How lovely."

"Where's Father?" Luke asked

"He's in the Library with Mark."

There was a screech from the direction of the kitchen.

"Amy! Have you got those platters?"

Amy rolled her eyes and called back.

"Coming, Erica."

She turned back to Luke and Sam.

"You'll have to excuse me. I'll see you later."

She rushed off, and they headed for the library to find Mark sitting on the floor wrapping presents.

Hugo was on a leather chair watching and Sam walked over and kissed him on the cheek.

"I'm so sorry about Daphne, Hugo."

He smiled grimly and sighed, but didn't say anything.

"How are the party preparations going?" Luke asked. "Can we help?"

"I wouldn't go near it if I were you," Mark said. "The plates haven't been delivered and Erica's on the rampage."

"What do you mean plates? Borrowham's got hundreds of plates."

"Yes, but not with 'Marion' monogrammed on them in gold. Erica's ordered them as a surprise, but Marion asked for an animal theme so I'm not sure how well they'll go down."

"Here's the nine-year-old now," Sam said, and they all turned to see Marion in an outfit that was interesting, to say the least.

It was a pink unicorn onesie.

"Oh, you're thinking this is for my party," Marion began, "But it's not, it's my extra-special chillax onesie. My party dress is awesome. Sam, will you help me when I need to get ready?"

She didn't wait for an answer before continuing.

"It's got spangles and stripes and there's an animal on it, but it's not a unicorn, it's a dog. Like Wilkins only not like Wilkins because it's pink and he's brown, which is lovely, but a brown dog wouldn't go with the rest of the dress. Would it, Wilkins?"

Wilkins tilted his head to one side as if to say '*What the hell are you talking about?*', then flopped onto the floor.

"My friends will be here soon, won't they, Mark?"

"Yes, they…"

Marion cut him off.

"Sally and Beatrice will arrive together because they live in the same village. Isla will be last. She's always last. I hope Benny comes."

"Is Benny your boyfriend?" Sam asked as Marion paused for breath.

"No. Yuk. He's okay I suppose, but he's not boyfriend material."

Sam smiled.

"Not boyfriend material?"

"No, but he's okay." She spotted what Mark was doing. "Oh!"

"Don't look," he said.

She turned away.

"I didn't see anything, Mark, except the wrapping paper, but I love it. Were those giraffes, because giraffes are awesome. Zebras are great too, but giraffes are the best." She looked back at Sam. "My whole party is going to be animal-themed, Sam. The invitations, the party bags, my dress, the plates, everything."

"Ah… how lovely."

"Yes, because I'm going to be a vet when I grow up."

"A vet?"

"Uh-huh. Wouldn't that be awesome? Although, I haven't ruled out being a ballerina or an astronaut."

"That's quite a spread of potential careers," Luke said.

Marion nodded, a serious expression on her face.

"I like to keep my options open."

Chapter 46

Josh tapped lightly on the door, almost wishing that his knock wouldn't be heard. That way he could make his escape without having to…

The door opened.

"Josh, hi," Nathan said. He looked around. "No Leanne?"

"No. She can't be here."

"Can't be here?" A worried expression appeared on his face. "Has something happened to her?"

"Oh no, definitely not. Well, not yet."

"Not yet? You're not making sense."

"The thing is, Nathan… Ah… Can I call you Mr Kemp?"

"Why would you want to do that?"

"It's more formal, more in keeping with what I'm about to ask?"

"Do you need money, Josh?"

"Eh?"

"Is that why you're here on your own? Are you in some kind of financial difficulty?"

"No. No. Nothing like that. The opposite."

"You've won the lottery?"

"Well, not the opposite but… Ah… Can I come in?"

"Of course."

Nathan opened the door and Josh walked in.

Nathan closed the door again and they remained standing in the hall.

"Well, what is it?"

Josh hesitated, maintained eye contact and tried to cover the silence with a smile, though he was conscious it might appear a touch forced.

He'd practised his speeches to both Leanne and her dad so many times that this part ought to be easy. All he had to do was say the right words in the right order. That was all.

"Are you going to speak, Josh, or just stare into my eyes?"

Josh cleared his throat, then started speaking, his voice slightly deeper than normal.

"You're beautiful."

Nathan took a step back.

"No!" Josh held his hand up. "Sorry. That's not right. I mean, you're not unbeautiful, but... What I meant to say was that Leanne is beautiful."

"Go on."

Josh swallowed.

"I love her with all my heart and I want us to spend the rest of our lives together. Ah... that's her and me, not you and me."

"I assumed you meant that."

"So, Nathan, ah... Mr Kemp, I'd like your blessing to ask for your daughter's hand in marriage."

Nathan smiled.

"That was lovely, Josh. Yes, I'm happy to give my blessing."

*

Josh had been nervous when he'd asked Leanne's dad for permission to propose, but that was nothing to how he was feeling now that the big moment was only an hour away.

In fact, he'd never been as scared in his life.

In his short career he'd encountered serial killers, abusive celebrities, murderous neo-Nazis and human traffickers.

But none of those had terrified him as much as this one woman.

Which was ridiculous.

It was only Leanne.

All she had to do was say yes, and he knew she would.

She loved him and he loved her.

They were meant for each other, so she was bound to want to agree to marry him, to spend the rest of her life by his side.

Wasn't she?

There was a bang on the bathroom door.

"Are you ever coming out of there?"

"Sorry," he called back. "I'm ah... I'm doing my hair."

"In there? But you always use the full-length mirror."

"Not my hair hair. My nasal hair."

"You haven't got nasal hair."

"No, but I like to check."

He opened the door.

Leanne smiled at him, then pirouetted.

"What do you think?"

She had on a figure-hugging crimson dress that he'd never seen before.

"Wowza!"

"I bought it during my lunch break yesterday and thought I'd keep it as a surprise for tonight."

"Wowza!"

She laughed.

"Are you going to say anything else, or are you just going to stand there gawping and saying 'Wowza' repeatedly?"

"No."

"No?"

"I mean yes. Later. Ah... I'll be saying something later."

She raised one eyebrow.

"What do you mean later?"

"Something else. I mean, we'll both be talking later, when we're at the restaurant. Not just me, obviously. You'll be talking too, eventually, when I've finished."

"You're not making any sense."
"Good."

*

An hour later, Josh and Leanne walked into The Olive Tree where a waiter in a black waistcoat and bow tie stood at a lectern. He looked up at Josh as they approached.

"Good evening, sir. Do you have a booking?"

"Yes. Josh Ogden. Table for two."

The waiter looked down at the open diary in front of him.

"Ah, yes. Mr Ogden. 7:30." He looked over at Leanne. "And you must be Leanne?"

She smiled. "That's me."

"Excellent."

He rubbed his palms together, then returned his attention to Josh.

"We have a special corner table for you, Mr Ogden." He winked before continuing. "Marianne will take your coats."

A young waitress appeared beside them as if by magic and took their coats away.

"Excellent," the waiter said again.

It was clearly his favourite word.

"Please follow me."

He winked again.

They sat at the table and Marianne returned with wine and food menus.

"He fancies you," Leanne whispered after the waitress had left.

"Who does?"

"The waiter. He winked at you twice. Didn't you notice?"

Josh felt suddenly panicked and decided to dodge the

question.

"Ah… Shall we have a Bordeaux, or do you want a red?"

"A Bordeaux *is* a red."

"Great. We'll have that then."

To his disappointment, it was the man in a waistcoat who returned to take their orders rather than Marianne.

Josh decided to keep his eyes down on the menu rather than look at the waiter and risk receiving another wink.

"We'll have the Bordeaux, please."

"Excellent."

"And the five-course '*Taste of the Season*' menu for both of us."

"Excellent choice, sir."

He took the menus away.

"He couldn't keep his eyes off you," Leanne said. "And the way he kept smiling. Didn't you think it was odd?"

"No."

The meal itself was delicious, and Josh managed to keep up his end of the conversation, which was nothing short of a miracle given the way his stomach was turning somersaults.

He'd practised, but now it was for real.

He was relieved when at last they finished their meat course. Once the plates had been cleared away, he grabbed both of Leanne's hands and looked deep into her eyes.

"Do you want me, sir?"

He looked up to see the waiter standing behind Leanne with a plate in his hand, on it a cake of some kind.

"Not yet."

"Excellent."

The waiter retreated.

Josh returned his attention to Leanne.

"What was that all…" she started to say.

"Ssh. I need to say something."

He swallowed.

"Leanne, you're beautiful. I knew from the moment we met that we should be together. I don't want this to end."

He stood up, walked around the table until he was standing beside her, and went down onto one knee.

The entire room went silent as people put their meals to one side to watch what was playing out in front of them.

Josh's heart was beating out of his chest, but he felt suddenly confident. This was his moment, their moment, and he wasn't going to make any mistakes.

"What we've got between us is wonderful. When I look into your eyes, I know that you love me as much as I love you."

He removed a small blue velvet box from his pocket, opened the lid and held it towards her.

"Leanne, will you do me the honour of being my bride?"

She put her hand to her mouth then, after a few seconds, removed it again, a broad smile on her face.

"Of course I will."

There was a round of applause from the other diners, and Josh stood up then bent forward to kiss Leanne.

"I love you, Joshy," she whispered when he pulled away.

"I love you too, Leanne."

Chapter 47

Maj watched as his daughter drenched her breakfast in maple syrup.

"Have you got enough there?"

She looked up at him, smiled, then squirted more out so that her waffles were almost completely submerged in a sea of liquid sweetness.

He returned her smile and shook his head.

"I don't know where you put it."

His daughter was tall and slim, taking after both her mother and father, and this was her regular Sunday morning treat to herself. If he ate something like that he was sure he'd acquire a pot belly in no time, but at fifteen Sabrina seemed to be able to consume whatever she liked with no impact whatsoever.

Mind you, she was going to be burning a lot of the acquired calories off later, and he was disappointed he was going to miss seeing her perform.

"Good luck today, Sabrina. Are you in the floor and vault competitions?"

She nodded, swallowed her mouthful and added, "And trampolining."

"I hope you do well, and I'm sorry I can't make it." He looked over at his wife. "Will you send me photos, Asha, and a video as well if you can?"

"Definitely."

"So, Dad," Sabrina said, another spoonful poised to be devoured, "what's the reason you're going undercover at Bristol Airport?"

"Undercover?" Asha said, then looked at her husband. "You didn't say you were going undercover. You're not going to be in any danger, are you?"

"It's not undercover, not really."

"You said you were going to be a baggage handler," Sabrina said. "Isn't that so that you can spy on criminals?"

"Maj?" Asha said before he could answer. "Well?"

"I'm not spying on criminals, all I'm doing is observing the extent to which We-Haul are looking after their staff. There's been a suggestion that they're not providing the proper protective clothing and, if that's the case, it means they're taking advantage of their employees. In all likelihood, though, it's a mistake, and all we'll need to do is ensure they update their procedures.

"It doesn't sound like an exciting assignment," Sabrina said.

"Just as well," Asha said.

Maj smiled. "I think you're right, Sabrina. It's going to be pretty boring. However, hopefully I'll be done in a couple of days, put my recommendations in and move on to the next job."

*

Traffic was light, and Maj was at the staff entrance before eight forty-five. His airside pass was checked, and he followed directions to Load Control as he'd been instructed.

Twenty or so men, and notably no women, were seated around tables, drinking coffee and chatting. Some already had some of their personal protective clothing on, and one of these looked up when Maj entered.

"This is for rampies, mate."

"Oh. I'm starting as a baggage handler today."

The man laughed, and the others nearby joined in, and he then called over to one of the other tables.

"Fraser!"

An older man looked over.

"What?"

The man gestured to Maj.

"New guy. First-timer."

Fraser stood up, walked over to Maj and offered his hand.

"Hi, I'm Fraser, shift supervisor."

He had a round, ruddy face, a jovial manner and an accent that made it clear he hailed from Scotland. It was harsher than Helen's, though, and Maj wondered if he might be from Glasgow.

They shook hands.

"I'm Maj, Maj Osman."

"Ah, yes. I was told to expect you. Temporary cover, isn't it?"

"That's right. I was worried I was in the wrong place when that man said this room was for rampies."

Fraser laughed.

"A rampie *is* a baggage handler, Maj. It's what we call ourselves, though officially we're called ramp agents. It certainly beats being called bag jockeys or luggage monkeys."

"I bet."

"Right. I need to get you some kit. What's your shoe size?"

"10."

Fraser nodded.

"I think I've got a pair that'll fit."

He walked over to a cupboard and pulled a stapled document out of the top drawer, brought it back and held it out.

"While I fetch your PPE you need to read through this and sign it." He grinned. "That way, if you get flattened by a Boeing 787 the airport can waive all responsibility."

The document was reasonable, making the distinction clear between the airport's responsibilities and his own. He signed and dated it and handed it to Fraser when he returned.

"Right. I've put your stuff over there." He gestured to a small table in the corner of the room. "There's a pair of kneepads, boots, gloves, a hi-vis jacket and ear protectors."

"Do I need to read something about procedures?"

"No time, Maj. I'm going to pair you up since it's your first day. You'll learn on the job."

He called over to one of the tables.

"Thomas, can you come here, please?"

A man in his early thirties stood up and walked over.

"This is Maj," Fraser went on. "It's his first day today so I want you to show him the ropes."

"Sure. No probs."

He nodded hello to Maj who nodded back.

"Right," Fraser said. "I'll leave you to it."

"It's not exactly complex," Thomas said once he'd left. "We'll be starting airside with an arrival, so you'll need your earmuffs. Get your kit on and we'll head out. The plane's due to land in thirty minutes."

Once they were outside, Thomas introduced him to the team leader, the dispatcher and the other six members of the team.

They stood back and watched as their plane landed and started taxiing towards the stand.

"This one's a Dreamliner," Thomas said, "which is why there are ten of us. It can go down to four for smaller planes. The dispatcher has an accurate count of how many bags are on board. We offload the bags from the hold into those dollies…" He pointed to several wheeled platforms. "…before driving them to the terminal and putting them onto the assigned baggage belt. Our aim is to put the last bag on the belt before the first passenger is through passport security."

Maj glanced around at the other members of the team. All seemed to be wearing the full PPE, including ear protectors. The fact that he hadn't been given any proper training, or even a set of procedures and standards to read through, was an omission, but hardly anything major.

The remainder of the morning alternated between departures and arrivals. After the first few, Maj felt he was beginning to get the hang of things and was pulling his weight. It wasn't as mind-numbingly boring as he'd feared, and he found Thomas and the others to be good company. There was the occasional dig at the powers-that-be, but it was all in good spirits.

He was amused when he recalled Asha's concern that he might be doing something dangerous. Nothing could be further from the truth.

They'd completed loading luggage for an Airbus departure, and Thomas and Maj were taking a break in Load Control, when Fraser wandered over.

"There's been a wee cock-up in Cargo, boys, and I need you two to work over there this afternoon. Means a late finish though. You both okay with that?"

"Overtime?" Thomas asked.

"Aye, there'll be overtime."

"Then I'm fine."

"Me too," Maj said.

"Good. Head on over after lunch and ask for Borys."

Chapter 48

Diana enjoyed bringing the family together for Sunday lunch.

It was something she tried to do at least once a month, an opportunity to share stories about school, friends, nights out and the like. Today, she had cooked roast beef, and it had been well received. Max, the younger of Apollo's children, had refused his green vegetables but soon succumbed after a smack around the ear from his father.

Once the social chit-chat had run its course, the plates would be cleared away and she and her brothers would retreat to the lounge to talk shop.

It was a system that had worked well while her father was alive, and worked well now, a way of keeping everyone functioning as one unit, both socially and when it came to the family business.

She looked over at her younger siblings and reflected on how, despite being twins, they were so different, in both appearance as well as manner. Apollo had a heavier build and was more laid back. Jay, the older by four minutes and a couple of inches taller, was far more impulsive, quick to react with violence if anyone went against him.

Diana sat at the head of the table, the position her father had always occupied, and watched as conversations continued in front of her.

Her son sat to her left while to her right sat Jay and beside him his latest girlfriend, Alicia, in her late twenties and ten years his junior. They were talking about football, or at least Roma and Jay were. Alicia, a bleached blonde with a dress so revealing it was almost indecent, was staring into space apparently ignorant of the fact that Roma could hardly keep his eyes from her breasts.

She was much the same as the ones before her, good in the sack no doubt, but with a brain the size of a peanut and a personality vacuum.

The woman next to her, Apollo's wife Beth, was so different from Alicia it was unreal, and it wasn't just that she was dressed sensibly and had an adult's IQ. Beth was a store manager, earning a decent income and happy in her work. She was aware of what her husband did for a living, but bright enough to say nothing and enjoy the rewards.

Next to her, at the opposite end of the table, was Apollo and beside him their sons Elliot and Max. As far as Diana could make out, they were talking about a school play.

She clinked her knife on her glass.

"A toast to Dad."

The others raised their glasses,

"To Dad," they said as one.

"Jay, Apollo, let's go to the lounge."

Her brothers stood up and they carried their drinks through to the front room.

Diana closed the door and took her usual seat on the cream upholstered armchair, while Jay and Apollo sat at either end of the pale blue recliner sofa, the former immediately pressing the button to raise his legs.

Jay took a sip of his red wine.

"Well?" he asked. "How did the new venture go?"

"Smooth as silk," Diana said. She looked over at Apollo. "Despite Milo."

"He didn't cause any problems, did he? I brought him in case we needed to demonstrate we meant business."

She gave a dry laugh. "I think Declan demonstrated that okay."

"What did he do?" Jay asked.

"Chopped the old woman's finger off. At the time I thought it was over the top, but I think it helps guarantee they don't breathe a word about what happened."

"And did you get the £200,000 you were aiming for?"

She smiled. "I doubled it. Got £400,000."

Jay nodded approvingly. "That's a good result. Going to do it again?"

"Kind of. I'm working on an idea which could be an even bigger earner."

Apollo sat forward on the sofa, clearly excited by this prospect.

"What is it, Sis?"

"I'll let you know when I've planned it out in detail. I need a couple of days to do more research."

"How much risk is there?" Jay asked.

"No more than this one, possibly less." She smiled. "It will require Declan's help again, but this time I'll direct what he does with that knife of his."

"I want in."

"I'm not sure I need you. I want to keep numbers down."

"This is a family business, Di. We need to cooperate on something as significant as this."

"Oh, yeah? I didn't see you coming to me for help when you extended your operation south of the river."

"That was different."

"Look, when I've worked up my plans, let's all three of us get together. I'd value your thoughts in any case, and if there's a part you can play all well and good."

"When do you think that'll be?" Apollo asked.

"A couple of days. No more than that."

"What about your protection business?" Jay asked. "Did it suffer because your attention was elsewhere?"

"Not at all. We missed a few days while Declan and Flynn were supervising the hostages in East Harptree Wood, but they caught up on Thursday and Friday."

"And is everyone paying up okay?"

"There was the usual resistance from some, but they always see sense in the end. There's only one still outstanding, a butcher in Redcliffe." She smiled. "Declan's paying him a visit tomorrow, so I don't think he'll be a problem for long."

"You need to be careful with that Irish thug, Sis," Apollo said. "He's got a short fuse."

"I think he attacked one of our dealers on Friday," Jay said.

Diana raised her eyebrows. "Declan did?"

"I can't be certain, but there's a rumour going around that this guy, his name's Flimsy, had snitched to the police on him. By all accounts, he was almost dead when he was found and may not make it through. Knife wounds across his face and internal injuries from being kicked repeatedly."

"But how would he even know Declan? He's in a completely different part of the operation."

"Reece is a mate of Declan's. Do you know Reece?"

"Yes. I know Reece."

"Well, Reece reckons Flimsy may have overheard Declan boasting."

"About the kidnapping?"

Jay nodded.

"For f…"

"Sis!" Apollo cautioned. "Language."

She gave a deep sigh and shook her head. "I'll have a word with Declan. He ought to keep his mouth shut."

"Yeah," Jay said. "You need to keep your guys in order."

"What about yours, Jay? I heard three of your guys were pulled in for questioning this week."

"The police are sniffing around, no more than that, and they're not stupid. They no-commented their way through the interviews so the police have nothing. And if they try to take it further by raiding their homes they'll find nothing, not now we're cuckooing."

"And you're sure none of them opened their big fat gobs under pressure?"

"Nah." He grinned. "They know what I'd do to them if

they did."

"Aside from that, Jay," Apollo asked, "how's business?"

Diana saw that he was trying to calm them down before their argument escalated, and decided to let it pass.

"Going great guns," Jay said. "University business is booming." He laughed. "Those kids can't seem to get enough. I'm looking to take on someone else to work alongside Reece, Tyrone and Mickey."

"Any names in the frame?"

"Not yet."

Diana looked over at Apollo.

"What about your operation?"

"Going well." He turned to Jay. "Borys is at the airport today for your consignment."

"What is it?" Diana asked.

Jay grinned. "Two thousand G of dark.'

"That's a lot of heroin."

"Sure is. Street value of two hundred k."

Chapter 49

"Do you work here on a regular basis?" Maj asked, as he and Thomas made their way to Cargo-1, a warehouse that lay beyond the areas of the airport that were devoted to passenger traffic.

"Not that often, maybe one day in ten. They have their own dedicated team and only call on us when they're short-staffed."

"Is the work very different?"

"Not really. Consignments tend to be a lot bigger, so we're using pallet carriers rather than dollies, but it's roughly the same process. We check what's coming in or going out against a manifest that the dispatcher provides, and then move it as appropriate. It's not exactly rocket science." He paused. "Between you and me, the biggest difference is that they're a bunch of twats."

"Who are?"

"The rampies in Cargo. Think they're the bees knees and look down on us. Like to call us bag smashers." He hesitated. "Arseholes, the lot of them. And this guy we're seeing, Borys, he's the worst."

"In what way?"

"He's rude and abusive. It's clear he thinks the likes of you and me are the dregs of the earth. God knows how he made it to supervisor."

"Borys is an unusual name."

"He's Polish. Surname's Dobrowski. Been here a few years, so his English isn't bad, but he doesn't say much."

A few minutes later they reached the warehouse, and Thomas led the way to a small kitchen come rest area in the near corner.

A few men in hi-viz jackets were seated around a table.

They looked up briefly, then returned to their conversation.

"Typical," Thomas whispered to Maj, then raised his voice and called over.

"Borys, we were asked to come and help you."

One of the men stood up slowly, turned and lumbered over to them. He was bulky and big around the chest and belly, though to Maj it looked more like he was bodybuilder large, rather than fat from over-eating. Not the most attractive of specimens, he had a large nose that seemed to be set between, rather than below, his wide-set eyes, and what looked to be a permanent scowl.

"I know you," he said as he drew near.

"Yes. I've been here several times. My name's Thomas."

Borys grunted and pointed at Maj while still keeping his eyes on Thomas.

"Him?"

"This is Maj."

Borys looked at Maj for the first time, and then turned and called to the men at the table.

"This one, he has girl's name."

"I was born in Somalia," Maj said. "Maj is short for Majid."

Borys turned back and scowled.

"I do not care. You are girl."

He walked away, pulled a clipboard down from a shelf, scanned it and said, again without looking up.

"FX4390. 15 hundred."

"Is that the time it lands?" Thomas asked.

"Yes," Borys said. "I will lead. You ramp rats do as Borys says. Yes?"

"Yes," Thomas said.

The more Borys talked, the more Maj got the impression there was hidden depth to the man. Although he spoke almost exclusively in monosyllables, there was a spark in his eyes that suggested every word was delivered carefully and with purpose.

He decided to keep a close eye on him in case he was using his abrasive manner to conceal something. Most likely a short-cutting of procedures rather than anything major but still, it was worthy of further attention.

"When do we need to be in position?" Thomas asked.

"Now," Borys said. "Follow me."

"What's the cargo we're unloading?" Maj asked.

"Boxes. Large boxes and small boxes."

"Of what? I was wondering how heavy they'll be."

"Chairs, machinery. Who gives fuck? Now, follow." He called back to the table. "Justin, Lance, we go now."

Two men stood up and the group of five left the warehouse and headed towards a stand where a FedEx plane was taxiing to a stop.

The next forty-five minutes comprised much shouting and pointing from Borys as the four men in his team transferred the plane's cargo to the warehouse.

Borys didn't help with the physical activities but, when he wasn't issuing orders, checked off every box against a list on his clipboard. He was clearly both ramp leader and dispatcher, but most definitely not a worker.

"Go to staff room," he said when they'd finished. "I will call when you are needed for next plane."

Maj and the other three walked into the staff room where Justin and Lance immediately turned their backs on them and returned to their seats at the table.

Thomas shrugged. "You see what I mean?"

Maj smiled. "Yes, although I can see why you said Borys is the worst. He seems to be continually trying to put everyone around him down, especially you and me."

"He's always like that. Did you notice how he doesn't do any physical work? That's been the case every time I've been in his team."

"I'm surprised he's not in here taking it easy now. What do you think he's up to out there?"

"He'll be double-checking the boxes against the

manifest."

"Why does he do that? He seemed thorough enough when we were out on the tarmac."

"I agree, and he's the only one who insists on doing it." Thomas laughed. "Maybe it's because he recognises how thick he is and is worried he'll get it wrong."

Maj wasn't so sure.

"Where's the loo?"

"Other side of the door we came in through."

"I'll be back in a minute."

Maj left the rest area but, rather than walk to the toilet, headed for the far end of the warehouse where they'd deposited the boxes from the FedEx plane. Something in his gut told him that Borys wasn't double-checking the cargo as Thomas thought but, if not, what was he up to?

He was forced to weave between pallets stacked ten or twelve feet high, but stopped about halfway across when he became aware of a regular banging, the sound of metal on metal. Whatever it was, it wasn't the sound of someone ticking boxes on a clipboard.

A few paces further on the noise stopped and he saw Borys. He was facing away and putting on his hi-vis jacket, a hammer visible on the box in front of him.

Maj tried to make sense of what he was seeing. Had Borys been hammering nails in because the consignment's lid had come loose in transit? But, if that was the case, why had he taken his jacket off? Was it because he was hot?

He stepped back out of view while he decided what to do, and almost jumped out of his skin when his phone pinged.

A split-second later he heard Borys shout out.

"Who is there?"

Maj stepped from behind the stacked pallets to find the Pole holding the hammer in his right hand, his arm raised as if he was about to attack.

He tried to talk casually but could feel his heart beating

against his chest.

"It's me, Borys."

He smiled, trying his hardest to make it realistic.

"I'm looking for the toilet and can't find it anywhere."

Borys held his left hand out.

"Give me phone."

"Why?"

"To see who sent message."

"It was my wife."

Maj stepped forward, hoping it was indeed Asha who had WhatsApped him, and not Luke asking how he was getting on.

He entered his passcode, and was relieved when a photo came up of his daughter mid-manoeuvre performing a handstand on a vaulting horse. He held the phone up so that Borys could see the screen.

"She sent me this."

Borys looked at the photo, wrinkled his upper lip and shook his head.

"You are dirty old man."

"What do you mean?"

"How old?" He stabbed his finger at the screen. "Your wife?"

"You're misunderstanding. My wife sent the photo, but that's my daughter. They're at a gymnastics event."

"Mmm." He paused. "Why you not ask Thomas where toilet is?"

"I know. Silly of me. I should have done."

Borys stared him in the eyes and seemed to be considering his options.

Maj only hoped those options didn't include beating him to death with a hammer.

After a few seconds, Borys raised his arm, but it was his left arm and he used it to point back towards the warehouse entrance.

"Toilet is beside door to come in. On other side to rest

area."
"Thanks."
Maj made his escape.

Chapter 50

It was five to nine when Luke and Sam walked into the Ethics Room.

Maj, Helen and Lily were already in, but there was no sign of Josh.

"I thought you were at the airport again today, Maj," Luke said as he hung his coat up.

"They decided they didn't need me, and said they'd let me know when I'm next needed."

"Did you find any evidence of bad practice?"

Maj shook his head.

"No, but I think there may be something else going on, possibly petty pilfering."

"Okay. Park it for now and we'll all get together after I've been to Filcher's Monday meeting."

"Have you heard from Josh, Luke?" Helen asked. "I noticed Leanne wasn't on reception. I hope that's not a bad omen."

"Not a word."

There was a noise behind them and a grinning Josh walked in, a carrier bag in his hand.

It was Sam who was first to react.

She smiled. "I take it congratulations are in order."

"You betcha. I got down on one knee, remembered all my lines, and she said yes."

Luke walked over and shook his hand.

"Congratulations, son."

"Thanks, guv."

Maj followed suit and then Sam, Helen and Lily stepped forward to kiss him on the cheek.

"You're going to be a married man," Helen said. "Next thing you'll be a grown-up."

"Ha, ha." Josh lifted his carrier bag up. "Leanne and I bought cakes." He turned to Luke. "Is it okay if we have them later on when Leanne can join us, guv? She's on a break from eleven to eleven-thirty."

"Sounds good, provided I've escaped Filcher by then."

"I've got a wee bit of news as well," Helen said. She had a broad smile on her face. "Becky's pregnant."

There was another round of congratulations.

Luke's phone started ringing and he stepped aside to take the call, looking down at the screen to see it was Pete.

"Morning, Pete. Have there been developments?"

"Yes, we're fairly confident we've identified who Jay is."

"Go on."

"Do you remember the Bill Curtis cartel?"

Luke gave a dry laugh.

"Difficult to forget that man, although I had managed to put him to the back of my mind. He was one vicious bastard, and did for Bristol what the Krays did for London's East End. Pity we could never bring him to justice."

"Jay's his son."

"What? I thought Curtis's business died with him."

"So did I, and it may well have done, but his son lives on Royal York Crescent, which is where Tyrone Goodwin told us Jay lives. And his registered name is Janus. You're not going to tell me you believe that's a coincidence?"

"No. He's got to be our man. Either he's continued the business, and been canny with it, or he's started up afresh." Luke paused. "Janus is an unusual name."

"Bill Curtis named all his children after Roman deities. He left a daughter, Diana, and another son, Apollo, who's Janus's twin. I don't know if you remember, but after he died it came out that he'd used the name Zeus as a cover for a lot of his activities. I guess he thought of himself as the king of the gods."

"Has Jay Curtis got a record?"

"Nothing, not even a caution."

"What about his siblings?"

"Clean as well, and there's no reason to think they're involved in any way."

"So, what's the plan?"

"DCI Franks wants to get him in for an interview, and she wants you to be there."

"She does?"

"Insists on it." Pete laughed and lowered his voice. "If you ask me, she must have had a cracking weekend, because it's like she's a different woman. She even thanked me when I held the door open for her earlier. I didn't think the word 'thanks' was even in her vocabulary."

"I hope she keeps it up."

"Me too."

"What's the pretext for getting him in?"

"Still working on our approach, but I'll be back in touch." He paused. "One other thing before you go. Flimsy McCoy didn't make it. He died in the night."

"We're looking at murder then."

"Yes, but because he was a drug dealer, the investigation has been rolled into Operation Tooting."

"Makes sense. So, Nicole is SIO?"

"Yes."

"Okay, Pete. Speak to you later."

He hung up and rang Misty.

"Have you heard about Flimsy?"

"No."

"He died in the night."

"Can't say I'm surprised given the state of him. Poor little fucker."

"That means this is a murder investigation now. Would you mind sniffing around to see if you can find out more about Declan O'Brien, the man Flimsy overheard?"

"Will do."

He hung up and a thought occurred to him.

He called over to Josh.

"Josh, have you got a minute."

He walked over.

"What is it, guv?"

"Declan O'Brien served eight years for grievous bodily harm, didn't he?"

"Yes, that's right. He attacked another man after an argument outside a nightclub."

"Can you remember if he used a weapon?"

Josh nodded. "A knife. Stabbed the man multiple times and, aside from being scarred for life, the victim was blinded in one eye."

"Okay. Thanks."

He looked at his watch, saw it was coming up to 9:30, and made his way upstairs to Filcher's office.

Gloria, Filcher's secretary, smiled as he approached.

"Good morning, Luke."

"Good morning, Gloria. Good weekend?"

"Fine thanks."

She handed him two sheets of paper, stapled together.

He scanned the top sheet, frowned, turned to page two and looked up at her.

"Seventeen agenda items! That's got to be a record."

She was still smiling. "It's not as bad as it seems."

"I don't even understand some of them," he said, and jabbed his finger halfway down page one. "What's Intercorporate Assessability when it's at home?"

"As I said, it's not too bad. You can go on in. The others are already here."

He walked in to find Fred, Glen and James seated at their usual places around Filcher's table, but with no sign of the man himself.

Fred looked up as Luke walked in.

"Take a seat, Luke. Filcher's at a breakfast event and asked if I'd chair the meeting." He grinned. "He told me to ensure we debated every point thoroughly, so with that in mind I prepared t' minutes."

He handed out copies of a four-page document which contained a paragraph of the team's conclusions against each of the seventeen agenda items.

"I prepared this when I got in this morning," he went on. "Only took me twenty minutes. Have a read through and let me know if owt needs changing."

It took them a couple of minutes to read it through.

"Item four should probably read HR rather than 'Internal Affairs'," James said when he'd finished.

"Good point," Fred said and made a note.

"And under item nine," Luke said, "you need to add Operation Tooting as a project the Ethics Team is helping Avon and Somerset Police with."

Fred made another note, then turned to Glen.

"Glen?"

"All looks fine and randy to me."

"Great." He stood up. "Thanks for your time, gents."

Chapter 51

Luke returned from Filcher's office smiling for once.

Sam looked up when he walked in.

"What happened?"

"Filcher's off somewhere so Fred chaired." He laughed. "He pre-wrote the minutes, and they were more comprehensive than when Filcher spends up to two hours pontificating."

"I rang Sebastian again, just to check on him."

"You seem to be ringing him every day."

"I feel the need to. This incident affected his family as well as him."

"How is he?"

"Still stressed, but he appreciated me calling."

He returned to his desk and reflected on Sam's use of the word 'incident'. Last time they'd spoken she'd said it was a personal issue, and he'd assumed it might be an illness of some kind.

'Incident' made it sound very different, as if it was a one-off tragedy. He couldn't help speculating what it might be. It had clearly upset Sebastian, and Sam had said it affected his family too. Had a close family member committed suicide or been in a traffic accident? Suicide was more likely, he thought, given the stigma associated with it and Sebastian's request that she keep it a secret.

*

At 10:30 Luke called the team together and Sam, Maj, Josh and Lily joined him at the meeting table while Helen stood at the whiteboard.

"I don't think this'll take long," he began, "but I think it's worth having a catch-up since a couple of things have happened since Friday. Helen, can you get rid of Stairway and Big Whopper, please?"

She erased them, leaving three columns for Tooting, Douglas and Rainbow.

"With regards to Tooting," he went on, "there have been two significant developments. First, the police have identified Jay, who Flimsy McCoy called 'the main man', as being Janus Curtis. Jay's father was Bill Curtis who led an organised crime gang called the Curtis Cartel until his death four years ago."

"Have they got enough to charge him, guv?" Josh asked.

"They've got nothing apart from the word of a low-end drug dealer. Talking of whom, that's the second development. Flimsy McCoy died last night, which means they've now kicked off a major investigation into his murder."

"Could it be Jay Curtis who killed him?" Sam suggested. "Given McCoy named him."

"It's a possibility, although Declan O'Brien is obviously in the frame as well."

Helen updated the whiteboard.

Luke turned to Maj.

"You said you may have come across petty pilfering by We-Haul staff, Maj?"

"Not by We-Haul staff, but by one of the team leaders handling cargo, a man called Borys. I could be mistaken, but he looked very suspicious."

"What did you see?"

"He was supposedly checking a consignment we'd just unloaded, but he was banging nails into the top of a box."

"Could it have been simply that it had come loose?"

"It could have been, but the way he confronted me when he saw I'd been watching was very aggressive. He's a nasty man, but even so it seemed over the top if that was all he was doing." He paused. "There was something else too. He's a large man, and he had a coat plus a hi-vis jacket on for the rest of the afternoon, but I could swear his waist was bigger."

"You think he may have stolen goods and secreted them around his waist?"

Maj nodded. "Yes. Perhaps in a bum bag."

"It would have to be high value to be worth taking that kind of risk," Josh said.

Maj gave a grim smile. "I went back later in the shift and checked the box. It had a despatch note stapled to the side with the Apple logo on it."

"Could be smart watches or even iPhones then. They'd be worth nicking."

"That's what I thought."

Luke scratched his chin. "All I can suggest is you keep a close eye on him next time you're working with him. If he does it again, ring me and I'll contact security at the airport. That way it won't have to be revealed that it was you who shopped him."

"Okay, Luke."

He turned to Lily and Helen.

"Any updates on FADS?"

"Rainbow," Josh said. "It's Project Rainbow." This earned him a glare and he held his hand up. "I'm just saying, that's all."

"Well, don't."

"Helen and I are going to a FADS session after work today," Lily said. "It's a first read-through and I've been given the role of Mandy, Gaz's ex-wife."

"Cumbria," Josh said.

Everyone turned to look at him.

"We could have called it Project Cumbria," he went on. "Since you're not so keen on Rainbow."

"Go on, son," Luke said, trying but failing to keep the

exasperation from his voice. "Explain yourself."

"He played Gaz, didn't he? In the film. Robert Carlyle. And Carlisle's in Cumbria."

"Is this really adding value?"

"Well, ah... no, but..."

Luke turned back to Lily.

"Carry on."

"Helen hasn't got a role in the play but she's going to say she wants to help."

"I might offer to be their prompt," Helen added.

"And there are still ten people who could be the troll?" Sam asked.

"Nine excluding Glen," Lily said. "Hopefully, we'll be able to rule some of them out tonight. Glen said the abuse started four months ago so it can't be anyone who's joined more recently than that."

"Okay. Well, good luck with it. Where are you meeting?"

"In the Royal Crescent Room downstairs, but that's only because it's a read-through. Inigo told me rehearsals will be at the Mission Theatre in Corn Street. That's where the productions are staged."

*

It was just gone eleven when Leanne turned up and, as with Josh earlier in the morning, she earned hugs and kisses all round.

"Where's Luke?" she asked, when she realised he wasn't there.

"He had to pop out," Sam said.

A couple of minutes later, Luke reappeared and looked over at Josh and Leanne who were smiling and holding hands.

"Congratulations, you two."

"Thanks, guv," Josh said.

Luke delved into his briefcase and pulled out a bottle of champagne

"I thought we ought to have some bubbly to celebrate." He put his hand back in and pulled out a stack of paper cups. "As long as you don't mind drinking out of these, that is."

"I'd drink bubbly out of a dog bowl," Helen said. She held her hand out. "Give it here. I'll be mother."

Luke passed the champagne and cups over and his phone started ringing. He looked down to see it was Nicole.

"It's DCI Franks. Excuse me a moment."

He moved away and accepted the call.

"Hi, Nicole."

There was a loud bang behind him as Helen opened the bottle.

"What was that?" Nicole said and laughed. "Have you been shot?"

"No, that was a Champagne bottle. Josh got engaged at the weekend."

"How lovely. Tell him congratulations from me, will you?"

This was a new Nicole.

"I will. How can I help?"

"It's Josh I'm ringing about. When you and I interview Jay Curtis, would it be okay with you if Josh sat in as well, primarily as an observer?"

Another surprise. She was consulting him on something rather than simply issuing orders.

"Of course. Can I ask why?"

"Two reasons. It would be good for his personal development, but more than that, he's got a way about him that puts suspects at ease. If he hadn't been alongside me when we interviewed Tyrone Goodwin we wouldn't have found out about Jay Curtis."

"I'll tell him. He'll be delighted."

"And don't forget to pass on my congratulations. His fiancee's a very lucky woman."

Luke hung up and stared at his phone for a few seconds, his mind struggling to process the change in the woman's demeanour.

Josh saw he'd finished and called across.

"What did she want, guv?"

"She wants you in the interview with Jay Curtis."

"She does?"

"Yes. You've impressed her, Josh, and that's not an easy thing to do. Well done."

Josh went a subtle shade of beetroot.

"She also asked me to congratulate you on your engagement and said that Leanne's a very lucky woman."

Josh's cheeks darkened a little bit more.

Luke looked at Helen who passed him his cup. He held it up.

"To Josh and Leanne."

"To Josh and Leanne," Sam, Helen, Maj and Lily replied in unison.

Chapter 52

Inigo was alone in the Royal Crescent Room when Lily and Helen arrived. He had placed copies of the script around the conference table and was sitting on the far side in the middle.

He smiled over at Lily when he saw her.

"Hello, my darling," he said, at the same raised volume he'd used when thdy's met in Costa Coffee. He turned his attention to Helen. "And you, my dear, must be Helen. How simply delightful to meet you."

"Thank you for letting me join."

"Ah. Do I detect a touch of Caledonian in your accent?"

"Aye. I'm from Edinburgh."

"How heavenly. Such a gorgeous, gorgeous city. Are you an act-or?"

He placed heavy emphasis on the last syllable and Lily smiled as it struck her what a tremendous Lady Bracknell he would make. His delivery of '*A Handbag!*' would be perfection itself.

"No," Helen said, "but I'd love to help in any way I can."

"That is most gracious of you. Please sit down."

As they were taking their seats the door opened, and two men walked in.

Inigo was all smiles again.

"Ah. George, Nev. Good evening."

He introduced them to Lily and Helen.

"Lorraine can't make it," George said. "She's got flu."

"That's a shame, the poor dear." Inigo looked over at Helen. "Would you mind reading the part of Jean tonight, Helen?"

"Not at all."

Glen was next in, followed by a group of five who were introduced as Sylvia, Mary, Anthony, Ian and Zachary. They moved to take seats.

"Ian," Inigo said. "Would you sit next to Glen, please? It makes sense, given the two of you are lovers."

Glen's teeth-baring grin, previously on full display, was wiped from his face in an instant.

"I'm not happy with the role of Linda," Sylvia said, looking pointedly at Inigo as she sat down opposite him. "I hardly have any lines. It was the same story last year."

"Don't you want to be my wife, darling?" Inigo said.

"Don't you darling me and, no, I don't much like the idea of playing your wife."

She looked daggers at him.

Lily decided to take advantage of the uncomfortable silence to narrow their suspect list down.

"What about you, Mary? Were you in last year's production?"

"Yes. This will be my eighth year."

"That's impressive," George said.

"Are you new then, George?" Helen asked, picking up on what Lily was up to.

"Yes. First year for me and Lorraine."

"Me too," Zachary said.

"And me," Nev added.

"We had several drop out after last year," Inigo said. "Most unfortunate. Jethro is particularly missed. Still, it's not surprising he didn't return. Not after what happened." He paused. "I think we had better get on."

He cast his eyes around the table.

"No need for a full performance, this is simply an opportunity for everyone to hear the story performed out loud and get familiar with the script. I take it you are all clear on which characters you are playing?"

They all agreed that they were, Sylvia grudgingly so.

"Wonderful. I will read the part of Gaz's son this evening. Anthony, your son is still happy to take the role, is he?"

"Oh yes, he's very excited."

"Good, good. We'll involve him once rehearsals are underway." He opened his script. "If you'll all turn to the first page." He waited until they'd done so before continuing. "Dave is the first to speak, so if you don't mind, George."

George cleared his throat, looked around the room and then read the first line.

"Gaz, who's gonna buy a rusty girder?"

Lily smiled to herself as the read-through continued. They had already eliminated four people, leaving only Inigo, Sylvia, Ian, Mary and Anthony in the frame. She hadn't warmed to Sylvia, who came across as a troublemaker, but that didn't mean much.

Inigo called a halt after they'd finished reading the first act.

"We'll take a break now. There's coffee and tea outside the room and we can all powder our noses."

"Oh," Glen said. "I didn't realise."

This received some odd looks, but no comments.

Lily sidled up to him as they left the room.

"We're not putting makeup on," she whispered.

"But Inigo said…"

"What he meant was that this is a chance for refreshments and to use the loo."

"Ah, because when I'm a Chippenmale, powder is essential. Not on my nose though."

Lily knew better than to ask where.

"Excuse me, Glen. I want a word with Helen."

She walked over to Helen and pulled her to one side.

"That narrows it down to five," she whispered.

"Seems to, aye. I've got Mary and Anthony sitting either side of me so shall I concentrate on them while you try to

Tiger Bait

get a handle on Sylvia and Ian?"

"That makes sense, and we can both watch Inigo. Look, Ian's on his own. I'll go over and see if I can engage him in conversation."

She walked over and smiled at him.

He stood upright when he saw her approaching and smiled back, but there was a nervous edge to it. In his late thirties, he was her height, perhaps 5ft 7 at a push, and slim with a very pale complexion. His wispy red hair was swept across to half-conceal a receding hairline.

"Hi, Ian. You must be pleased to be playing Lomper?"

"I, ah, yes. Yes. Very pleased."

"Did you have a large role in '*Mamma Mia*' last year?"

"I played Bill, one of Donna's ex-boyfriends."

"The Australian?"

He nodded. "I wasn't going to take part this year, then Inigo said he wasn't returning so I decided to come along."

"Who wasn't returning?"

"Him," He gestured to a group of three standing together.

"Anthony?"

"Yes, Anthony."

"Why?" Lily lowered her voice. "Did you fall out?"

"I wish it were that simple." He sighed. "It was after one of our live performances. The whole business with Jethro was really unpleasant, and then when Anthony…"

"Time to go back in, dears," Inigo said, loudly enough to make Carys on reception turn her head. "Come on. Chop, chop."

The remainder of the read-through went smoothly.

"Thank you, everyone," Inigo said when they'd finished. "We'll meet on Wednesday evening at The Mission Theatre for our first rehearsal. 7:30. Don't be late, and please, please, please, do your absolute best to learn your lines for the first act beforehand."

Lily wanted to speak to Ian, but he was out of the door

and away before she could catch him. She called to Sylvia.

"Sylvia, have you got a moment?"

She turned and looked down her nose at Lily before replying.

"What is it? I have a bus to catch."

"I wonder if you could give me some advice?"

"If you're quick."

Lily led Sylvia away so that they were out of earshot.

"I'm concerned about trolling."

"Trolling?"

"Yes. Abuse on social media. I heard that FADS members have been targeted."

"You mean Facebook and Insta-thingy?"

Lily nodded. "And Tik-tok."

"I don't use any of them. They're full of porn."

"And you haven't received any abusive emails?"

"No." She raised one eyebrow. "Who's been on the receiving end?"

"Inigo for one."

Sylvia sneered. "I'm not surprised after that nasty business with Jethro." She looked at her watch and gave an exasperated sigh. "I'll have to rush now if I'm going to catch my bus. Excuse me."

She pushed past and walked rapidly to the exit.

Lily turned around to find everyone had left except Helen and walked over to her.

"Well, what did you think?"

"Ach, at least we've got it down to five."

"I think we can rule Sylvia out. She told me she doesn't use social media, and I believe her."

"That's good. Down to four then."

Lily wrinkled her nose.

"I'm not so sure. It could be someone who's not participating this year but holds a grudge. Did anyone mention Jethro to you?"

"No."

"He was in 'Mamma Mia', and Ian and Sylvia indicated something unpleasant had happened after one of their performances. It could be that Jethro holds a grudge and is the troll."

"I guess we'll have to do a wee bit more digging at rehearsal on Wednesday."

"You're going to be in the production, then?"

"Aye. Inigo grabbed me on his way out. He wants me to play Linda, Gerald's wife."

"So, Sylvia's got her wish."

Helen laughed.

"She won't be happy though, not when she finds out her character has to pee standing up in a men's urinal."

Chapter 53

Diana sat at the kitchen island, a glass of chardonnay in her hand, and glanced, for the umpteenth time, at the wall clock.

Where the hell were they?

Apollo and Jay had promised to get to hers for eight and it was now nearly half-past.

She took another sip of her wine and resisted the urge to ring. They probably had good reasons for being late. Apollo was most likely putting his boys to bed, while Jay's enterprise was always busiest in the evenings.

The trouble was that she was proud of the plan she'd come up with, and itching to present it to them. The rewards were considerable and would make the money taken from Sebastian Thatcher seem like petty cash.

There were risks of course, but she'd seen how well her team had performed, even that idiot Milo who Apollo had brought in against her better judgement. Not one of them had revealed their face, nor had they referred to each other by name.

Even a single slip-up would have meant taking extreme action, but she'd been ready for that eventuality. There would have been a car accident, Sebastian taking his parents and their friend out for the day and losing control of the vehicle. She'd even chosen the place where the accident would take place, Holcombe Quarry near Shepton Mallet.

Luckily, it hadn't come to that and, after paying her team, Diana had a couple of hundred thousand tucked away in her offshore account, a tidy sum but nothing to the several million this latest venture should bring in.

This time it was even more essential that the team keep themselves unidentifiable. Unlike the kidnapping and ransom, there was no question of their crime being a secret once the money was theirs and, with such a large amount taken, the police would be doing everything in their power to catch the perpetrators.

The front doorbell rang, and she put her glass down and went to open it.

It was Apollo.

He kissed her on the cheek.

"Sorry I'm late, Sis. Is Jay here?"

"Not yet."

She opened the door wide. Apollo walked through, and she was about to close it when she saw Jay storming up the drive.

He rushed through the door.

"Fucking Tyrone! I'll kill the bastard when I get hold of him."

"Shush," Diana said. "Roma's in his room upstairs."

"I don't give a flying…" He paused. "I need a drink."

"Help yourself. You know where it is."

She and Apollo exchanged a look and Apollo shrugged, making it clear that he didn't know why their brother was so angry.

Jay was pouring himself a large measure of whisky when they got to the kitchen.

He looked up at his brother.

"Want one?"

"No. I'm good, thanks."

Apollo fetched himself a beer from the fridge.

"What happened?" Diana asked.

Jay knocked back a decent slug, then slammed the glass back onto the counter.

"He shopped me."

"Tyrone?"

"One of them. He's the most likely." He took another sip from his tumbler. "The police have called me in for interview. It's voluntary, but I'll have to go in to get them off my back."

"Did they give a reason?" Apollo asked.

"That peddler, Flimsy, the one I told you about on Sunday, died in hospital and they're looking for his killer. The police are saying I might have information that could help them with their enquiries, which is shit. I've never even met the tosser." He drained his glass. "They've got nothing to connect me with it. I think they're fishing, and it can only be because Tyrone, Reece or Mickey gave them my name."

He reached into the cupboard for the whisky and poured himself another double.

"What are you going to do?" Diana asked.

"I'm going to have a word with the boys, find out which one it was." He took another sip. "Won't take me long to get it out of them."

"I meant about the interview. Are you taking a solicitor?"

Jay shook his head. "No. That'll make me look guilty." He sighed. "Anyway, I didn't come here to talk about my problems. You going to tell us about your new idea?"

"It's simple really." She took another sip of her chardonnay. "I'm going to persuade an innocent member of the public to steal money, between two and three million, and then hand it over. What's more, his colleagues will help him."

Jay's eyebrows shot up. "Have you been taking magic mushrooms? How are you going to do that?"

"A tiger kidnap."

"A what?"

"It's a technique the IRA used in the seventies and eighties, only they used it to plant car bombs rather than for money. We need to observe and stalk our prey before pouncing, hence the name."

"I don't understand," Apollo said. "If we kidnap someone, how are they going to steal money for us?"

"They don't, their family does."

She could see that her brothers were still confused.

"Have either of you heard of Faversham's?"

They shook their heads.

"It's a bank for the very rich, much like Coutts. I know the name of the man who runs their cash holding centre."

"And you're planning to kidnap him?" Jay asked.

She smiled again.

"No, and here's why the plan's foolproof. We're going to kidnap his daughter. Then, when I give this guy a photo of her, he'll do anything I ask. Our success with the Thatchers shows that we can handle the abduction and imprisonment of our bait, and this approach takes all the risk away from the theft itself."

Jay nodded approvingly.

"Sounds good. I want in. This will be the biggest thing the family has ever pulled off and we should all be involved."

"Consider it done. You too, Apollo, but don't bring Milo this time, okay? I don't trust him to keep his mouth shut."

"No problem."

Diana ran them through her plan and, after discussion, fine-tuned a couple of details.

"It's now a case of stalking our prey and grabbing her when it's safe to do so," she said when she'd finished.

"Who's going to do the stalking?" Jay asked.

"Declan. Flynn's preparing the van."

Chapter 54

Maj was frustrated. He was keen to return to the airport but hadn't heard anything since he'd been in at the weekend.

He decided to ring Fraser.

"Fraser Bruce."

"Hi, Fraser. It's Maj here, Maj Osman."

Fraser laughed.

"Are you tapping into my thoughts?"

"Why?"

"I was about to ring around, and you're on my list. I don't suppose you're available for an evening shift today, are you?"

"Yes, definitely."

Maj had been in work since eight that morning, but decided a white lie was in order.

"I've been sitting on my backside all day so that would suit me down to the ground."

"Good man. It's in Cargo. Do you mind?"

Couldn't be better.

"With Borys?"

"I'm afraid so. I can ring round the others…"

"No, that's fine. He's not so bad."

Another chuckle.

"Aye, lad, aye. I'll believe you, but thousands wouldn't. Shift is five until midnight. Can you be here for five?"

"Shouldn't be a problem."

"Grand. Go straight to Cargo. Thomas'll be there as well."

Maj hung up and rang his wife. She didn't answer so he left a voicemail.

"Asha, it's me. Sorry, but I've been asked to work at Bristol Airport this evening. I won't be back until about one in the morning. Love you."

He hung up and walked over to Sam.

"I've got a shift at last." He looked at his watch. "It starts at five, so I need to head off smartish."

"That's great. I'll tell Luke. Good luck."

"Thanks."

He'd brought more appropriate clothes just in case, jeans and a jumper, and changed quickly in the bathroom before heading downstairs. It was nearly four, so he was cutting it tight.

He was approaching reception when he heard a voice behind him.

"Not good enough!"

He assumed this was directed at someone else until the next words. They were barked out much as a sergeant major might address the weakest member of his squadron.

"Mange! Stop there!"

Maj hadn't met Luke's boss many times, but enough to recognise the stop-start, hawkish voice.

He sighed and turned around.

"Maj, Mr Filcher."

Filcher looked around, momentarily confused.

"Where?"

"No, what I mean is that I'm Maj. That's my name. Not Mange."

"Mmm." Filcher gestured at Maj's clothes. "What's this?"

"What's what?"

"Your clothes. Not good enough. Pullover, denims." He shook his head in disgust.

"I needed to change before leaving."

"Are you part-time, Mange?"

Maj didn't bother to correct him again.

"No, Mr Filcher. I'll be working at Bristol Airport until midnight."

"Moonlighting! Pah!"

"No. I'm working undercover on an investigation."

Maj noticed that Filcher had his briefcase in his hand.

"Are you working this evening as well, Mr Filcher?"

Filcher followed his gaze to his briefcase and pulled his arm back so that it was partly hidden by his body.

"Ah… Yes."

At that moment his secretary, Gloria, appeared behind him.

"Mr Filcher, Peter Dobson rang."

Filcher swung around, then glanced back at Maj before answering.

"Yes. Our meeting. On my way."

"I told him, but he's worried you won't have enough light for nine holes and said he'll meet you on the first tee."

Maj took the opportunity to turn and head rapidly for the exit.

An hour later he parked in the staff car park, rushed through security and headed straight for Cargo-1.

It was just gone five when he walked in to see Borys standing in front of half a dozen rampies. He saw Maj and scowled.

"You are late."

"Sorry, Borys. I was stuck in traffic."

He joined the others and Thomas looked over at him and nodded hello.

"We have three this evening," Borys said. "One in, two out."

He gestured to a corkboard on the wall where a handwritten notice was pinned up.

"You start now to prepare for first consignment." He looked down at his clipboard. "Most of it is in dock number one and marked for DHK3444. It needs moving to dispatch area. Delivery of remainder is running late."

"What time are we expecting it?" the man at the end of the line asked.

"Driver told me 17:35 so must work hard, no slacking."

The line dispersed and, while the Cargo rampies headed straight for dock one, Thomas and Maj walked to the cork board to check the evening's timings.

Today's Schedule

DHK3444	**OUT**	**18:00**
FX9201	**OUT**	**20:30**
SNC528	**IN**	**23:30**

"There's a long gap between the last two," Maj said.

Thomas was about to answer when Borys spoke from behind them.

"Always lazy, you baggage monkeys. No need to study list, simply do as Borys says."

"We were seeing what's expected of us this evening, that's all," Thomas said.

Borys spat on the ground and advanced until his nose was almost touching Thomas's.

"Do as told. Understand?" He turned to Maj. "You too."

Thomas shrugged.

"Come on, Maj, better do as he says."

They went to join the others, and Thomas shook his head as they started moving a box onto one of the forklifts.

"The bastard's even worse than normal."

Maj wondered what this meant, if indeed it meant anything. Borys had been as rude on Sunday, and what he'd done that day had been suspicious, to say the least. Did his attitude today mean he had plans for this evening as well? He was determined to keep a close eye on him.

The first two consignments went off without a hitch. The second FedEx flight was delayed slightly, but that was due to the late arrival of the pilot rather than anything the rampies got wrong.

It was nearly half-past nine when they finished loading FX9201, and they then spent an hour and a half in the rest area awaiting the arrival of SNC528, a Transnational Shipping plane flying in from Amsterdam. As on Maj's first shift, he and Thomas were snubbed by the cargo rampies and resorted to playing cards to while away the time. It at least enabled Maj to gently probe his colleague about PPE, and any slackness in looking after staff, but he was left with the impression that We-Haul and the airport ran an efficient operation.

They were midway through a hand when Borys clapped his hands together.

"Out, everyone. The plane is about to land."

They joined the other rampies in taking the pallet carriers to the stand. Five minutes later the plane, a Boeing 737-400 which had been converted to transport cargo, taxied in and they began unloading. As was always the case, Borys barked orders, and marked boxes off on his clipboard, but did no physical work.

The team transported the cargo to dock number four where a large lorry had reversed into position, its rear doors open and its tail-lift down. They transferred the pallets to the truck, both sides of which bore the words 'South West Freight Haulage' in large blue capital letters.

It was tiring work, and it was half past midnight before they finished. Borys passed a note to the driver, they exchanged a few words, and the lorry left.

"We're done," Thomas said with a sigh. "And about time too. I'm knackered."

"You go on without me," Maj said. "I need to use the loo."

"Okay. See you next time."

This time Maj was telling the truth. He'd had three coffees before the last plane arrived, and was desperate for a wee, so it was with much relief that he relieved himself.

As he washed his hands he wondered if he'd been wrong about Borys. Yes, he'd been rude and abrasive, but that seemed to be par for the course and he'd done nothing suspicious all evening.

He headed for the exit and had walked a hundred paces when he remembered he'd left his coat in the rest area. It was the last thing he needed. He was shattered, having already worked a sixteen-hour day, and he still had an hour's drive ahead of him.

Muttering to himself, he turned around and retraced his steps. As he approached the warehouse, he heard a voice and stopped immediately. It was Borys, and it sounded like he was around the next corner.

Maj stepped forward slowly and silently as far as he could without being seen, stood with his back to the wall and listened carefully.

"…at 12:35," Borys said, his voice quieter than normal, and Maj realised he was on the phone.

There was a short pause.

"Yes, SWFH."

Another silence.

"He is taking the Failand route."

Yet another pause.

"Good. Let me know."

Maj's stomach sank as he recognised this as the end of the conversation.

It wasn't that there was necessarily anything sinister in what had been said. In all likelihood, it was part of the dispatcher's job to update the logistics company, to tell them that their driver had left and was on his way.

But that didn't mean that Borys, an unpleasant man at the best of times, wouldn't be apoplectic with rage if he found that Maj had been prying on him for a second time. And what was to say he didn't have the hammer, or worse, in his coat pocket.

Maj looked back at the direction he had come. The path was straight for at least fifty yards with no side alleys.

If Borys walked towards him and turned the corner, he had nowhere to hide.

Should he brazen it out? Walk forward as if he hadn't heard a thing, feign surprise at seeing the Pole and tell him he had forgotten his coat?

No.

The idea was ludicrous.

He'd told more or less the same story on Sunday, and there was no way Borys would believe him a second time.

There were footsteps.

The man was moving towards him.

Then Borys's phone started ringing and the footsteps stopped.

Maj saw his chance, but he had to move quickly.

He turned and walked as quietly as he could back towards the exit and safety, hoping and praying he could reach the turning before the conversation ended.

"Hello," he heard Borys say. "Yes, it is…"

Maj was ten yards along the pathway now and could no longer hear the words.

He upped his pace.

Twenty yards.

He started running, confident he was now of earshot, reached the corner and raced around it.

He paused for a moment, panting, then started running again, fearful that the Pole had heard something and might even now be chasing him, a weapon in his hand.

Maj was still shaking when he climbed into his car, but relieved that his wallet and keys had been in his trouser pockets and not in his coat.

He allowed himself five seconds to regain his breath before turning the engine on and starting his drive back to Bath.

Chapter 55

Becky was smiling to herself as she got off the bus.

The sun was shining, not a common occurrence in Bristol in March, and everything felt right with the world.

The baby would change their lives forever, but for the better, she was sure of it. The timing was good too. She and Ronnie had stable jobs, and he seemed to have fully recovered from the problems that had plagued him for the past few years.

She'd loved telling their families. Her mum and dad had been over the moon, keen for her to keep them up to date with developments. They'd offered to buy the buggy before spending considerable time deliberating what they wanted to be called by the little one, eventually plumping for Grandad and Grandma.

Helen, who was going to be 'Nanny', had been delighted as well, but that was Helen for you, always positive and upbeat.

Becky walked towards the butcher's shop, hoping that this time she would find Mr Khan awake. A flat had come up less than half a mile away which would be ideal for him. It was on the ground floor and, most importantly, within his budget. She was looking forward to telling him about it.

As she drew nearer to the entrance, it occurred to her that she might encounter the Irishman again. It was unlikely though. Five days had passed since she'd seen him confront Abdul, and she was sure that the gambling debt would be settled by now. After all, it was only a hundred pounds.

She walked into the shop to see Abdul behind the counter. He had his back to her and was cleaving a large slab of meat into chops.

He turned around and she saw that he had a plaster

stretched across the top of his right cheek.

Abdul saw her looking and laughed.

"Excuse this." He put his finger to the plaster. "I cut myself shaving."

He was the kind of man with a permanent five o'clock shadow, but even so, the plaster seemed well above the area she'd have expected him to shave. However, she decided to let it pass.

"Is Mr Khan in?"

"Yes, and he's awake this time."

She made her way to the old man's room at the back of the house.

"Hello, Mr Khan."

"Hello, Becky. Would you like a cup of tea?'

"I'd love one, but I'll make it."

He smiled.

"Thank you, my dear."

She made them both drinks and then showed him the apartment on her iPad.

"Thank you so much for finding this," he said when she'd finished. "It's lovely and the sooner I can move out the better. I don't like being a burden to my son and his family."

"With any luck, it'll be within the next few weeks. I'll do my best to get it through as soon as I can."

"Thank you," he said for the third time.

"I'll be back when I've got the forms for you to sign."

"Goodbye, dear."

"Goodbye, Mr Khan."

She stood up and returned to the shop to find Abdul taking payment from a customer.

Becky waited until the woman had left before speaking.

"I've found your father a flat, Abdul, and he loves it."

"That's excellent. The sooner he can get out of this place the better."

This took her aback.

"Oh."

He saw her reaction and held his hand up.

"No, I didn't mean... I'm happy for my father to stay here, but, well, you were here on Friday. You saw that man." He put his hand to the wound on his cheek without seeming to realise what he was doing. "I'd hate to think what he might do to Dad if I'm not here."

"You've paid him though?"

"For this month, yes."

"This month? I thought it was a gambling debt."

Abdul swallowed and stared at her for a few seconds.

"I'm, ah... The amount I owed was £200. I'm paying it in two instalments."

"I see."

"Becky, you won't tell anyone about this, will you? It's very embarrassing."

"Of course not, Abdul. Your secret's safe with me."

She left the shop to find the sun had vanished, the sky now a blanket of grimy grey clouds which held the regrettable promise of rain. The temperature had dropped by several degrees as well, and she tightened her coat around her neck before starting the walk back to the bus stop.

Poor Abdul. He'd built up a gambling debt and was clearly struggling to repay it.

But the more she thought about it, the more she wondered why. Was £200 really a struggle for him to pull together?

When she reached the bus stop, she had the sudden sense that someone had been following her. Spinning around, she caught the tail-end of a coat as someone darted down a side alley.

She stepped forward and looked down the narrow track between the backs of two rows of shops. The man was moving quickly, almost running. He was tall, and for a moment she wondered if it might be the man who'd threatened her the week before.

But, no. That was a ridiculous thought.

As she watched, he darted left and disappeared from view. She hesitated, then shook her head. This was nonsense. Even if it was the Irishman, the one who'd been demanding payment from Abdul, he had no interest in her. She was a customer in a butcher's shop, nothing more, nothing less.

She turned, castigating herself for being paranoid, then paused as she heard a soft shuffling, almost as if someone was creeping up on her.

Suddenly panicked, Becky swung back around to see who was making the noise.

And that was when she saw him.

Chapter 56

Luke looked up from his paperwork when he heard Maj enter the Ethics Room and could immediately see that he was shattered. His eyes looked drawn, and it was obvious that he hadn't shaved.

"Sorry I'm so late, Luke," Maj said as he hung his coat up and walked over.

"Don't be ridiculous. After the day you had, I assumed we wouldn't see you at all today."

"You got my text then?"

"Yes. What time did you get home?"

"About half past two this morning."

"And was it worthwhile?"

Maj shrugged.

"I'm not sure. As far as I can see, both We-Haul and the airport run a tidy ship. There are individuals who might forego one or other piece of PPE, but that's down to them. The procedures seem tight enough."

"That sounds conclusive, so why not stop now, tell June Fairbanks her accusations are unfounded, and close the investigation?"

"It's that Polish guy I told you about."

"Borys?"

Maj nodded.

"As I told you, he's a nasty piece of work, but it's not just that. There's something off about him."

"Has he done something else that you found suspicious?"

"Not really. After we unloaded the last plane's cargo onto a lorry, I overheard him calling the logistics company to tell them the driver had left." He paused. "It wasn't so much what he said as the way he said it. It was almost as if he was sharing a secret."

"Is there anyone you could speak to, to see if calling the logistics company is standard practice?"

"That's a good idea. I could ask Thomas. He's the rampie I've been working alongside."

"Okay. Let me know how you get on."

"Will do."

"And don't stay late. You need a good night's sleep."

"Thanks, Luke."

"And now, you'll have to excuse me. Mr Ogden and I need to leave for Portishead."

He called over to the youngest member of the team.

"Are you ready to leave, Josh?"

"With you in two tics, guv."

*

This was the third time Luke had given Josh a lift to Portishead.

And he was again regretting it.

"We haven't agreed on a venue," Josh said, moving on from the previous fifteen minutes which had been spent speculating on the best time of year to get married.

Luke tried to feign enthusiasm.

"Haven't you?"

He would have given anything for the chance to listen to the last thirty minutes of '*Isle of the Dead*'. Bone was near to identifying the villain of the piece, and he was itching to see if his suspicions had been right.

"…a barn," Josh said.

Luke glanced over at him, having not taken in the first part of the sentence.

"What?"

"Leanne wants to get married in a barn."

"What, with chickens and cows all over the place?"

"No, guv. They keep them out of the way I think. She says they can be quite posh. Expensive too."

"Right."

"I'd prefer a hotel. Not a swanky one, but a small one, maybe a converted farmhouse."

"Uh-huh."

"Although they can be expensive too."

"I dare say."

"What do you think?"

"About what?"

"The venue."

"I can't say I really mind, son."

Josh turned to gaze out of the side window and for a wonderful moment Luke thought he'd finished speaking.

However, the peace only lasted a few seconds.

"I'm going to be a father."

Luke almost slammed the brakes on in shock.

"Why didn't you say?"

"No, guv. Leanne's not pregnant."

"But…"

"It's what happens next, isn't it? After we're married, we'll have a family." He shook his head. "I don't feel old enough to have children."

"You're not. You're much too young. Wa-ay too young."

"You think so? How old were you when Ben and Chloe were born?"

"I was…"

He had to think for a moment, then realised he'd been twenty-four, less than two years older than Josh was now, and decided to change the subject.

"I'm surprised you haven't been asking me questions about this interview. Last time you didn't stop."

"I have got a few actually."

Shit.

"What do we do," Josh went on, "if the perp says 'No comment' to every question?"

Luke chose to ignore his use of 'perp'.

"He won't."

"Eh?"

"We're confident he is, as Flimsy put it, 'the main man'. His name was put to those three mid-level dealers we interviewed, and their reactions made it blindingly obvious that they work for him. He's got no record though, and he'll have gone to great pains to distance himself from day-to-day operations. I guarantee he'll come in playing Mr Innocent and won't bring a lawyer with him. Every question we ask will be played back with a straight bat and he'll smile his way through it."

"So, what line of interrogation will you take?"

"We'll be questioning him, son, not using bright lights and Chinese water torture."

"Gotcha. Questioning, then. How will you approach it?"

"It'll be a case of playing it by ear. Throw a few names at him, see how he reacts and go from there."

"What about me? Will I have a role to play?"

"We won't be playing good cop, bad cop if that's what you mean. This guy's going to be too smart for that to work, but that doesn't mean you have to stay quiet throughout. DCI Franks was impressed with you when the two of you interviewed Tyrone Goodwin. If you think we've missed anything, or there's something we should probe a little deeper on, you should speak up."

"Gucci."

"Provided DCI Franks agrees, that is. She's the SIO and will take the lead in the interview."

"Gotcha, guv. Exciting, isn't it? Mucho intrigo."

Luke smiled.

"It's certainly going to be interesting, Josh, but I'll be surprised if we catch Jay Curtis out. If he's as high up as we think he is, he's going to be a hard nut to crack."

Chapter 57

DCI Franks was waiting for them in the corner office of Operation Tooting's incident room when Luke and Josh arrived.

"I've had a call to say Jay Curtis is here," she said. "He turned up half an hour early."

"Trying to impress us with his cooperative attitude, I dare say," Luke said.

She smiled. "Probably. Take a seat. No harm in keeping him waiting."

They sat down.

"How are you going to play it, Ma'am?" Josh asked, then corrected himself. "I mean, DCI Franks."

She smiled again, and Luke was beginning to understand what Pete had meant earlier in the week. She seemed like a completely different person, more relaxed and comfortable in herself.

"Don't worry about it, Josh. Call me whatever you like, as long as it's not rude."

"I wouldn't…"

She held her hand up to stop him and looked over at Luke.

"I'd like you to take the lead. You've got more experience than me, and I'll come in when necessary."

"If you're sure."

"Yes. I think that'll work well. Josh, you stay out of it unless you've spotted something you think we may have missed, and even then, I think it's best if you ask for a word outside. Okay?"

Josh nodded.

They went downstairs to the interview suite to find Sergeant Fowler was again the officer on duty.

"Hello, Sergeant," Nicole said.

"Ma'am."

She looked at Josh, tapped the open book on the counter and handed him a pen.

"Fill it in."

"Ah… thanks."

He entered his details below the most recent entry and passed the pen to Luke who did the same.

"Thanks, Sergeant," Luke said as he passed the pen back."

She didn't acknowledge this but gestured down the corridor.

"Room 3."

Josh put on his best smile.

"Thanks, Sergeant. Lovely to talk to you as ever."

This was met with a haughty sniff and a death stare, but he continued smiling before turning to follow the others down the corridor.

Luke opened the door for Nicole and followed her in, Josh at the rear.

Jay Curtis was relaxing at the table, a coffee mug in his hand and a broad, knowing smile across his face. He had a strong jawline, neatly trimmed black hair, and smart business-casual clothes.

Luke took an instant dislike to him.

"Thanks for coming in, Mr Curtis," Nicole said.

"Not at all." His smile widened even further. "If I can help the police in any way…"

She took a seat opposite him, and Luke sat next to her.

Luke could see that Josh was struggling to know where to position himself, and waved his hand towards a seat in the corner of the room behind Curtis.

Josh nodded and took the seat.

"New recruit, is he?" Curtis asked.

Nicole ignored the question.

"Thanks for agreeing to come in, Mr Curtis."

"Not at all. Always ready to help the police, especially when they're as pretty as you."

Luke was pleased to see that she didn't react to this in the slightest.

"I'm DCI Franks and this is Luke Sackville."

Curtis looked over at Luke.

"Not in the police then?"

"No. I'm a consultant."

Curtis gestured over his shoulder with his left thumb.

"What about him?"

"That's Josh Ogden," Nicole said. "He's also a consultant."

He shook his head in mock horror.

"Terrible, this understaffing. Having to bring consultants in left, right and centre. The government ought to give our police forces more budget, keep us safe in our beds."

This was all accompanied by the same broad smile and knowing look.

A look that said to Luke, *'You know I'm a criminal. I know I'm a criminal. But you've got bugger-all chance of catching me out.'*

"Mr Curtis," Nicole began, "are you happy to proceed with this interview without a solicitor present?"

He took a sip of his coffee before answering.

"Of course. I've got nothing to hide. It's awful what happened to that poor man, and I'm not sure how I can help, but I'll do what I can."

Nicole clicked the record button.

"Interview with Janus Curtis in interview room 3 at Avon and Somerset HQ. The time is 14:20. Also present are DCI Nicole Franks, Luke Sackville and Josh Ogden."

"Nicole's a nice name. It suits you."

Again, she ignored him.

"Mr Curtis," she began, "I'd like to start by capturing some background details for the recording."

"Of course."

His smile was now really getting on Luke's nerves.

"Full name?"

"Janus Augustus Curtis."

"Date of birth?"

"28th of July 1985."

"And your home address?"

"13, Royal York Crescent, Bristol."

"What do you do for a living, Mr Curtis?" Luke asked. "It must pay well to afford a house there."

The cocky smile returned.

"Yes, I've been lucky. I dabble in a number of areas, but most of my earnings come from investments."

Luke nodded as if he was completely happy with the answer.

"As you were told when you were invited to interview, Torquill McCoy, otherwise known as Flimsy, was viciously assaulted on Friday evening. He fell into a coma and passed away on Sunday night."

"Awful. That poor man."

"How well did you know Flimsy, Mr Curtis?"

"Not at all. I've never met him, and the first time I heard his name was when the police rang me."

"That surprises me, because DCI Franks and I interviewed Mr McCoy last week and he claimed that you are, and I quote, 'the main man'."

Curtis furrowed his brows.

"Main man for what?"

"For drugs. That you're the leader of the Bristol drug cartel."

"What?" He gave a dry laugh. "You mean he accused me of being a drug dealer? That's utter nonsense." He held both hands up in supplication. "I swear on my father's grave, Mr Sackville, I'm an innocent man."

"Your father was Bill Curtis, is that correct?"

"Yes, that's right. He died an awful death from cancer a few years ago."

"And was he also an innocent man?"

"Of course."

"Do you know Tyrone Goodwin?"

"No."

"Reece Stevens?"

"No."

"Michael, known as Mickey, Wright?"

"No. Who are these men?"

"We suspect them of being drug dealers, and one of them told us he works for you."

"Which one?"

"Why do you ask?"

"Interested, that's all, but I've never heard of any of them."

Over his shoulder, Josh had his hand raised high in the air and Luke took the hint.

He turned to Nicole.

"Is it okay if we take a short break, DCI Franks?"

She nodded.

"Interview paused at 14:39."

She pressed the stop button.

Chapter 58

"It was Tyrone who told us he works for Curtis, wasn't it?" Josh asked in hushed tones, once the three of them were in the corridor.

Nicole nodded. "He said he did odd jobs for him."

"Why, Josh?" Luke asked. "What are you thinking?"

"I was wondering about circling back to it. Maybe ask other questions then come at it from the other end, ask if he uses handymen at all."

Luke turned to Nicole.

"What do you think?"

"It's a good idea." She paused. "I also think that returning to the subject of Bill Curtis might be productive. He was on the defensive when you asked about him."

Luke considered this for a moment.

"I'll take the handyman angle, but it might be better if you probe on his father. It's more of a personal matter and I think you might be able to engage him better on it than I would."

"Because he's been trying to flirt with me?"

"He wasn't exactly subtle about it."

"Yes, okay. I'll ask him about Bill Curtis." She smiled. "Don't expect me to flutter my eyelashes at him though."

"Good, and when we've had enough of his rebuttals and denials, I'd like one of us to be more aggressive and open up with what we think he's up to. Do you want to do it, or shall I?"

"She's great at 'bad cop'," Josh said and turned to Nicole. "You can use your look again."

"Okay," she said. "I'll do it."

"Your look?" Luke asked.

"I'll explain later."

Tiger Bait

They returned to the interview room and Nicole pressed the button.

"Interview resumed at 14:48."

"Have you put more make-up on, DCI Franks?" Curtis said. "Or is it the way the light's catching your face?"

Luke was pleased to see that, yet again, Nicole didn't react.

"Torquill McCoy also told us," Luke began, "that he'd overheard someone talking about killing three people."

"How awful. Was it one of those three dealers you mentioned?"

"No. McCoy said it was Declan O'Brien. Does that name mean anything to you?"

Curtis shook his head.

"Another blank. I'm so sorry. I'm not being of much help, am I?" He paused. "Are you sure you can trust the word of poor Mr McCoy? Drug dealers must lie all the time to protect themselves."

"I didn't say McCoy was a drug dealer."

There was a momentary hesitation before Curtis replied.

"Oh. I assumed he was, given that's all you seem to have been talking about."

"As it happens, he *was* a dealer. Perhaps that's how you came across him. Do you use drugs?"

"No."

For almost the first time, Luke believed one of Curtis's answers. He pretended to consider his denial for a moment.

"Is there a chance he worked for you in another capacity? Your house must be very big. Did he help with decorating or around the garden?"

"Definitely not. I'd remember his name if he had."

"And yet you don't remember Tyrone Goodwin's name, even though he's done a number of handyman jobs for you. The way he was talking it's clear that the two of you are on first-name terms."

Curtis hesitated, but only for a second, then flicked his fingers.

"Ty, that's who it is. Sorry, I should have recognised the name, but he introduced himself as Ty and he's never told me his surname."

"Isn't it on his invoices?"

"It's always been cash in hand." He laughed. "Oh dear, I'm not going to be in trouble with the tax man, am I?"

"What, like Al Capone?"

Curtis glared at Luke and there was a few seconds silence.

Nicole saw her opportunity.

"Do you mind if I ask you a couple of questions about your family, Mr Curtis?"

He smiled at her in a way that made Luke, and doubtless Nicole, feel slightly nauseous.

"Are you keen to know if I'm single or married, DCI Franks?"

Yet again, she ignored him.

"Are you aware that your father was well known to the police, and was suspected of being a drug trafficker?"

"Of course I am. It was ridiculous. Someone high up had it in for him, but neither of us could ever understand why."

"So, he was an honest man?"

"Very much so. More than that, he supported local charities and he was a wonderful father."

"I see."

She smiled and managed to hold it firm when he returned his smoothness-personified grin back at her.

"I wonder if this is all confusion on McCoy's part," she went on.

"It must be."

"Because you've got a twin brother, haven't you?"

"Yes, Apollo. What of it?"

"I wonder if McCoy might have confused the two of

you." She paused. "What does Apollo do for a living?"

"He doesn't deal drugs, if that's what you're implying. He works in logistics."

"I believe you, Mr Curtis."

"Good."

She hesitated.

"The reason I believe you is because if he did deal drugs then he would be messing on your patch."

"What do you mean?"

"Come on, Mr Curtis, we're not stupid."

Luke saw Josh gesticulating and looked over to see him mouthing, "Her look. She's doing her look."

"We've spoken to four people in the last week," she went on, her voice slightly raised, "who are clearly scared at the very mention of your name. One of them lost his life as a result of speaking out."

"I don't…"

She held her hand up.

"Let me finish. It's clear to me that you are not only a drug dealer, you're the kingpin, the scum that's risen to the top. You've taken on the drug cartel from your father, and you're running a series of operations that are spreading misery and disaster across Bristol."

He shook his head.

"This is farcical. You've got nothing."

"I may not have much now, but I've got an excellent team and believe me when I guarantee we won't stop until we've put you behind bars."

He sneered and couldn't bite back his next words.

"Dig too deep and you'll find yourself in trouble."

"Are you threatening me, Mr Curtis?"

He didn't respond.

She glared at him for a few seconds, then said, "Interview concluded at 15:06," and pressed the stop button.

Chapter 59

Helen got off the 522 at Bath bus station and pulled her phone out of her handbag as she began the short walk to Corn Street.

Her son answered straight away.

"Hi, Mum. You sound like you're on the move."

"I am. I'm in Bath for a rehearsal."

"A rehearsal?"

"Don't laugh. I've joined an amateur theatre group."

He laughed.

"Stop it, Ronnie."

"I never had you down as a drama queen, Mum."

"Very funny. It's a wee work thing. I thought I'd call to check you're both okay, well, to check Becky's okay. Any morning sickness?"

"We're both fine and no, there's no morning sickness. Not yet anyway. Becky's at The Grapes in the city centre this evening, meeting up with a few friends to tell them about the baby. She went straight from the office and I'm expecting her home at any minute."

"That's nice. I hope she had a good time."

There was silence at the other end, and she could sense he was troubled by something.

"Are you okay, Ronnie?"

"Yes, but I'll be pleased when she's back safe and well."

"Why do you say that?"

"You remember she told you about that incident at the butcher's shop?"

"Of course I do."

"Well, she was due to go back today to see Mr Khan because she's found him a flat. I'm sure nothing happened, but I'd like to speak to her to put my mind at rest."

"Have you tried ringing?"

"Yes, but it's going straight to voicemail."

"Try not to worry. I'm sure she's fine."

"I know, Mum, but I can't help it."

"Ring me when she's home, won't you?"

"Yes. I'll let you know as soon as she's back."

She hung up.

"Good evening, my dear lady."

The booming voice could only belong to one man, and sure enough, when she turned around Inigo advanced towards her.

"Hi, Inigo."

"On time, I see. Bodes well. I dislike bad timekeepers. It makes things very difficult when one is directing."

"I'm sure."

They passed McDonalds and headed down Corn Street to number 32, a grand Georgian building.

Inigo saw that she was admiring it.

"Splendid, isn't it? Originally built as a Catholic chapel. Ah, here's Ian."

The three of them made their way inside where Lily was deep in conversation with Mary, Zachary, George and a woman who Helen assumed was his wife, Lorraine. Anthony stood to one side talking to a young boy who had to be his son.

The only person on the stage was Glen, who was doing push-ups and alternately counting and grunting.

"Ugh… Forty-two elephants.… Ugh.… Forty-three elephants… Ugh…"

A few minutes later the others arrived.

"Ah, the full ensemble," Inigo said. "Wonderful. Come around, my friends."

"Five more for the fifty," Glen said between elephants.

They all watched in patience as he finished five more push-ups then stood up and wiped sweat from his brow. He was displaying all his teeth, evidently pleased with himself.

"Not sure I'll want to kiss you when you look like that," Ian said.

Everyone laughed.

Except for Glen.

"Nice one, Ian," Nev said, patting him on the shoulder."

"Today," Inigo began, "we will embark together upon the adventure that is Act One. I hope you have learned your lines."

There was some mumbling, and a whispered, "Nearly" from George.

"I have," Mary said.

"It's disgraceful," Sylvia said.

"What, that I've learned my part?"

"No. My character. I have to urinate."

"Pretend to urinate," Ian said.

She huffed and blew out her cheeks. "Obviously, Ian."

"Ladies and gentlemen," Inigo said, attempting to bring them together. "We need to start. I don't want us to concentrate on movement tonight so much as our characters and your accents. You need to unleash your inner Sean Bean."

"Madonna," Glen said, nodding his head.

Everyone turned to look at him.

"What?" Nev asked.

"Madonna," Glen repeated, his ivories back on full display mode. "They were married."

"That's Sean Penn," Lily said.

Glen nodded again.

"That's right." He turned to Inigo. "I've been practising."

He stepped forward and said, in his best John Wayne accent, "Get off your horse and drink your milk."

Inigo sighed.

"Sheffield, Glen. The play is set in Sheffield."

Helen could see that Glen was struggling with this.

Tiger Bait

"You need a Yorkshire accent, Glen, not an American accent."

He nodded slowly as he grasped what she meant.

"Like Fred Tanner's?"

"Exactly."

"Right," Inigo said. "George, Anthony and, sorry, what's your son's name?"

"Martin," Anthony said.

"Please can the three of you move onto the stage."

He waited until they were in position.

"Excellent. Let's start."

"Gaz, who's gonna buy a rusty girder?" George asked.

"Come on," Anthony said.

"Dad, it's stealing," Martin said.

And so it went on.

Inigo cringed a few times at the accents, understandably so, Helen felt, given they ranged from completely absent to unintelligibly overdone, but seemed to be prepared to let things flow.

It was only when the first scene was finished that he called a halt.

"Well done, everyone. Now, George, when you…"

He proceeded to give comments and advice, then asked them to start again. They did so and Helen could already see that there was some improvement.

Rehearsals continued for an hour at which point Inigo called a halt.

"Break time, everyone. We'll resume in twenty."

Helen walked over to Lily.

"I'm going to corner Mary if I can," she whispered.

Lily nodded.

"I'll see if I can talk to Sylvia, and perhaps Anthony, although it's difficult. His son's hanging onto him like a limpet."

Helen headed over to Mary.

"Mary, have you a got a moment?"

"Yes. Why."

Helen pulled her to one side and lowered her voice.

"I heard a rumour that you were being trolled online. Is it true?"

"Yes. It's been awful."

Mary turned out to be a chatterbox, and the next twenty minutes were taken up by detailed descriptions of every insulting email and Facebook post she'd seen.

It was disappointing, because Helen had hoped to corner at least two others, but she did notice that Lily managed to circulate, moving on from Sylvia to Ian, Nev and finally Anthony.

"Time's up," Inigo called. "I'd like another run-through of the scene where Gaz and Dave hear Lomper trying to start his car. George, start with the line, 'You need a hand?'."

George, Anthony and Ian mounted the stage.

"You need a hand?" George asked, then paused. "Yeah, it's your HT leads, I reckon."

Lily sidled across to Helen as they continued delivering their lines.

"I know who the troll is," she whispered.

"You do? Who…"

"Ladies," Inigo called. "Silence, please."

"Sorry," they both said.

"I'll tell you later," Lily whispered and moved away.

"From the top," Inigo said.

"You need a hand?" George repeated. "Yeah, it's your HT leads, I reckon."

Chapter 60

"Well done everyone," Inigo said. "I think that's enough for tonight. We'll continue with the first act next week but Nev, Sylvia, please, please, my dears, try to learn your lines."

"I'll do my best," Nev said.

"It's not easy when you've changed my character," Sylvia said haughtily.

He ignored this and turned to Helen.

"Well done, Helen. I think you'll make an excellent Linda."

"Thanks."

She called across to Lily as the others started to move towards the exit.

"I need to ring my son. I'll be with you in a tick."

"Okay. I'll see you outside."

She turned her phone on and was horrified to see that she had a series of missed calls, all from Ronnie.

She hit callback, and as it rang, she couldn't stop the awful thoughts going through her head. It was nonsense, of course it was, but if he didn't answer should she go straight around to check everything was okay? What if…

"Hello, Mum."

"Ronnie. Thank goodness. I had five missed calls. Is everything okay?"

"That's why I was trying to ring. I said I'd let you know when Becky got home."

"So, she's home?"

"She got here about five minutes after we spoke." He paused. "I forgot. You were in a rehearsal, weren't you? Is that why the phone was turned off?"

"Yes." Helen heaved a sigh of relief. "She didn't encounter that awful man again then?"

"No. She ran into one of her old school friends though. Hadn't seen him since sixth form. That's why she was late."

"Why wasn't she answering her phone?"

"It had died. She's always forgetting to put it on charge so I shouldn't have been surprised." He paused. "How was your rehearsal?"

"It was good thanks."

"Great. I'd better go."

"Okay. Bye, Ronnie."

She hung up to find she was the last one remaining besides Inigo, who was standing by the exit door and had clearly been waiting for her to finish her call.

"Sorry, Inigo."

"Not a problem, my dear. Not a problem at all."

He gestured for her to go first, then followed her through the exit, locking the door after him.

They emerged onto Corn Street to find George and Ian talking to each other, but no sign of Lily.

"Have you seen Lily?" Helen asked.

"She had to rush off," George said.

"Did she say why?"

"No, but from the look on her face it was something serious."

"We were chatting to her," Ian said, "when she got a text. Her face went white as a sheet when she read it."

"She didn't say what the message was?"

"No. She just said, 'Excuse me, I'll see you next week,' and headed off in that direction." He waved his hand towards the western end of Corn Street. "Practically running, wasn't she, George?"

George nodded. "Practically running."

"Okay, thanks. I'll ring her."

She gave them all a wave and started walking towards the bus station. As she did so, she called Lily's number. After five or six rings it went to voicemail.

"Hi, Lily. It's Helen. I hope everything's okay. Give me a

call when you can."
　She hung up.

Chapter 61

Lily was walking as quickly as she could towards Avon Street. The Dark Horse was in Kingsmead Square, which meant it was only a five-minute walk.

She was worried sick. Her dad had had high blood pressure for several years, and his doctor had repeatedly advised him to lose weight. However, he'd failed to stick to every diet her mum had planned for him, and it was almost inevitable this would happen.

At least he had had the good fortune to be near a doctor when he collapsed.

'My name is Doctor Carol Ingram,' the message had said. 'Your father has suffered a heart attack but is still conscious. We are at The Dark Horse cocktail bar.'

She glanced down at her iPhone in case there had been another message and saw that someone had left a voicemail. For a second she wondered why it hadn't rung, before realising she'd left it in silent mode after the rehearsal had ended. Annoyed with herself, she clicked the action button on the side of the phone, then called voicemail in case it was the doctor ringing with an update.

She listened to Helen's message and hung up, deciding she'd ring her back later. Right now, her priority was her father.

Lily turned onto Avon Street. It was deserted and she speed-walked along the middle of the road. She was about halfway along when she heard an engine. Turning, she saw a van heading her way.

Thinking how stupid she was, she darted sideways onto the pavement, but was shocked when the van veered in her direction, then mounted the kerb and continued towards her. There was a split second where her eyes met those of the driver, but his eyes seemed to be floating in space, no other part of his face visible.

The only good news in all of this, if you could call it good news, was that the van was moving slowly. It was still gaining on her though and she had to act quickly.

Lily veered around and saw a footpath to the left between two large blocks of flats.

This was her chance, her only chance. For some reason, whether it was to mug her or something worse, the driver was pursuing her. At any moment he might leap out of his van and she needed to act quickly. She was a fast runner, so with luck she'd be able to outrun him if he chased her on foot.

She turned into the footpath and increased her pace. There was no noise behind her and, after she'd covered twenty or so yards, she stopped and turned around.

The van had parked across the end of the footpath, but there was no sign of the driver.

But that didn't mean she was safe. For all she knew, this path was a dead end. And, even if it wasn't, he might even now be running around the other side of one of the blocks of flats so that he was ready for her when she emerged.

What was certain was that she was in danger and she needed help.

She decided to call the police and turned her phone to enter 999 on the screen.

She'd typed two 9s when she thought she heard a noise. Before she could react, a bag was thrust over her head, coming down almost to her elbows. At the same time, a hand clamped hard against her mouth, and something sharp dug into the left side of her waist.

This was followed by a hissed voice in her right ear, the accent unmistakeably Irish.

"Don't make a fucking sound."

His hand was held so tight to her face that she couldn't have screamed if she'd tried.

"Walk to the van."

He released his hand from her mouth but prodded her again with what she could only assume was a knife.

She walked forwards.

"Stop."

He paused, then spoke again, slightly louder this time.

"All clear?"

Another man responded. "All clear."

Her assailant then lifted her up and slung her over his shoulder, walked a few paces and then dropped her unceremoniously onto the floor of the van.

She heard him climb in. A few seconds later the doors were closed, and she started to sit up.

"Why have you…"

Before she could finish the sentence, his boot connected with her thigh and she let out an involuntary yelp of pain.

"Don't speak, and don't fucking move."

She lay back down again.

A few seconds later the engine started and the van headed off.

Chapter 62

Luke looked up when Helen walked in.
"How did you get on yesterday evening?"
"Lily thinks she knows who the online troll is."
"That's great news. Who is it?'
"She didn't have a chance to tell me."
She paused and he could see the concern on her face.
"What's wrong?"
"I'm worried about her, Luke. She said she'd meet me outside the theatre, but when I came out she'd gone, and now she's not answering her phone."
"Any clue as to why she left?"
"George and Ian told me she received a text message and seemed upset by it."
"Hopefully, there's a simple explanation. Look, it's only half-past eight. Let's give it an hour and, if Lily hasn't appeared by then, and hasn't been in touch, let's talk again and decide what to do."
"Aye. Okay."
Luke returned to the monthly report. He'd almost finished and was desperate to see the back of it.
He nodded hello to Josh when he arrived a few minutes later, and Maj some ten minutes after.
There was still no sign of Lily, and he noticed Helen looking disappointed each time it wasn't her walking into the Ethics Room.
Could it be that the troll was onto her? Had he or she sent her a text to divert her away and then set on her, either verbally or physically?
It was unlikely, but there was always the chance. He decided he'd ring Pete to see if anything had been called in that might shine a light on it.

However, he didn't want to do it when Helen was in earshot, and walked over to Sam.

"I'll be back in a few minutes. I need to ring Pete."

"Okay."

He left the office and found an empty meeting room further along the corridor.

Pete answered straight away.

"Morning, Luke."

"Hi. I wonder if you could do me a favour?"

"Shoot."

"Do you remember Lily?"

"Yes. Is she working with you again?"

"Yes, and yesterday she…" He stopped speaking when his phone pinged. "Just a second, Pete. This might be her."

He opened the WhatsApp message and saw that it was indeed from Lily.

Sorry, Jethro. I won't be able to come into the office today. My father has had a heart attack.

"Was it her?" Pete asked.

"Yes."

"You sound hesitant."

"She got my name wrong, that's all, but yes, it's from Lily. Sorry, Pete. False alarm."

"No worries."

He hung up and stared at the message for a few seconds.

Why had she put Jethro instead of Luke? It certainly couldn't have been the fault of autocorrect.

Then he realised what must have happened. Lily would have sent a few messages off quickly, wanting to minimise time away from her father. He would only be one recipient with others going to friends she'd arranged to meet, her agent, possibly even the director of '*The Proposal*', the play she'd been given a part in.

In her stressed state, it was no surprise she'd got the names mixed up.

He returned to the Ethics Room and walked over to Helen.

"I've had a message from Lily."

"Oh, thank goodness."

"She's fine, but her father has had a heart attack."

"The poor man."

"She only lives down the road from me, so I'll pop around when I get home today and see if she needs anything."

"She might be at the hospital if they've kept him in."

"That's true. Still, no harm in trying."

Chapter 63

Maj realised he was staring at the screen, his mind doing cartwheels but no progress being made. He turned to the next desk.

"Josh, can I run a couple of thoughts by you?"

"Is this about Project Douglas?"

"Yes. I'm convinced the guy in Cargo is up to something, but I'm too tired to work out what to do next. I don't want to disturb the others, so do you mind if we chat in the canteen?"

"No problem."

Five minutes later they were seated at a table by the window, Maj with a flat white and Josh cradling a hot chocolate.

Maj watched as Josh put his drink down on the table, pulled a bag from his pocket, opened it and tipped mini-marshmallows into his cup.

"They don't have them here," he said when he saw Maj's raised eyebrow, "so I asked if I could bring my own."

He raised the cup to his mouth, took a sip, then grinned.

"Delicioso."

He wiped his mouth with a paper napkin.

"Right. I'm all yours."

"As you know, I've only been on two shifts, and both times I've seen the shift leader acting suspiciously."

"This is the Polish guy, Borys?"

Maj nodded. "That's him. The first time it looked like he'd taken something from a crate and hidden it around his waist."

"The crate with Apple's logo on it?"

"Yes. The second time was after the shift on Tuesday

night. We'd loaded boxes from an incoming plane onto a lorry and Borys rang someone to tell them the lorry had left."

"That doesn't sound very suspicious. It's probably standard practice, isn't it?"

"Apparently not, but it's not unknown. I spoke to Thomas, the guy I've been working alongside, and he says some dispatchers ring the logistics company as a courtesy."

"That's what he must have been doing then."

"Yes, but why do it so secretively? Everyone else had gone home, and yet he was talking in hushed tones as if he was worried he'd be overheard. Why would he do that if all he was doing was ringing the logistics company? And, as for it being a courtesy call, believe me, Borys doesn't do courtesy."

"Okay. Let's go back a step. Can you remember exactly what he said on the phone?"

Maj thought about this for a second.

"He said it had left at 12:35, and he confirmed it was SWFH when he was asked."

"SWFH?"

"It's the name of the logistics company. South West Freight Haulage. I saw it on the side of the lorry."

"Nothing odd so far. Did Borys say anything else?"

"Yes, he told them the route it was taking. I assume that was so they'd know when to expect it to arrive. He was going via Faulkland."

"Faulkland near Norton St Phillip?"

"I assume so." Maj laughed. "I doubt he'd be going via the Falkland Islands."

"Where are South West Freight Haulage based?"

"I'm not sure."

Josh picked up his phone and googled the company.

"I thought as much."

"What?"

"They're in Avonmouth. No way would he drive from

Bristol Airport to Avonmouth via Faulkland. It's well out of the way."

"What could that mean though? I'm sorry, Josh, the lack of sleep's catching up with me and I'm not thinking straight."

"Could he have had another consignment to pick up? Or perhaps..." He paused. "Maj, is there any chance you misheard him?"

"What do you mean?"

"Are you sure he said 'Faulkland'?"

"I thought he did, but I'd been working since eight that morning so I could have got it wrong."

Josh was back on his phone.

"I saw something this morning. It was only the headline, but I wonder if..."

He tapped a few more times and then looked up triumphantly.

"Could it have been Failand?"

"It could have been. Why?"

Josh read what was on his screen, swiped up a couple of times and then passed the phone over.

"I've got Somerset as one of my special interests on the BBC News app. Read that."

Theft near Failand

Avon and Somerset Police estimate that over £0.5m worth of goods were stolen when a lorry was flagged down in the early hours of Wednesday morning on the B3128 outside the village of Failand.

The driver was tied up by three masked men who then transferred much of the contents to their own vehicle. Among items stolen were a large quantity of Stihl and Makita power tools and medical training supplies.

If you have any information, contact police on 101 quoting reference number 5220706508.

"That's got to be it," Maj said. He shook his head. "I knew Borys was up to no good."

He pushed his chair back and stood up.

"Thanks, Josh."

"No problemo."

"Come on. We need to tell Luke."

A few minutes later they were standing in front of Luke as he read the news article.

"What do you think?" Maj asked when he'd finished.

Luke sat back in his chair.

"I don't think there's any doubt now about what Borys was doing in that phone call you overheard, Maj."

"Tipping off his thieving mates?" Josh suggested.

"Absolutely, and it should be easy enough for the police to ring the haulage company to confirm they didn't receive a phone call from the dispatcher." He scratched his chin. "The big problem is the lack of any evidence."

"I heard him make the call," Maj said.

"Yes, but he'll deny it and might well say that you've got a grudge and made it up. That would make it a case of your word against his, and I can't see a jury finding him guilty beyond reasonable doubt on the back of that."

"What then?"

"He needs to be brought in for questioning, to see if anything can be prised out of him. Leave it with me. I'll find out who's leading the investigation and have a word."

Chapter 64

Diana was pleased she didn't have to spend any time with their hostage.

The riskiest part with the Thatchers had been the handover, because Diana had to be there for the funds to be transferred, but the beauty of this venture was there was no need for her presence, and it would appear to have been an all-male gang. The girl's ignorance of the fact that a woman was involved minimised the chances of the police catching up with them.

This time it would be someone else obtaining the money for her.

But that was in the future. Right now, she needed to concentrate on the next stage of her plan.

She pulled the car up beside one of the entrances to the woods and was pleased to see there were no other cars. The lack of visitors had been a prime reason for the choice.

She pulled out her phone and called Declan. He answered straight away.

"Hello."

"I'm here. Can we meet?"

"Yes. Flynn's in with her."

"Good. I'll see you by the boundary marker."

She got out of the car, took off her shoes and pulled on her Wellingtons, knowing from her earlier visit that the path was bound to be muddy, then retrieved the carrier bag from the boot and followed the track south.

After a couple of hundred yards, she spotted the eighteenth-century stone plinth that was their agreed meeting point. Declan was leaning nonchalantly against it, a cigarette in his mouth.

"Hello, Diana."

"Ssh."

"There's no one around. Haven't seen a soul all morning."

"Where have you parked the van?"

"Where we agreed." He pointed west. "It's only a hundred yards in that direction, but it's hidden by the trees and well away from the tracks."

"Here are your sandwiches and drinks." She passed him the carrier bag. "How's the girl? Is she causing any trouble?"

"She put up some resistance when I demanded the pin for her phone."

"What happened?"

He chuckled. "She didn't resist for long."

"What did you do?"

"Threatened to cut her ear off."

"But you didn't do it?"

"Of course I did. I thought it might help persuade her wee daddy to cooperate."

Diana fell silent.

He chuckled again. "Only joking, but I can do it if you want me to."

"No, Declan. There's no need. Did you message her father from her phone to say that she'd decided to stay with a friend overnight."

"Yes."

"And her boss?"

He nodded. "I did exactly as you asked. Told him her father had had a heart attack."

"Good. What's her pin?"

"280518."

He took out a silver iPhone, tapped the code in and passed it over.

"There's the photo."

Diana looked down at the screen. The image showed an attractive young woman in her early twenties. She was bound by rope to a plastic garden chair and was glaring into the camera, a defiant look on her face.

"Why the rope?"

"I told you. She's trouble."

"Fair enough, but I don't want you to harm her unless it's essential."

"Unless her wee daddy tries to say no, you mean?"

"Yes, or..." She paused, not wanting to share every element of her plan with him. "Or unless I say otherwise."

He took a drag from his cigarette, then flicked it away.

"I'll get back to the van."

"Ring me if there are any issues."

"Don't worry." He grinned. "There won't be anything I can't handle."

She watched as he disappeared into the trees, then turned and walked back to the car where she changed back into her shoes and climbed into the driver's seat.

It only took a few seconds to find the WhatsApp chat between the girl and her father, and she used it to send the photo, gave it a few seconds, then selected '*Deep Man Voice*' on her voice changer app and phoned his number.

He answered immediately.

"Lily, what the hell's that photo all about?"

She waited for a few seconds.

"Lily?"

"I am not your daughter."

There was hesitation at the other end.

"Who... Who are you?"

"Can you be overheard?"

"No. I'm in my office. What is this?"

"My name is Zeus, Mr Newport. You are going to do something for me and, in return, your daughter will be freed unharmed. If you do not do exactly as I ask she will die."

She paused to ensure this had sunk in, and heard him swallow before replying.

"I'm not a rich man. I haven't…"

"Be quiet." She paused. "I know that between nine-thirty and ten tomorrow morning, a large amount of cash is being delivered to the cash holding centre, and that access to the safe requires two fingerprints, yours and your deputy's. I believe her name is Sharon Hedges. Is that correct?"

"Yes."

"Tomorrow morning, after the delivery drivers have left, you will show Sharon the photo of Lily. You will make it abundantly clear that if she does not assist you in taking the cash to your car your daughter will die. You will also explain that she must not tell anyone what has happened until you contact her to tell her that Lily is safe."

There was silence at the other end.

"Is that understood?"

"Yes. I understand. What then?"

"Once the money is in the boot of your car, you will drive to Tesco's car park in Wells, leave the vehicle unlocked with the keys in the glove compartment, and walk to Cafe Nostra on Broad Street. You will stay there until your daughter contacts you to say she has been released."

She was conscious that he was in a state of shock.

"Tell me what you have to do, Mr Newport?"

"Leave my car unlocked in Tesco's car park and walk to Cafe Nostra."

"Do not even think about contacting the police. Your daughter's life depends on it. Is that clear?"

"Yes, it's clear."

She hung up.

Chapter 65

Luke's phone buzzed and he looked down to see a message from Pete.

DS Croker is your man for the lorry theft in Failand. His number is 07805 665822

Luke called the number and it rang a few times before being picked up.

"Detective Sergeant Croker."

"Hi, this is Luke Sackville."

"Ah, Mr Sackville. Detective Inspector Gilmore said you might place a call to me. I believe you have information relating to the appropriation of high-value items from a heavy goods vehicle during the early hours of Monday 10th March."

Luke couldn't help smiling. The man spoke in a very deep baritone, but it was more than that. He used words that might have been found in an over-formalised police report.

"That's right. Please call me Luke, though."

"Certainly, sir. What exactly is the nature of this information?"

"I believe you're the lead for the investigation, DS Croker?"

"That is correct, although I am working closely with a colleague from NaVCIS, the National Vehicle Crime Intelligence Service, a police unit that collates, analyses and disseminates road freight crime information across England and Wales."

"I'm familiar with it."

"You are, sir?"

"Yes. I was a serving police officer until just over a year ago."

There was silence at the other end.

"DS Croker?"

"Were you Detective Chief Inspector Sackville, sir?"

"That's me, although I'm not so sure I like the past tense. Have we met?"

"Only once. I joined your team briefly when you were leading the Oliver Penman investigation."

It came back to him now.

"Garret Croker, isn't it?"

"That's me, sir." He hesitated. "Otherwise known as Noosey."

"Of course. How could I forget? Your contribution was invaluable."

"Thank you, sir."

"Okay, Garret, let's stop the formality. It's Luke from now on. I wanted to talk to you because I know the name of one of the people involved in the robbery."

He described how Maj had overheard a man tipping his colleagues off about the route the lorry was taking after leaving Bristol Airport.

"The man's name is Borys Dobrowski," he concluded. "Unfortunately, it's one man's word against another. However, I believe it would be worthwhile interviewing him to see if he slips up."

There was another pause at the other end.

"Garret?"

"I am sure that would be a good idea, ah… Luke. The problem though is that I find my approach to interviewing can be less productive than is optimum. I have been told that I tend to be a touch on the formal side which makes it a challenge catching interviewees off-guard. Whether I would be effective is questionable." He hesitated. "It's a shame you cannot help. I recall that you had a reputation for being a highly effective questioner and interlocutor."

Luke leapt on this.

"Why don't you and I interview him together, Garret?"

"But you're a civilian."

"I am, but I'm also contracted as a consultant to Avon and Somerset. Most recently, I've been assisting with Operation Tooting."

He explained how the contract worked.

"Thank you, Luke. I'll be in touch."

Luke hung up.

Chapter 66

Lily's captors stood at the other end of the van, watching her every move through the slits cut into their black balaclavas.

She wasn't hungry, but knew she needed to keep her energy up, and took a tentative bite of her ham and cheese sandwich.

Should she try again to engage them in conversation? So far, her attempts had been fruitless. They'd said the odd word to issue commands, enough for her to know that one was from Northern Ireland and the other from Australia, but had refused to answer questions.

They didn't seem at all on edge, as if kidnapping and imprisonment were routine, part of their everyday lives. However, she got the feeling they were hired thugs, rather than one of them being the mastermind behind whatever was going on.

That didn't make them any less scary though.

The Irishman's reaction, when she refused to provide the code for her phone, had been the most frightening experience of her life. She had totally believed him when he threatened to cut her ear off, and was sure he would have done so if she'd resisted further.

Saying that her boss's name was Jethro had been a last-minute thought. It wasn't much, but it left her with a glimmer of hope that Luke might see what she had done and recognise it as a call for help.

It was only a glimmer though.

She tried to make sense of everything that had happened. It was clear this wasn't a sexually focused abduction, thank goodness, but was it a random kidnapping or had they targeted her? The more she thought about it, the more she thought it had to have been planned.

But why? Her parents weren't rich. Surely, it couldn't be the online troll at FADS behind it, having realised that she knew his name. No, that was ridiculous. The nature of his abuse, hiding behind fake email addresses and invented Facebook identities, made it clear he was a weak man, the sort of person who acted alone, a stalker type, not the sort who would have these brutes at his beck and call.

Then who?

And more importantly, why?

Staying silent wasn't getting her anywhere, so she decided to make another attempt to get something useful out of them, risky though it might be to rile them.

"Why am I here?"

There was no response.

"Where are you from, Sean? You don't mind if I call you Sean, do you? It's an Irish name and I can see you're Irish. Are you from Londonderry or further south? Belfast perhaps?"

"It's Derry not Londonderry."

"Ah. So, you're a catholic, are you? Isn't keeping me prisoner a mortal sin?"

His eyes widened.

"Shut your mouth, bitch."

He took a step forward and Lily sat back in the chair, suddenly fearful that she'd overstepped the mark.

Fortunately, his colleague put out his arm to stop him.

"Ignore her."

She breathed a sigh of relief. That was close, but she needed to press on. She was already in fear for her life and this was her chance, while both men were there, to try to make them slip up. With luck, the Australian would continue to protect her if the Irishman advanced again.

Lily tried to keep her voice light, but her heart was beating nineteen to the dozen.

"It's good to hear you speak, Bruce. Let me guess.

Tiger Bait

You're from Sydney, right?" She swallowed, looked the Irishman in the eye, and added, "Or should that be Londonsydney?"

This time he stormed forward too quickly for the other man to stop him, grabbed her hair in his massive fist, pulled it back so that her head was bent backwards over the chairback, then bent his face down to hers.

"You've asked for it now."

He pulled his knife from his pocket and pressed a button on the side of the handle. A six-inch blade shot out of the end and he put the point to Lily's neck.

"No, Declan! Don't!"

This made the Irishman look up.

"You stupid…"

The other man realised his mistake.

"Oh, fuck!"

Declan turned back to Lily. He was sneering now.

"You had a chance, but now…"

He shook his head, then pulled back hard on her hair, causing her to yelp in pain, before letting go and returning to the Australian's side.

"There's no choice. I'll have to tell the boss."

Lily watched as he opened the van door, descended onto the ground beyond and then slammed it shut.

She looked into the Australian's eyes, hoping for some sign of sympathy for her situation, but there was nothing. He simply stared back, his lips pursed and his eyes cold.

It was clear she'd totally misjudged the threat these men posed. She'd thought she was doing the right thing trying to make them slip up, but now realised she'd been wrong, terribly wrong.

Chapter 67

Roma rubbed his eyes, sat up in bed and looked through fog-filled eyes at the alarm clock on his bedside table.

It was well after eleven, almost half-past. He yawned, briefly debated lying back down for another thirty minutes, then decided that no, he would show initiative as he'd promised himself he would.

His mum was going to be proud of him.

He staggered to the bathroom, washed his face and brushed his teeth, then threw on the denims and the black hoodie he'd worn the evening before.

His uncle was going to be pleased too.

Roma's plan was simple. He was going to head to Annie's, pick up some gear and head for the corner of Brentnall Way and Manor Road in Fishponds. It was a prime spot with easy sales, mainly to the students who had lodgings in that part of Bristol, and he'd had a successful few hours there two evenings earlier.

By rights he should be at school, but once his mum had said she was going to be leaving early he was unable to resist the idea of an extra few hours sleep. School was for knobheads and losers anyway. The sooner he could start working for the family business the better.

He put on his backpack, pulled the hood of his hoodie up, wheeled his bike out from the garage then mounted it and headed towards Lawrence Hill.

After thirty minutes, he turned off Stapleton Road and dismounted outside Wharfside, a multicoloured block of 1970s flats that had seen better days. As he wheeled his bike to the entrance, he wrinkled his nose as he caught the ever-present smell of dog piss.

He pressed the buzzer for Flat 1-3.

"Hello," a cheery woman's voice said. "Who's there?"
"Harry Potter."
She giggled and there was a click as she unlocked the metal entrance. He pushed the door open, leaned his bike against the wall, then made his way up the stairs to the first floor and knocked on her flat.

She opened the door and beamed at him.
"Hello, Roman."
"It's Roma, Annie."
She giggled again.
"Oh, yes. Silly, silly, Annie. It's Roma. It's Roma."
She banged the side of her head as if forcing the word to stick.

"Roma," she repeated and banged her head again. "Roma." Another bang. "Roma."

Seemingly happy now, she smiled at him.
"Are you staying for a cup of tea, Roma?"
"I won't, ta. Just need to fetch some stuff."
"Tyrone's here."

He immediately changed his mind and pushed past her. Tyrone was an important player, one of Uncle Jay's top boys, and he was excited at the thought of talking to him.

The dealer was lounging back on Annie's scruffy brown sofa, a roll-up in his hand. He looked across as Roma walked in.

"How ya doin', man?"
"Fine, Tyrone. How are you?"
"Cookin' on gas, my man. Know what I mean?"
Roma didn't but that wasn't going to phase him.
"Sure I do."
"Good on ya. Been busy?"
Roma was about to answer when the intercom rang.
"Oh," Annie said, staring at the door entry handset on the wall. "How exciting. I love having visitors. I love it, love it, love it."

She picked up the handset, listened for a second and

then pressed the button to open the door.

"Who is it?" Roma asked.

She smiled. "Harry Potter."

A minute or so later there was a loud double knock on her door. She pulled it open and Jay stormed in, almost knocking her over as he pushed the door wide open.

"Hello, Jay," she said.

"In your bedroom!" he ordered, his eyes fixed not on her but on Tyrone. "Now!"

She turned without saying a word and did as he asked, closing the door behind her.

Tyrone was no longer leaning back, but was perched on the front edge of the sofa.

"You's rare here, Jay. All okay?"

Jay advanced on him and raised his right arm to reveal he was clutching a baseball bat. He slammed the end into his left hand.

"No, Tyrone. Everything's not fucking okay."

Tyrone started to get to his feet, but Jay shoved him in the chest and he fell back down again.

Jay swung his arm with all his force and there was a crack as the bat connected with Tyrone's left knee.

Tyrone yelped in pain and Jay swung again, hitting him on the same spot as the first blow.

"You're a snitch, a grass, you…"

He lifted the bat yet again.

"I didn't say nuffin."

"Fucking liar."

It came down again, on the right knee this time.

"Argh!" Tyrone screamed.

Jay turned to Roma.

"Out!"

"I came for gear, Uncle Jay. I'm going to Fishponds."

"Get it and fuck off."

Roma moved quickly to the kitchen where he pulled several bags out from one of the wall cupboards and stuffed them into his backpack.

He raced through the lounge to the front door, darted downstairs, released the metal entrance, wheeled his bike out, climbed on and headed in the direction of Fishponds.

After a few seconds, he was smiling.

Tyrone was hard. He had a reputation for being one of the toughest around, so seeing his uncle deal with him like that was awe-inspiring.

What a man!

Twenty minutes later, he reached the junction of Brentnall Way and Manor Road, leaned his bike against a lamppost and sat back on a low garden wall.

Five minutes after that he made his first sale and the second soon afterwards.

A third man approached him. He was in his twenties and shaking slightly. Roma wondered if he was crashing after a previous high.

"What do you want?"

"China White. A double."

"Cost you sixty."

The man extracted his wallet from his back pocket and peeled out three notes.

Roma reached into his backpack, withdrew two small clear bags and exchanged them for the money.

"Thanks," the man said and turned away.

"Any time, mate. Any time."

His customer turned away and it was then that the sirens started.

Roma turned to see a blue and yellow police Volvo speeding towards him along Manor Way. He grabbed the handles of his bike only to see a second car coming from the other direction.

Both vehicles screeched to a halt and within seconds both Roma and his customer were pushed against the wall, handcuffed and read their rights.

Chapter 68

Luke hit send, and there was a whoosh from his laptop as the email disappeared into the ether.

It was a relief to finally see the end of his monthly progress report. The blessed thing had wasted several hours of his time, and in all likelihood it would be printed off for Filcher but never read.

He decided to pop to the second floor and see how Fred dealt with the marketing department's report. Fred was canny and would doubtless have found a way of expending minimal effort on it.

Halfway up the stairs, his phone rang.

"Luke Sackville."

"Good afternoon, Luke. This is Detective Sergeant Croker. We have arrested Borys Dobrowski and he is on his way to the Keynsham Custody Suite. I have also had approval for you to assist in interviewing him. Are you available this afternoon?"

Luke looked at his watch. It was a quarter past twelve.

"Could I aim to be there at 2 o'clock? I'll need to grab some lunch and tidy up a couple of things."

"That works for me."

"How did he react when you arrested him?"

"He was displeased."

"Displeased?"

"Perhaps that is an understatement on my part." He paused. "Actually, it is a gross understatement. Mr Dobrowski was extremely aggressive and abusive. Despite his first language being Polish, he was able to utilise a number of Anglo-Saxon expletives, addressing me as a fart-filled turd on one occasion."

Luke smiled.

"Did he indeed?"

"And worse, might I add. Considerably worse."

"I can imagine. I'll see you later, Garret."

He hung up.

Still smiling, he decided Fred could wait for another day and returned to the Ethics Room where he went straight over to Maj.

"Maj, Borys has been arrested."

"That's good news."

"I'm going over to Keynsham to interview him this afternoon."

Josh was seated at the next desk and heard this.

"Can I help, guv?"

"Not on this occasion, Josh, but thanks for offering."

He turned back to Maj.

"I'm hoping I'll be back in the office afterwards. If not, I'll give you a call to let you know how DS Croker and I got on."

"Thanks, Luke."

"I think you should assume you won't be doing any more shifts at Bristol Airport. If he hasn't already, Borys will soon realise that it was you who informed the police about his phone call."

He moved over to Helen.

"Any more news from Lily?"

She shook her head. "No, but I'm not surprised. Knowing her, she'll be focused on helping her dad."

"Please let me know if she does get in touch."

"Will do."

Lastly, he approached Sam.

"I heard what you said to Maj," she said, her voice slightly flat. "Don't worry, I'll cover."

"Are you okay?"

"I'm fine, but I rang Sebastian, and he's had some bad news."

"About him or is it one of his family?"

"Neither. It was another person who got caught up in what happened."

"Is he or she going to be okay?"

"No, but Sebastian said he saw it coming. She was nearly eighty and the stress was too much for her."

"Are you saying a woman's dead as a result of this incident?"

She nodded.

"Was this someone he was close to?"

He saw her hesitation, and held his hand up by way of apology.

"Sorry, I know you can't talk about it, but if you need to see him…"

"No, it's fine, Luke. I don't think I can be of any help. What's done is done, but thanks."

"Do you want to grab a sandwich in the canteen before I leave?"

"Yes, that would be nice."

*

Thirty minutes later, Luke climbed into his BMW.

He'd enjoyed their lunch break, but then he always enjoyed Sam's company. They'd managed to avoid talking about either Sebastian or work, and she'd seemed a little more relaxed when he kissed her goodbye.

But now, he needed to turn his mind to Borys Dobrowski. From what both Maj and DS Croker had told him, the man was pugnacious. He was likely to be hostile and argumentative in the interview, but that could be turned to advantage. If the man was riled, he might well speak without thinking and reveal something useful.

The trouble was that he knew very little about him other than that he was Polish and worked as a shift leader in Cargo at Bristol Airport. DS Croker would have mentioned it if he had a record so there was nothing to build on there.

After a few minutes thought, he decided the best bet would be to begin by exploring areas the man would be comfortable with. He'd ask him where in Poland he was from, when he'd come to the UK, how long he'd been at Bristol Airport, that kind of thing. Once he was warmed up, he'd let loose with both barrels.

He was wondering how exactly to do this when his phone rang, and he accepted the call without seeing who it was.

"Hello."

"You're not going to fucking believe this."

He couldn't help laughing.

"Good afternoon, Misty. I take it you've found something out?"

"Too right I have."

"About Jay Curtis or about Declan O'Brien?"

"Both. They're linked."

"Do you mean O'Brien works for Curtis, or the other way around?"

"Neither. They're both part of a complex web. It's a fucking Mafia if you ask me."

"You're losing me now. Did you just say they work for the Mafia?"

"Not literally, but we're talking a family business. Declan O'Brien's an enforcer and a little bird told me that he works for Jay Curtis's sister."

"Enforcer for what?"

"A protection racket covering a large part of Bristol."

"And you're sure she's at the head of this?"

"I'm not positive, but that's what I've heard."

Luke recalled what Pete had told him about Bill Curtis's three children.

"As well as a sister, Jay Curtis has a twin brother. Did your informant mention him? His name's Apollo."

"He didn't, no. Want me to ask him? I left him in a cafe

with a mug of hot chocolate and he's probably still there."

"Please."

"Okay. I'll call you back."

Five minutes later, Misty rang back.

"It cost me another fifty, but he told me. Yeah, Apollo's the third leg of this evil fucking clan."

"What's his speciality?"

"Theft to order. Luxury goods and the like."

"From people's homes?"

"No. Lorries mainly."

Chapter 69

DS Croker was waiting outside the custody centre when Luke arrived.

"I'm glad you're here. He's been complaining about being kept waiting."

"I can't say I'm bothered. Has he asked for a solicitor?"

"Yes, and he's here. He's complaining as well."

"Great. Should be fun then."

They walked inside and a red-faced man in a too-tight blue suit immediately walked over.

"About time!" he said, then backed away slightly when confronted with Luke's nine-inch height advantage.

"Hi," Luke said and offered his hand. "I'm Luke Sackville. I assume you're Mr Dobrowski's solicitor?"

The man shook hands and nodded.

"Maxwell Broughton from Dersden, Hound and Ratherscoop."

"And you understand why your client has been arrested?"

"On hearsay as far as I can gather."

Luke didn't respond but turned to the sergeant.

"Where are we interviewing him, DS Croker?"

"Room 2."

They made their way to room 2, a windowless space inside which were a table, four chairs, a recording device and an unhappy Pole.

Borys Dobrowski was standing behind one of the chairs, his arms folded across his chest and his brows so furrowed they almost met the end of his nose.

"I am busy man," he said. "This is outrage."

"We'll be as quick as we can," Luke said with a smile. "Please take a seat."

Borys grunted, but sat down. His solicitor sat to his left while Luke and DS Croker took the seats opposite.

"We're going to record this, Mr Dobrowski," Luke went on, "but if at any time you want a pause or need a break, please let me know."

There was another grunt.

Luke pressed the record button.

"Interview with Borys Dobrowski in room 2 at Keynsham Custody Centre. The time is 13:55. Also present are Detective Sergeant Garret Croker, Luke Sackville and Mr Dobrowski's solicitor, Maxwell Broughton."

The formalities out of the way, Luke sat back and looked the interviewee in the eyes.

"How long have you worked at Bristol Airport, Mr Dobrowski?"

"Three years."

"And I believe you're originally from Poland. Is that correct?"

"Yes. I am here ten years now."

"Warsaw?"

"No. A village. You would not know it."

"But now you live in a big city with a different language to cope with. You must find it challenging."

Borys turned to his solicitor.

"What is point of this? Is not relevant. Do I need to answer?"

Broughton lowered his voice.

"There's no harm, Mr Dobrowski. I'll advise you if you need to remain silent."

"I'm sorry," Luke said, holding both hands up. "All I'm trying to do is put you at your ease."

"So that you can trick me?"

Well, yes, was Luke's honest thought.

"Of course not. I want this over with as much as you do, but I want to make sure you're comfortable and not stressed in any way."

This was greeted with yet another grunt and a scowl.

"Okay, let's concentrate on why you were arrested. The reason you were brought in has been explained to you, I trust?"

"Yes. Someone lied about me."

"We have a witness who told us that he overheard you on the phone. He said you were telling someone that a lorry had left the airport at 12:35 and was taking the Failand route to Avonmouth. That lorry was held up and the cargo taken about half an hour later."

Borys shook his head.

"That is lies. Your witness invented this story."

"You deny making the phone call?"

"Yes. Check my phone if not believe me."

"Your personal phone or the burner phone?"

There was a momentary hesitation, but no more than that.

"What is burner phone?"

Luke smiled.

"Ignore me. I was thinking out loud."

As he said this, he remembered what Maj had seen on his first shift. Borys had hammered the lid of a crate shut, and looked as though he might have something around his waist. It could be a theft to order for Apollo but, given this was a family business, might it have been drugs for Jay?

It was a long shot, but worth a go.

"Do you have two bosses, Mr Dobrowski?"

"Only one. Dominic Price. He is Cargo Manager."

"I forgot him. That would be three then?"

"What do you mean?"

"This cargo theft was for Apollo Curtis, wasn't it?"

Borys's eyes widened for an instant before he pulled himself together.

"I have never heard that name."

Luke nodded, trying to give the impression that he believed every word.

"What about last Sunday? Who were you working for then?"

Borys looked confused.

"Last Sunday?"

"Yes. You were at Bristol Airport so clearly you were working for Mr Price, the Cargo Manager, but who did you take the drugs for?"

Borys swallowed but didn't say anything.

"Was it Jay Curtis, Apollo's brother?"

It was his solicitor who spoke next.

"What's this all about? I wasn't told about a drugs theft."

Luke ignored him.

"I'm right, aren't I, Mr Dobrowski? You work for both Jay and Apollo, don't you?"

"I advise you not to answer," Broughton said, but Borys was now glaring at Luke and wasn't listening.

"This is nonsense. You make this shit up. I do not know these two men."

"What about their sister? Are there occasions when you work for her as well?"

"No. Is more shit."

"Are you sure?"

"I have never even met Diana."

Luke smiled and sat back in his chair.

"You've never met her?"

"No."

"And yet you know her name."

Broughton sat up.

"Can we take a break. I'd like a word with my client."

"Of course. Interview paused at 14:23."

Luke stopped the recording and he and DS Croker left the room.

Once outside he pulled the sergeant to one side.

"He's going to say no comment to everything from now on, I guarantee it."

"How did you know about the Curtis family?"

"Jay Curtis is now the main person of interest in Project Tooting and I heard at lunchtime about his brother and sister being involved, though not in drugs."

"If Apollo's focus is theft, what's the sister's?"

"She runs a protection racket." He paused. "Look, would you mind finishing off the interview? I could do with updating the Tooting team on this."

"Yes. I'll do that."

"Thanks, Garret."

Luke returned to the BMW, deciding he'd ring on the way back to Bath.

Pete answered straight away.

"Good timing yet again, Luke."

"Why?"

"We arrested Jay Curtis's nephew about an hour ago. He was caught red-handed in Fishponds, along with a punter who'd bought two bags of heroin from him."

"That's good news. Is he Apollo's son?"

"No, Diana's. We're trying to contact her so that we can interview him. He's only fifteen so we need a responsible adult."

"I'm not sure she counts as responsible."

"What do you mean?"

"I think the three of them, Jay, Apollo and Diana, have continued where their father left off."

"You think all three are involved?"

"Not in the drugs side of the operation, that's Jay, but I have it on good authority that Apollo's into large-scale theft, while Diana's running a protection racket across Bristol."

"Good authority?"

"Misty Mitchell."

"I'm not sure DCI Franks will think much of that."

"It's not just that though."

He explained what had happened when he and DS

Croker interviewed Borys Dobrowski.

"I see," Pete said when he'd finished. "I'll talk to DCI Franks and see what she wants to do next."

"Good. Tell her to ring me if she wants to."

"Will do."

Chapter 70

Diana had driven back to the woods as soon as Declan rang.

She met him at the stone plinth again. This time he was pacing up and down in front of it, a cigarette in one hand and his balaclava in the other. He was clearly less relaxed than on her previous visit, but didn't seem to be on edge. No, it was more that he was fired up with adrenaline.

The Irishman was enjoying himself.

He looked up as she approached, drew on his cigarette and exhaled a thin stream of smoke before speaking.

"We have a difficult decision to make."

"Why? What's so urgent you needed to drag me back here. The less I'm around the better."

He took another deep drag, then flicked the cigarette to the ground.

"The girl can't be released."

"I have no intention of releasing her, not until we have the money."

"You don't understand. Flynn told her my name. She mustn't be allowed to tell anyone. She can never be released."

She gave a dry laugh. "We can't keep her here forever."

He stared back at her, and it was only then that she realised what he meant.

"Did he reveal your whole name?"

"No, only my Christian name, but it's enough." He paused. "I have no problem doing it. Flynn and I can bury her deep in the woods and she'll never be found."

"You said there was a difficult decision to make, but it sounds like you've already made it."

"She has to die, there's no choice. The question, Diana,

is when? Is her father demanding more photos like Sebastian Thatcher did?"

"No, he isn't."

"In that case, why not do it now? Keeping her alive only increases the risk of being spotted."

She considered this for a few seconds.

"I think you may be right."

He nodded and started to move towards the trees.

"Just a second."

He turned back. "You haven't got cold feet, have you?"

"Not at all, but…"

Her phone started ringing and she looked down to see 'Caller Id Withheld' on the screen.

"Wait while I get this."

She accepted the call.

"Hello."

"Am I speaking to Diana Parkhouse?"

"Yes. Who is this?"

"This is Detective Constable Robbie Hammond. I'm sorry to have to break this to you, Mrs Parkhouse, but your son, Roma, has been arrested and is now in custody."

Her heart leapt into her mouth.

"That can't be right. Roma's only fifteen. What's he been arrested for?"

"Possession of Class A drugs with intent to supply."

Fuck, fuck, fuck.

"We intend to interview your son, but need an appropriate adult present because of his age. How soon can you be here? We're at the custody centre in Keynsham."

She looked at her watch.

"I could probably get there by four-thirty."

"Thank you. Do you need the post code?"

"No. I'll google it."

She hung up.

"Who's been arrested?" Declan asked.

"My son, and I need to be with him when he's

interviewed." She hesitated. "I've changed my mind. Don't deal with the girl yet. There's always the chance her father will ask for a photo when I ring him tomorrow morning."

"So, we do it after that?"

"Yes. I think it's safest that way."

He headed off again and she started walking back to her car, shaking her head at her son's stupidity. It sounded like Roma had been dealing in the open in full daylight. Had Jay not taught him anything about how to be secretive and ever-aware?

Chapter 71

Luke threw his coat onto his chair, marched over to the whiteboard and then called back to Helen.

"Is it okay if I clear this?"

"I'll do it. Give me a minute."

"What's up, guv?" Josh asked, as Helen took a photo of the board and then started to remove Post-its.

"We've made progress on Operation Tooting, thanks to Misty, and I want to get my thoughts in order."

"Do you want help?"

"Actually, yes, that would be good." He turned to the others. "Can I pick your brains, guys?"

They all moved to the meeting table and Luke turned first to Maj.

"I'll be especially interested to see what you think."

Maj raised one eyebrow.

"Why's that, Luke? I've had next to nothing to do with Tooting."

"Borys is tied into it."

"Borys?"

Luke smiled.

"It'll become clear in a moment."

"I'm ready," Helen said. She was standing in front of the whiteboard, a marker pen in each hand.

"I love doing the crazy wall," Josh said, before adding, "Whoopsio. I didn't mean to say that out loud."

"Okay," Luke said. "Let's make a start. Helen, please can you write three names along the top. Janus, Apollo and Diana."

She did as he asked.

"As you all know, we believe that Janus, or Jay as he likes to be known, runs a drugs operation in Bristol. If you remember, his father, Bill, led what became known as the Curtis Cartel until he died a few years ago."

He pointed to the names of the other two siblings.

"We had assumed Apollo and Diana hadn't taken on the mantle from their father and are innocent of any crimes. However, based on what Misty told me, it seems likely that Borys Dobrowski, the man Maj came up against at the airport, works for Apollo who is running a theft-to-order gang. His focus is large scale, principally targeting road haulage."

Helen added Borys's name below Apollo's.

"What about Diana?" Josh asked.

"She's in the protection racket, charging people to 'look after' their businesses."

"So, Reece Stevens works for Jay," Sam said, "while Declan O'Brien most likely works for Diana. That explains how they know each other."

"Exactly."

"I bet that's who he was," Helen said under her breath.

"Who?" Luke asked.

"The man who shoved Becky in the butcher's shop. I bet it was nothing to do with gambling. He must have been one of Diana's enforcers."

"Didn't you say he was Irish?" Josh asked.

"Yes, why? Are you thinking it might be O'Brien?"

Josh smiled and nodded. "You betcha. I've got a photo of him on my phone. If I send it to you, could you ask Becky if that's him?"

"Aye, I can do that."

Luke rubbed at his chin. "There's also evidence that the three legs of the family work together." He turned to Maj. "That package Borys removed from the Apple box was likely drugs for Jay. Also, Diana's son, Roma, was arrested this lunchtime for intent to supply."

"Roma?" Josh said. "Bill Curtis chose some properly odd names for his children, and now it looks like his daughter's carrying the tradition on."

"They weren't so much odd as narcissistic. Janus, Apollo and Diana are all Roman deities. Bill Curtis had a god complex, and after he died the police found out that he'd used Zeus as a cover name on more than one occasion."

Sam sat up when she heard this.

"What did you say?"

"I said he had a god complex."

"No, the cover name?"

"He called himself Zeus? Why?"

She looked at him for a moment, picked her phone up from the table and stood up.

"Will you excuse me? I need to make a call."

"Yes, that's fine. Helen perhaps you could contact Becky while Sam's out to see if it was Declan O'Brien in the shop?"

"I've just sent you the photo," Josh said.

"Thanks," Helen said. "I'll message her now."

Luke's phone pinged and he looked down to see another message from Lily.

My father's still bad so I'll be off tomorrow as well. Sorry, Jethro.

He typed out a reply.

Don't worry, Lily. I hope he feels better soon. Jethro.

He stared at the message, wondering if he should add a smiley emoji after 'Jethro' before sending it. She'd called him that twice now, so it had to be deliberate, some kind of joke that he wasn't quite getting.

It was an odd time for humour though, given what had happened to her father. Perhaps he should ignore it and just put 'Luke'. He was about to do this when Helen walked over.

"Becky's confirmed it's him." She saw the perturbed expression on his face. "Are you okay?"

He smiled.

"It's nothing. I've had another message from Lily, and she called me Jethro again. I was wondering how she'd managed to get it wrong twice. It's not like her."

"Jethro?"

"Yes. Unusual name."

"Can I see?"

"Sure."

He raised his phone and she looked at the screen and then called to Josh.

"Josh, have you got a second?" She pointed to the phone. "Luke's had this from Lily."

He read the message.

My father's still bad so I'll be off tomorrow as well. Sorry, Jethro.

"Well?" Helen said.

Josh shook his head. "It's not from Lily."

"Because it says 'Jethro'?" Luke suggested.

"Well, that, but also Lily would never call her dad 'father'. She'd say 'dad'. Anyone under thirty would say 'dad'."

Luke suddenly felt awfully old, but that wasn't what was bothering him. His gut was telling him something was wrong, that he had to read between the lines.

"There's something else," Helen said. "Jethro could well be the troll in FADS."

"That makes even less sense. I can't see any reason why she'd be texting him to say her father's had a heart attack."

"Dad," Josh corrected. "She'd say 'dad'."

Luke ignored this.

"You don't have her father's number, do you, Josh?"

"Sorry. I don't even know his name."

"Do you know where he works?"

He shook his head. "No. I think he works for a bank, but I couldn't swear to it."

Luke grabbed his coat.

"This doesn't smell right. Tell Sam I'll be back for her in an hour or so."

"Where are you going, guv?"

"Norton St Phillip. I'm going to call in on the Newports. Hopefully, Lily's there with her father but I want to be sure she's okay."

Chapter 72

"Why won't you tell me your name?" Lily asked. "I know your friend's called Declan, so what's the problem?"

He stared back at her, but didn't respond.

"Come on," she pleaded. "I can't keep calling you Bruce. Unless your name is Bruce, of course. Is it?"

He ignored her again.

"Okay. I'll stick with Bruce."

She had to persevere in the hope that she could find out something useful. Extracting even one word from him was like squeezing blood from a stone, but she was determined to keep trying.

She forced a smile.

"How much are they paying you, Bruce? Is it as much as Declan?" She paused. "I bet it's not. He's the one in charge, isn't he? You're very much the minor player here, a bit of brawn, that's all."

"Shut your mouth."

That was good. She'd forced a reaction. Now she had to keep him talking.

She was about to ask another question when she heard a rat-a-tat-tat on the outside of the van. A few seconds later, Declan climbed in and closed the door behind him.

To her surprise, he wasn't wearing his balaclava.

"Where's your mask?" the Australian said.

"I don't need it."

He turned so that his back was to Lily and started talking, too quietly for her to make out the words.

"When?" the Australian asked when he'd finished.

"Tomorrow morning, once he's delivered the money."

"What are you talking about?" Lily asked, trying to keep the rising panic from showing in her voice. "Who's this man you're talking about? What money?"

They both turned to face her, and the Australian removed his balaclava.

She looked at him and then at Declan. They were like peas in a pod or, more accurately, devils in a horror movie. They were hired thugs and their faces told of many violent encounters.

But it was their insensitivity that scared her most. They looked at her as if she was an object. No, worse than that, as if she didn't matter, a means to an end.

They no longer cared that she knew what they looked like.

Which could only mean one thing.

Chapter 73

Sam had to ring three times before Sebastian answered.

"Hi, Sam. Sorry, I was in a meeting."

"Sebastian, I think I know who abducted your parents."

"Are you going to tell me it was a woman?"

"Why do you say that?"

"I finally managed to reverse-engineer the calls from Zeus. The voice generated was high-pitched and almost certainly a woman's."

"It'll be Diana then," Sam said half to herself.

"Diana?"

"We've been helping the police investigate organised crime in Bristol, and have uncovered a gang we believe is run by two brothers and a sister. The sister's name is Diana, and their father used Zeus as a cover name before he died."

"In that case, it was probably her who held the laptop open while I transferred the ransom money. At the time I thought she was an assistant. I didn't dream she'd be the person in charge and the one who'd rung me to demand the ransom."

"We believe Diana runs a protection racket, and is likely to have used men from that side of her operation for the kidnapping. I take it neither you nor your parents caught sight of any of them or heard their names?"

"No. They were very careful. My dad did say their accents were distinctive though. He also got the impression that the man who forced Barbara to take the video was the leader. He had a Bristol accent."

"It's possible he's one of the brothers. What about the others?"

"There were three. One had a rural Somerset accent, one was Australian and the third was Irish. Dad said he sounded a lot like Gerry Adams, the ex-president of Sinn Fein, so he must have been from Northern Ireland. He was the one who pulled a knife when your dog appeared."

"We might have a name for him too."

Sebastian paused for a moment before replying.

"So, this woman Diana and her cohorts are going to be arrested, are they?"

"I imagine so, but this news has only just broken. The police still have to gather evidence against them."

She could sense the concern in his voice.

"Don't worry, Sebastian. Your secret's safe with me."

"I know, Sam, but if these people get wind that the police are after them who knows where they might seek retribution."

"I'll keep you up to date on progress."

"Thanks."

She ended the call and returned to the Ethics Room to find Helen, Josh and Maj at their desks but no sign of Luke.

She walked over to Helen.

"Where's Luke?"

"He's gone to Lily's house. He said he'd be back in an hour or so."

"Why the rush? He said he was going to pop in after work."

"He was worried about her. It's probably nothing, but she texted him again, and got his name wrong for the second time. It's probably down to the stress she's under after her father's heart attack."

"Probably." Sam looked up at the whiteboard. "How did you get on?"

"It was a useful session. I think we're making progress."

She scanned the board. The siblings were at the top with several names underneath, and she noticed that the word 'Belfast' had been added next to Declan O'Brien's name. This tied in with what Sebastian had said about one

Tiger Bait

of the abductors being from Northern Ireland.

Her eyes moved above him to Diana, then above that to Bill Curtis, where she saw Helen had added the word 'Zeus'.

Running a protection racket was bad enough, but this woman had to be ruthless to kidnap three innocent people, a crime so brutal that it had resulted in someone's death. It must have been a terrifying experience.

A thought occurred to her but, no, surely that was ridiculous.

However…

She turned back to Helen.

"You said Luke's worried about Lily?"

"Yes. She called him Jethro, which was probably because she had him on her mind, but she did it twice."

"Who's Jethro?"

"He's ex-FADS and, before Lily left, she told me she knew who the baddie was. It could well be him."

Sam's head was spinning. Lily was level-headed, very on the ball, and she couldn't imagine her confusing names like that. And if it she'd done it deliberately she must have been sending some kind of message.

She decided to ring Luke.

Chapter 74

Luke was a few miles from Norton St Phillip when his phone rang. He was pleased to see Sam's name come up.

"Hi, Sam. Sorry I dashed off like that."

"Are you at Lily's yet?"

She spoke quickly, almost snappily, and he wondered if he'd done something to upset her.

"No. I'm five minutes away. Why?"

"Helen said you're concerned about her."

"I am a little. Her messages were odd, but it's probably nothing. I'm sure she'll laugh them off when I tell her she got my name wrong."

"Probably, but... If she's not there, but you manage to speak to one of her parents, can you mention Zeus?"

"Zeus? As in the alias Bill Curtis used?"

"Yes."

"Why, Sam? Do you think they're mixed up with the cartel in some way?"

"I don't think they're criminals, but..." She hesitated. "Are they wealthy?"

"I wouldn't have thought so. They've got a detached house in the village, but it's not what I would call grand. Why does that matter?"

"As I said, it's probably nothing, but would you mind throwing the name at them to see how they react?"

"Of course not."

"And please can you ring me when you leave?"

"Will do."

He hung up, confused by what Sam had asked him to do.

What connection could there possibly be between Lily's family and an organised crime gang who made money from

Tiger Bait

drugs, theft and a protection racket? Had Sam come across a piece of evidence that he'd missed? But if she had, surely she'd tell him.

Could it be that Lily had confided something to Sam and sworn her to secrecy? No, he was sure that the only secret she had from him was in relation to Sebastian Thatcher.

Was it that then?

The more he thought about it, the more he decided it had to be. The name Zeus must have cropped up in the incident that had so upset Sebastian.

He parked outside the Newports' house, an Edwardian brick building with bow windows on both the ground and first floors. It was pleasant but, as he'd said to Sam, not grand or ostentatious.

After ringing the bell, he stepped back, hoping that it would be Lily who answered.

A moment or two later, the door was pulled open by a woman who had to be Lily's mother. She was slim and striking to look at, with high cheekbones similar to her daughter's. Her face was pale though, and her eyes were rimmed with red. It was clear that her husband's heart attack had taken its toll.

"Mrs Newport?"

"Yes. Can I help you?"

"I'm sorry to bother you. I'm looking for Lily."

"Ah... She's not in at the moment."

"Is she at the hospital?"

"The hospital?"

"Yes. Sorry, I should have said. I'm Luke, Luke Sackville. Lily's been working for me at Filchers in Bath."

"Yes." She swallowed. "Lily's mentioned you."

"She messaged me to say she wouldn't be in, and I thought I'd pop around to see how things are."

"I see. That's very good of you. We're fine, Carl's fine. Ah... I'll tell Lily you called."

She started to close the door, but Luke put his hand against it to stop her. As he did so, she glanced backwards as if to ensure no one had come up behind her.

"Is everything okay, Mrs Newport?"

She seemed to find it hard to reply, and he could see her eyes were becoming moist.

"Yes. Yes... As I said, we're fine."

"And Lily's at the hospital?"

"Yes."

"The RUH?"

She nodded and started to close the door again, but again he stopped her.

"Mrs Newport, does the name Zeus mean anything to you?"

Her eyes widened. A split-second later they started to close, and her shoulders began to sag. Luke could see she was about to faint and reached forwards to support her. As he did so, he heard a noise from inside the house.

After quietly lowering her so that she was seated on the floor, her back propped up against the wall, he pushed the door open and stepped as silently as he could down the hall.

The noise came again and he realised someone was in the room to his left. He crept to the door and was about to put his ear to it when it was jerked fully open.

Luke stepped back and raised his arms to defend himself, then realised that the man in front of him was unlikely to be a threat. A slightly overweight, middle-aged man, he wore black rectangular glasses and a scared expression.

"Who are you? Where's Tara?"

"Your wife's fine, Mr Newport, but she fainted. She's in the hall."

The man pushed past Luke and went up to his wife, who opened her eyes as he approached.

He turned back to Luke.

"What happened?"

"Zeus."

Carl took an involuntary step backwards, then looked up at Luke and scowled.

"Is that who you are?" he hissed. "You monster! Where is she? What have you done to my daughter?"

"I haven't done anything, and I'm not Zeus."

"Then…"

"My name's Luke. Your daughter's been working for me."

"You need to go. I can't…"

"I'm not going anywhere." Luke looked down at his wife. "Tara, are you okay to stand up?"

"I think so, yes."

He helped her to her feet, then turned back to her husband.

"Why don't we sit down and talk this through?"

"I can't," Carl said. "You don't understand."

"No, but I'm beginning to."

"I think we need to tell him everything," Tara said, seeming to recognise that Luke wasn't going to simply walk away.

She turned to her husband.

"I'm feeling a little better now, Carl. Why don't I make us all a cup of tea? You and Luke go into the front room, and I'll be with you in a minute."

Chapter 75

The lounge of the Newports' house successfully combined modernity with tradition, the ceiling adorned with decorative plaster mouldings while there were colourful abstract paintings on three of the cream walls.

It was bright too, a room to relax in with family and friends, though such a scene was hard to imagine given the state of the man now perched on the end of one of the tan leather armchairs.

Carl was beside himself with worry and wound up almost to breaking point with tension.

Luke looked down at him.

"You need to tell me everything."

"I can't." He gave a deep sigh. "He said if I told anyone…"

"Is this Zeus?"

"Yes."

"Lily's in danger, isn't she?"

Carl shook his head.

"I can't tell you. I can't."

"You have to. I'm ex-police and …"

His eyes widened. "No." He started to stand up. "You need to leave."

"Please, Carl. You have to trust me. I promise I won't involve the police without your say-so."

"We have to tell him," Tara said as she entered the room carrying a tray of drinks. She put it down on the coffee table and passed one mug to Luke and a second to her husband. "He's promised he won't tell anyone, so what have we got to lose."

Luke waited for a few seconds before prompting again.

"What happened, Carl?"

Tiger Bait

After another sigh, the words started flowing freely.

"I was sent a photo of Lily this morning. It came from her phone. She was tied to a chair. Then, a minute or so later, he rang and told me…" He hesitated and took a sip of his tea before continuing. "He told me she'd die if I didn't do as he asked."

"Can I see the photo?"

Carl clicked on his phone a couple of times and passed it over.

Luke looked at the image for a few seconds.

"What time was this?"

"About a quarter past ten. I was in the office."

"What else did Zeus say?"

"He knew we've got a cash delivery tomorrow morning and…"

Luke held his hand up.

"We?"

"Sorry. I work for Favershams, a private bank. I manage the cash holding centre." He took another sip of his tea and continued cradling it as if it was a life support system. "Zeus knew our safe needs two fingerprints to be opened, and told me that I have to show the image to Sharon, she's my deputy, and persuade her to help me open the safe once the delivery men had left. I then have to put the money in my boot, leave the car in Tesco's car park in Wells, and wait in a cafe until Lily rings to say they've freed her."

"And they gave no clue as to where she was being held?"

Carl shook his head.

"No. None."

Luke looked down at the photo again.

"It looks to me like it's a van or lorry."

"Yes," Tara said. "We thought the same." She paused. "What do we do, Luke?"

This was an excellent question, and one that Luke found hard to answer. He didn't want to give them false hope, and there was very little to go on.

"I need to talk to my partner, Sam. She's the one who told me to mention Zeus to you and may have more information that we can use to pull together a plan."

"How did she know about Zeus?"

"I'll tell you after I've spoken to her. Please excuse me for a moment."

He stepped outside, closed the door and walked down the hall to the kitchen where he wouldn't be overheard.

Sam answered immediately.

"Well? Did you speak to Lily?"

He answered with a question of his own.

"Did Sebastian's incident involve kidnapping?"

"Oh, no! Have they got Lily?"

"Yes." He hesitated. "Sam, I know you promised him you'd keep it secret, but now you have to tell me everything so that we can find her."

He explained what Zeus had ordered Lily's father to do.

"That's very different," Sam said when he'd finished. "And you're right. I'm sure Sebastian will understand why I have to tell you what happened to him." She paused. "Sebastian's parents and a neighbour were abducted and only released after he paid a ransom of £400,000."

"Was it the neighbour who died?"

"Yes."

She hesitated and he could tell there was something else on her mind.

"What is it, Sam?"

"They cut off the end of her finger and posted it to Sebastian to show they meant business."

This sent a shiver down his spine. It was clear that they were extremely ruthless and would stop at nothing.

"Okay, let's agree what we know. First off, the name Zeus proves it's the same gang, the Curtis Cartel. Agreed?"

"Yes, and more than that, we know it's Diana."

"How? Isn't it more likely that Zeus is Jay or Apollo?"

Tiger Bait

"No. Diana's using a voice changer app."

Luke didn't bother asking how she knew this. There wasn't time to mess about.

"Okay, so it's Diana. Triumphant after her windfall from Sebastian, she's building on her success by using Lily as bait to get Carl to commit the theft. The next question is where they're keeping her prisoner. From the photo sent to her father it looks like she's in a van."

"The Thatchers and Barbara were held in a van too. In East Harptree Wood."

"Isn't that where you took Wilkins for a walk?"

"Yes, it was. I wanted to be nearby when Sebastian paid the ransom. I was there for over an hour, and must have covered every trail, so the van must have been very well hidden."

"Mmm. I suppose it's possible they're using the same place for Lily, although it's unlikely."

"What are we going to do, Luke? Is the only way to guarantee her safety to let the theft go ahead?"

"That won't guarantee anything. Look what happened to Barbara."

It occurred to him that it might even now be too late, but he tried to banish that thought to the back of his mind.

"Do we tell the police?" Sam asked. "Diana's at the custody centre now for her son's interview. Couldn't they arrest her and force her to tell them where Lily is?"

"Too risky, although…"

"What?"

"I've got an idea. It might work but I need to make a few phone calls."

"What should I do?"

"Ring Sebastian, explain what's happened without giving specifics, and ask if there's anything he or his parents can think of that might help us locate the van."

Chapter 76

Luke decided he'd ask DCI Franks rather than DI Gilmore. Pete would do as he asked, no question about it, but instinct told him Nicole would be more likely to get a response.

He called her number.

"DCI Franks."

"Nicole, it's Luke. I've got an enormous favour to ask.'

"Ask away. I owe you one."

"Is Roma still there, the lad who was arrested for intent to supply this lunchtime?"

"Yes, we're still waiting for his mother. Pete and Robbie are going to interview him once she's here. Why?"

"Okay, this is going to seem a little odd, but bear with me. Can you take him in a drink, chat to him informally and ask him if he and his mother go for walks and, if so, where?"

"For walks?"

"I said it would seem odd, but believe me this is extremely important."

"It seems… Just a second."

He heard her say, 'Thanks, Robbie,' then she came back on the line.

"His mother's arrived. Should I ask both of them about their walks?"

"No. It's vital she isn't there when you ask."

"You're not making sense, you know that?"

He didn't reply, but mentally crossed his fingers.

"All right, Luke," she said after a few seconds. "I'll ask him and ring you afterwards."

"Thanks, Nicole."

He hung up, breathed a sigh of relief, and called up

another number. It was a woman who answered.

"Good afternoon. This is PC Drummond in the chief constable's office. How may I help."

"Hello. I'm Luke Sackville. Is the chief in?"

"She's in a meeting at the moment, Mr Sackville. Can I take a message?"

"Sorry, but this is extremely urgent. I'm sure she'll speak to me if you tell her who's calling, and tell her it's a matter of life and death."

There was a moment's hesitation before the reply came.

"Stay on the line."

He waited for a minute or so before there was a click and he heard Chief Constable Sara Gough's voice.

"This had better be good, Luke."

"I was serious when I said it's a life and death situation."

"Go on, then. How can I help?"

"A message was sent from a phone at 10:15 this morning and I need to know the location."

"Why?"

"There is a very serious crime being committed and someone's life is in danger. I need to find them as soon as possible. I'm sorry, but I can't tell you more than that."

She paused and he held his breath while she considered this. After a few seconds, she spoke again.

"I'll see what I can do, Luke. What's the number?"

He gave her Lily's phone number and she promised to be back in touch as soon as she could.

He returned to the front room.

"Did you manage to speak to your partner?" Carl asked.

"Yes, and I phoned two other people as well, but don't worry, I didn't tell them what had happened or give them your names."

"What do we do now?" Tara asked.

"We wait." He looked down at his untouched mug of tea. "I don't suppose you've got any coffee, have you?"

She stood up.
"How do you like it?"
"Strong, no milk or sugar. Thanks, Tara."

Chapter 77

Diana was annoyed. She'd been sitting in the waiting room for over half an hour and was keen to see Roma.

She left the room and stormed up to the sergeant at the duty desk.

"When am I going to be allowed to see my son?"

"What is his name, madam?"

She sighed in exasperation.

"He's only fifteen. This is ridiculous."

"I can try to find out what the delay is, but I'll need his name."

"Roma Parkhouse."

"Roman with an 'n'?"

She sighed again, even more deeply this time. "No. It's Roma. R-O-M-A."

"Give me a moment."

He looked down at his pad, found the name and then looked back at her.

"It shouldn't be long now."

"How long?"

"We are waiting for the interviewing officers to become available, and then you'll be called in."

"I can't hang around all day."

He half-smiled.

"It's inconvenient, I know, but I'm sure they'll be down soon."

She turned and returned to the waiting room, then pulled her phone out, keeping a wary eye on the door in case anyone came in.

Declan answered after a couple of rings.

"Hello."

"Is everything okay, Declan?"

"Not really, no. The bitch keeps mouthing off, trying to wind us up."

"You can cope with that, can't you? That's what I'm paying you for."

"Sure we can, but I don't see the point. Her wee daddy's not going to ask for another photo, that's obvious, so why wait until tomorrow? If she carries on like this, Flynn and me, we're going to be awake all night. Plus it'll be dark soon, much easier to dig when it's daylight."

Diana considered this and looked at her watch. It was five-thirty. If her father was going to make any demands, which she thought unlikely, he would probably have done it by now.

"All right, Declan. Go ahead."

She ended the call just as the waiting room door was pushed open.

"Mrs Parkhouse?"

"Yes."

"I'm DC Hammond. Sorry for the delay."

"You're finally ready, are you?"

He smiled.

"Yes. Please follow me."

Chapter 78

Luke's phone rang and Carl and Tara almost jumped out of their seats.

"It's my partner," he said. "Excuse me a minute."

He returned to the kitchen and accepted the call.

"Hi, Sam. Did you get anything else out of Sebastian?"

"Unfortunately not. He said he'd ring his parents to see if there was anything else that he could remember and ring me back." She paused. "I was wondering if it's worth going to East Harptree Wood on the off chance they're using it again."

He was about to answer when he saw that DCI Franks was trying to ring.

"Sam, there's another call coming in. I'll put you on hold."

He switched calls.

"Hi, Nicole. Any joy?"

"Yes. He's a nasty piece of work, that kid, but none too bright. Didn't take much to get the information out of him. Have you got a pen?"

Luke looked over to Carl and Tara.

"Have you got something I can write on?"

Tara walked over to the mantelpiece, picked up a notepad and pen and passed them to Luke.

"Ready when you are, Nicole."

"Okay. Here goes. There are five. East Harptree, Harridge, New Row Farm, Beacon Hill and Loocombe."

"Thanks, Nicole."

He jotted the names down, ended the call and Sam came back on the line.

"That was DCI Franks," he said. "Diana has taken her son on walks to four woods in Somerset in addition to East

Harptree. I suspect they were all visits to check their suitability. Could you look them up?"

He read them out to her.

"Thanks. I'll google them."

Luke waited.

"I've found three of them," Sam said after a few minutes. I can't find Locombe though."

"It's Loocombe. L-O-O."

"Oh, right." She paused. "Got it. All four are in the same area of Somerset, north of Shepton Mallet." Another pause. "I don't think it would be Loocombe Wood though, it's very small without easy access. I can't see how you'd get a van there. Just a second... Yes, the same goes for New Row Farm."

"So that narrows it down to Harridge Wood and Beacon Hill Woods?"

"Yes, and it could be either by the look of them. Harridge Wood is near a village called Nettlebridge about 3 miles north of Shepton Mallet."

"And Beacon Hill?"

"About 2 miles south of Harridge."

"Okay. Just a second."

He entered Harridge Wood into the maps app on his phone and clicked for directions.

"Harridge Wood is only twenty minutes from here. I'm going to head there first. If I don't have any luck I'll move on to Beacon Hill."

"Good luck, Luke, and be careful, won't you?"

"I will. Love you."

"Love you."

He hung up and returned to Carl and Tara.

"I may know where Lily is being held."

"Where?" Tara asked.

"In one of two woods near Shepton Mallet. I'm going to head there now. I don't suppose you've got a decent torch, have you? It's going to be getting dark soon."

"Yes, we've got one," Carl said. He stood up, left the room and returned a few seconds later.

"Thanks," Luke said as he took the torch from him. "What's your mobile number?"

Luke added it to his contacts then gave Carl his own number.

"Ring me if you hear anything."

"Let me know when you find her," Tara said.

"I will."

Though he worried it was more an 'if' than a 'when'.

Chapter 79

"How long have you been a criminal, Flynn?"

The Australian glared at Lily from the plastic chair at the other end of the van, but didn't respond. He no longer bothered to wear his balaclava, and didn't seem bothered that she now knew his name.

She wasn't sure why she was continuing to bait him, but she had to do something. Perhaps it was her way of trying to delay what she now feared was inevitable, or perhaps it was simply to keep her mind from thinking about what these men might do to her.

Whatever the reason, she wasn't going to stop.

"How much am I worth to you personally, Flynn? Twenty thousand? Fifty thousand? I bet you're getting less than anyone else, but then all you are is muscle. It's not as if you're being paid to use your brains."

He spat on the ground by his side.

She decided to change tack.

"I've got friends on the outside who are very intelligent. A lot more intelligent than you. Some of them are ex-police. They'll know I've been taken, and I bet they're on the scent right now. You'd better watch your back, Flynn. Any moment now…"

There was a rat-a-tat-tat on the van door and it gave her a lift to see Flynn jump to his feet in shock. It proved she had got to him. That was something.

Not much, but something.

The door opened and Declan climbed in. He sneered at her, then grasped Flynn's shoulder and turned him so that they were both facing away. He started talking, but he was almost whispering and all she could make out was the word 'deep'.

When he'd finished speaking, Flynn moved to the side of the van, picked up a long roll of dirty grey blanket that she assumed contained tools, then stepped down out of the van, closing the door behind him.

"What's he doing, Declan?"

Declan sat in the chair but rather than remain silent, as his colleague had done, he grinned, happy to reply.

"Flynn's preparing the ground." He paused. "And I mean that in the literal sense."

He reached into his pocket, pulled out his switchblade and pressed the button on the handle. She shrunk back in her chair as he stood up and walked towards her.

He bent down so that their noses were almost touching, and pressed the point of the blade against the skin below her left ear.

"Listen to me, bitch. If you want to keep these pretty wee ears of yours, you'll shut the fuck up. Understand?"

She nodded.

Without adding to this, he returned to his chair, pulled out his phone and started scrolling.

A few seconds later she heard a thump outside the van, then a few seconds later another.

Then another.

Flynn was preparing the ground.

Chapter 80

Luke was trying his hardest to cut the journey time to Harridge Wood from the satnav's twenty-minute prediction to fifteen minutes or less.

At the speed he was travelling, he hoped he didn't encounter the police en route, though he was driving on country lanes so thought it unlikely.

Sam rang when he was five minutes into the journey.

"I've found detailed maps of the woods. Both Harridge and Beacon Hill are over a hundred acres so it's going to be like finding a needle in a haystack. Harridge is closed to the public at the moment because of ash dieback."

"That could be a good reason for Diana to choose it."

"Yes, I thought the same."

"Is there a parking area?"

"No. You'll have to park on the road. I'll send you the maps for both woods."

"Thanks."

He hung up.

Ten minutes later he passed a thick copse on his left, and a hundred yards further on the satnav announced that he'd reached his destination. He pulled over onto a narrow patch of muddy ground in front of a five-barred gate bearing the sign 'No Entry - Closed to the Public'.

After parking, he retrieved the torch from the passenger seat and climbed out of the car. It was still light enough to see, but only just, so he needed to move quickly. The gate wasn't padlocked, and he was able to push it open. He bent to study the ground but saw no signs of any recent tyre tracks in the mud.

He set off at a rapid jog. After fifty yards or so the track forked. Looking down at the map, he saw that he could take a circular route leading back to this point.

There were two challenges which meant it would take him at least an hour to cover the entire wood.

First, the total distance he had to cover was at least a couple of miles, and he would have to stop regularly to check for tracks leading off the main one.

Second, the map showed that there was access from five roads, in addition to the one he'd parked beside, so he would need to veer off the main track to take in those entry points and see if there was any evidence of a vehicle entering.

He ran on, and after another two hundred yards or so his phone started to ring. Cursing himself for not putting it on vibrate he stopped running and accepted the call.

"Hello."

"I've got the general location for you, Luke."

"That's great, Ma'am."

"Don't hope for too much. All I can give you is an area of about half a mile square. It's in the countryside, north of Shepton Mallet."

"How far north?"

"About a mile."

"Fuck."

There was a moment's hesitation before she spoke again.

"I take it that wasn't what you were expecting?"

"No. Was the phone used in Beacon Hill Wood?"

"Just a second." She paused. "Yes, almost certainly. Either that or on one of the roads close by."

"Okay." He started jogging back to the beemer. "Will they be able to come back to you with GPS coordinates?"

"You know that pinpointing the exact location usually requires a warrant?"

"Yes, but as I told you, someone's life is in danger."

"And you can't tell me more?"

"I'm sorry, I can't."

"I'm putting a lot of trust in you, Luke."

"I know you are, Ma'am."

She sighed.

"I'll see what I can do."

He ended the call as he reached the BMW, climbed in, started the engine and accelerated away.

Four minutes later he reached Beacon Hill Wood and saw a sign for parking. He pulled in, set his phone to vibrate, and called up the map Sam had sent.

The wood was perched on the top of a hill and was L-shaped, the longer part of the L running east to west parallel to the road, while the shorter leg ran south towards Shepton Mallet, following the course of Fosse Way, an old Roman road.

The car park was at the corner of the L and the shape made it impossible to take a circular route, as had been his plan at Harridge Wood.

He decided to head south first. The map showed steep embankments after a half a mile or so which would be impossible for a vehicle to traverse. He'd follow the track to that point, then double back and head east.

It was now dark, and he was wary of using the torch in case he was spotted, so half-covered the beam with his palm. This gave him enough light to see the way ahead, and to spot any gaps in the trees wide enough for a van to pass through.

Chapter 81

Flynn opened the van door, and Lily saw that it was now dark outside.

He climbed in, a torch in his left hand.

"It's done."

Declan turned to face him.

"How deep?"

"Four feet, maybe five."

"I said six feet."

"Come on, Declan. Five feet is plenty. There's no dog going to dig that far down."

"Yeah. You're probably right."

Lily watched them wide-eyed. The two men were talking matter-of-factly, as if they were undertaking a home DIY project together, not planning someone's burial.

Her burial.

She had to do something, but what?

"I'll check it out," Declan said and held his hand out for the torch. "Stay here with her."

He climbed down, closing the door behind him, and Flynn sat down on the plastic chair and looked over at Lily.

She swallowed and was about to speak when Declan opened the door, climbed back in and shook his head at Flynn.

"What were you thinking, you fucking moron? It's no more than three foot deep!"

"Do you want me to…"

"No. I'll do it." He gestured towards Lily. "Keep a close eye on her."

He climbed back down and closed the door.

Now was her chance.

Her last chance.

It was clear Declan had no conscience. Hell, the man seemed to be enjoying the whole thing.

Flynn hadn't been as bright and sparky though. Perhaps, deep down, he was uncomfortable with what they were about to do.

She heard a thump outside, then another a few seconds later. The interval was shorter than when Flynn had been digging. If Declan was now thinking five feet was deep enough it wasn't going to take him long.

This was it, her one opportunity.

"Have you got a family, Flynn?"

He said nothing.

"A sister, perhaps?"

Again nothing.

There was another thump outside.

"What would you think if it was your sister sitting where I am, if she was about to be murdered and thrown into a freshly dug grave?"

Still no response.

"You'd be upset, wouldn't you? You'd…"

"Shut your mouth!"

Another thump.

"Declan, the way he talks to you. Surely, that winds you up, doesn't it? Don't you want to show him you're a man not a mouse? Stand up to him rather than cower in a corner?"

He looked her in the eyes, then at the van door, then back at her.

Was she finally getting to him?

Might there be a chance she could persuade him to help her escape?'

He stood up and walked slowly towards her.

Another thump.

He stopped a couple of feet away, his face expressionless.

"Are you going to untie me?"

Flynn moved behind her and she felt a sudden jolt as he pulled the chair back so that it fell to the floor.

He leaned down and sneered.

"Tell it to the ceiling, bitch."

He continued glaring at her for a few seconds, and then returned to the other end of the van.

Chapter 82

It was taking Luke much longer than he'd anticipated.

Above him was the slenderest of crescent moons, and he daren't expose the full beam of the torch.

This meant that he could no longer run or even jog. He was having to walk at a normal pace, peering left and right to try to see any gaps in the trees, and using the torch only when it was essential. Even then, he held his hand loosely over the bulb to minimise the glare.

Suddenly a gap in the trees opened up, and he was greeted with a view of twinkling lights on a far-off hill. He shone the torch down to see he had been close to stepping off an almost vertical slope.

These were the embankments he'd seen on the map. He needed to turn east now and follow them along. A few hundred yards should see him reach the Fosse Way. He'd then have to retrace his steps almost to the car before turning east.

He took a couple more steps, felt his phone vibrate in his pocket and pulled it out to take the call.

"Hello.'

"I've got the GPS coordinates for you."

He breathed a sigh of relief.

"Thank you, Ma'am. Just a second."

He switched to the Maps app on his iPhone.

"Okay. What's the latitude?"

"51.21136."

He entered the number, then a comma.

"And the longitude?"

"-2.51908."

He typed this in and hit return. The display zoomed to a point along the longer flank of the wood, the stem of the

L. He switched to the map Sam had sent through and saw that the location was about fifty yards north of an ancient stone plinth, and no more than a couple of hundred yards from where he was standing.

"Have you got it, Luke?"

"Yes. Can I ask one more favour?"

"Go on."

"DCI Franks' team is interviewing a fifteen-year-old boy, Roma Parkhouse, in Keynsham. They've arrested him for selling drugs and his mother, Diana, is there as a responsible adult. I'm hoping she hasn't left yet, in which case can you ask them to find an excuse to keep her there until I get back to you?"

"Is she implicated in whatever this is you're up to?"

"Yes, but at the moment the evidence is only circumstantial."

"You're asking a lot, Luke."

"I know, Ma'am." He paused. "Thank you."

He ended the call, retraced his steps north to the main west-to-east track, then turned right and switched off his torch. After allowing a few seconds for his eyes to adjust to the near-total darkness he started jogging.

A minute or so later he almost stumbled into the standing stone, shielded his phone to ensure it couldn't be seen and looked down at the Maps display.

He studied the screen for a moment, returned the phone to his pocket and stepped past the stone for about five paces before turning left.

There was a gap between the trees ahead of him that was wide enough for a vehicle to go through.

He bent down, took out his torch and, shielding it again, shone it on the ground. Sure enough, there were tyre tracks.

After turning it off, he stood up and stepped through the gap and forwards. After thirty yards or so the trees closed in but widened to his left, again creating a passage wide enough for a vehicle. He followed the gap, which then bent to the right, and stopped dead in his tracks when he saw a van no more than twenty yards ahead of him.

It was facing directly towards him. Given the narrow confines, it meant they must have reversed it into position.

He crouched down, now on high alert, adrenaline firing through his veins.

Then he heard a voice, the accent unmistakeably Australian.

"Is it done?"

An answer came back immediately, and this time the man was clearly Irish.

"Yes. The wee girl's done for."

Chapter 83

Luke pressed on as silently as he could towards the van.

The men's words had sent a shiver down his spine and fired him up. He was going to make them pay for what they had done. Surprise was on his side, and he intended to use it to its full potential.

That and seventeen stone of pent-up fury.

He approached the left-hand side of the van and, when he reached the driver's door, heard the Irishman again.

"We'll lift the girl out together. It'll make it easier to drop her in."

He was inside the van.

"Okay," the Australian said, and Luke heard him climb in to join the other man.

He crept along until he was level with the back of the vehicle, and the next words he heard both shocked and delighted him.

"No! Leave me alone!"

It was Lily.

She was alive.

Luke's heart was thumping even harder now, but he was ready. These bastards wouldn't know what hit them.

"Shut the fuck up!" the Irishman demanded.

"No, I…"

Luke heard a loud slap and a scream of pain from Lily.

"You get that side of the chair," the Irishman said. "Right, lift."

She had to be tied to it, which meant they would need to put her down at the back of the van, climb down, then pick her up again.

Or at least that was what he hoped.

That was when he would strike.

He heard the sound of the chair being set down, then two thumps as the men stepped from the van.

This was his cue.

He rounded the corner to see soft light spilling from the rear of the vehicle and the two men poised to reach for Lily.

Luke lifted the torch so that the beam shone full in their faces, roared and shoulder-charged the nearer man, who toppled into the second causing him to fall backwards to the ground.

The first man managed to stay on his feet and started to turn, but Luke was too quick for him, drew back his right fist and swung with all his might. There was a crack as knuckles connected with jaw, and the man fell back against the rear door before sliding to the ground.

Luke turned to see the second man climbing to his feet and reaching into his pocket.

"You're a dead man," he snarled.

It was the Irishman.

"Watch out!" Lily screamed. "He's got a knife."

The knife appeared and there was a click as the blade shot from the handle. The Irishman dived forwards, aiming for the stomach, but Luke was too quick and twisted left to avoid the blow, simultaneously grabbing the man's wrist with his left hand as his arm flew past.

The Irishman tried to break free but Luke's grip was too strong.

Keeping hold of the man's wrist, he swung his right hand down. There were two loud cracks as the radius and ulna in his arm fractured.

"Aagh!"

He dropped to his knees.

Luke turned to check on the Australian and saw that he was now sitting up, tentatively feeling his jaw but showing no signs of climbing to his feet.

Luke retrieved his torch from the ground and swung it

in an arc around the back of the van, revealing a deep hole some five paces away. A spade was embedded in the ground beside it.

He retrieved it, returned to the two men and held the spade in the air.

"Get in the hole!"

The Australian looked up at him, then at the spade, and bent forwards, crawled to the hole and dived in.

Luke turned to the Irishman.

"You too!"

"No!"

Luke swung the spade down into the man's left leg.

There was another scream of pain.

"In! Now!"

The Irishman held his functioning arm up.

"Okay! Okay!"

He started to get to his feet.

"On your hands and knees like your friend!"

He crawled to the edge and fell head-first into the open grave.

Luke stepped forwards, shone the torch into the two men's eyes and held the spade in the air again.

"Make one move, either of you, and I'll use this again."

Keeping his eyes on them, he leaned the spade against his thigh, retrieved his phone and dialled the last number on his call list.

"Hello, Luke."

"Ma'am, please can you send officers to those coordinates you gave me? There are two men here awaiting time at his majesty's pleasure. Oh, and an ambulance would be a good idea too."

"What about Diana Parkhouse? We kept her waiting for a solicitor."

"She needs to be arrested and cautioned."

"What are the charges?"

"Kidnapping, conspiracy to commit extortion and

attempted murder. Probably others too, but that should get the ball rolling."

"Did you get there in time?"

Luke looked over at Lily and smiled.

"Yes, Ma'am. I got here in time."

Chapter 84

Luke's phone rang.

"Is it him?" Sam asked.

"Yes."

He accepted the call.

"Hello, Pete. All set?"

"We're about ten minutes away."

"Great. I'll fetch the others, and we'll see you in reception."

He hung up and turned to the rest of his team.

"They're on the way."

"I hope it goes smoothly," Helen said.

"Good luck, guv," Josh added.

"Thanks."

He stood up and made his way to Glen's office, knocked once and walked in.

The Head of Security looked up from his desk, his words punctuated by the regular clack-clack of the Newton's Cradle.

He pointed at it and grinned his all-teeth-on-display grin.

"Look. It's still working."

"That's good. Listen, DI Gilmore's just rung. They'll be here in a few minutes."

"To arrest and cushion him?"

Luke smiled. He knew what he meant.

"Yes, Glen. Let's go and get Ambrose."

The seventy-five-year-old founder of Filchers was standing outside his office talking to Ellie, his secretary, when they approached. As ever, he was stylishly dressed and looked much younger than his years, despite his near-white hair.

"Ah. Hello, Luke. Hello, Glen. Are they here?"

"On their way," Luke said.

"Good. I can't say I'm looking forward to this, but I'd rather be there when it's done."

They made their way to reception.

Glen turned to Ambrose as they waited.

"I've got a perpetual motion machine."

"Have you indeed?"

Glen nodded.

"It's a Newton's Cradle. As long as you keep lifting the balls and letting them drop, it goes on forever." His grin returned. "Perpetually."

"Fascinating."

"Ah, they're here," Luke said.

Pete walked over, nodded to Luke and Glen, and shook Ambrose's hand.

"I don't know if you remember me, Mr Filcher. I'm Detective Inspector Gilmore. We met last year."

"Of course I do, Pete."

Pete turned to the uniformed constable beside him.

"This is PC Walker."

"Good to meet you, sir," the constable said.

"And you too, constable." Ambrose sighed. "Right. Let's get this over with."

He led the way to the stairs and they walked up to the first floor, entered the area used by the Vericomm team and headed for the client director's office.

As they approached, his secretary looked up from her desk and took in this unusual group comprising the CEO, three other men, one of them a giant, and a police officer.

"Are you looking for Matthew, Mr Filcher?"

"No. Jethro Mansell. Do you know where he sits?"

"Yes." She turned and pointed. "He's in the third cubicle along."

"Thanks."

Ambrose moved to one side to let Pete take the lead,

Tiger Bait

and Luke saw Mansell turn when he heard them approach.

He was an unattractive man, in his forties, with a pudgy face and eyes that were too close together.

Luke saw his jaw drop when he saw that one of the group was in uniform.

"What is this?"

"Are you Jethro Mansell?" Pete asked.

"Yes. Why?"

"I'm Detective Inspector Gilmore from Avon and Somerset Police, and I'm arresting you for cyber-bullying under the Malicious Communications Act 1988 and the Protection from Harassment Act 1997. You do not have to say anything, but it may harm your defence if you do not mention when questioned something which you later rely on in court. Anything you do say may be given in evidence." He paused. "Do you understand, Mr Mansell?"

He swallowed and nodded.

"PC Walker."

The constable handcuffed Mansell, and the group, now six in number, returned downstairs, accompanied by muttering voices as they passed other employees.

"Thank goodness that's over," Ambrose said, once the two police officers had taken their prisoner away.

"I'd better return to my office," Glen said, "to see if my cradle's still perpetualising. The last thing I want is trouble with my motions."

He left and Ambrose turned to face Luke.

"Helen and Lily did a great job discovering Mansell was the troll. What put them onto him?"

"Lily was talking to another actor, Nev, during a break in rehearsals, and he revealed that Mansell had sent him a nasty email before he left FADS. It wasn't as vicious as the later communications, which was why he'd forgotten about it, but when Lily saw it she recognised phrases that were in the anonymous social media posts. That was enough for the police to get a search warrant, and what was on his laptop is going to be enough to convict him." He paused. "Ironically, he started trolling because of something relatively minor, an argument with the director and the cast over how often they should rehearse."

"And how is Lily faring after that awful business last week?"

"Very well, Ambrose. It was a stressful experience, and she's got a nasty bruise on her cheek, but other than that she's physically well."

"And her mental state?"

"Surprisingly good. She's travelling to London today for rehearsals for a part she's got in a West End play."

"Good for her. What about the gang that abducted her?"

"All in custody. The leader was a woman and she, one of her brothers and three others have been arrested. One of them, an Australian, has already provided information that should lead to successful convictions."

"You said 'one of her brothers'?"

Luke nodded. "She's got two. One of them, Apollo, is facing charges of theft in addition to kidnap and false imprisonment. The police are convinced her other brother, Jay, is the leader of a drugs operation in Bristol, but he's proving harder to bring to justice."

"Is that Operation Tooting, the case we're providing consultancy for?"

"Yes. Josh and I have been helping them. Our best chance of bringing Jay to justice is a mid-level dealer called Tyrone Goodwin. There are rumours that Jay beat him up, and the SIO's hoping that if we lean on him he'll open up."

Ambrose smiled. "Well done, Luke. Keep up the good work, and please tell your team that I think they're doing a fantastic job."

"Thanks, Ambrose. I will."

"Actually, why don't I tell them myself? Would you mind?"

"Of course not."

They made their way to the Ethics Room to find Sam, Helen, Maj and Josh seated at the table in the centre of the room.

They all turned when he entered.

"Well, guv?" Josh asked, then spotted Ambrose behind him. "Oh!"

"They've taken Jethro Mansell away," Ambrose said, "but the reason I've popped my head in is to say what a great job you're all doing."

"We've got a great manager," Maj said.

"You have indeed. Right, well I'll leave you to it. Keep up the good work."

"Nasty wee bawbag," Helen said after he'd left.

"That's not a nice thing to say about our CEO," Josh said with a smile.

"You know who I mean." She turned to Luke. "Will Jethro Mansell go to prison?"

Luke nodded. "Hopefully. He could be looking at up to six months."

"It should be longer," Sam said. "I've seen what he posted online. It was horrible." She paused. "Oh, I nearly forgot. James popped in while you were out. He's sorted a new car for you, a Mercedes E Class Estate." She turned to the others. "We need it to keep Wilkins under control."

Luke's phone rang.

"Excuse me."

He stepped away and accepted the call.

"Good afternoon, Ma'am. Thanks for calling back."

"You're not asking for another favour, are you?"

"No. I rang to thank you for putting so much faith in me last week. I know I was out of order asking for your help like that, but I didn't know how else to locate the van where they were holding Lily."

"I knew from the tone of your voice you were in desperate straits, Luke, and, to be honest, I enjoyed having a part to play. So much of my job is directing others, I have few opportunities these days to get my hands dirty."

"Thank you anyway, Ma'am."

"I should be thanking you. Your team too. I gather they've all played a part in bringing the Curtis family to justice. Please pass on my personal thanks."

"I will."

He hung up and turned to the others.

"That was Sara Gough, the chief constable of Avon and Somerset Police. She asked me to pass on her personal thanks to all of you for helping to catch the Curtises."

"Gucci!" Josh said, a broad grin on his face.

"Right, guys," Luke said. "It's 12:30 and I'm hungry. Lunch is on me, and I'm not talking the staff canteen."

"KFC, guv?"

"No, Josh. Let's drive to the Boathouse. I fancy a decent steak."

Afterword

As with all my books, this is a work of fiction. However, some of the scenarios and crimes are based on real life, and I thought it worth explaining where I drew inspiration from.

Tiger kidnapping is a twist on the IRA's tactic of abducting people to force their family to plant car bombs. The criminals' goal is to have their risky business done by someone else.

A prime example of a tiger kidnap is the 2009 Bank of Ireland robbery. A man, his five-year-old nephew, his girlfriend and her mother were held overnight by six heavily built masked men, dressed in black and carrying handguns. In the morning, the two women and the child were taken away and the man, a bank employee, was ordered to collect cash from his workplace. He was given a photo of the rest of the family at gunpoint to convince his colleagues that their lives were under threat.

He obtained the money, put it in his car in four laundry bags, and drove to a railway station where a gang member took the keys and drove the car away. The family were then freed.

A member of the Irish Parliament remarked after the Bank of Ireland robbery that "tiger kidnappings are taking place in Ireland at a rate of almost one per week".

Cuckooing is becoming increasingly common, especially in the South of England, and is the term used by the police to describe a situation where the home of a vulnerable person is taken over by a criminal, usually to deal, store or take drugs. The term comes from the cuckoo's practice of taking over other birds' nests for its young.

A number of MPs are calling for cuckooing to be criminalised as part of a review of the 2015 Modern Slavery Act.

Protection rackets involve criminals demanding regular payments from businesses, claiming to protect them from harm. The Kray twins famously ran protection rackets in the East End of London in the 1950s and 1960s, and there are also more recent UK examples in areas controlled by gangland firms.

In Italy, government officials say that 80% of businesses in the city of Palermo in Sicily pay pizzo, or protection money, to the Mafia.

The Bill Curtis Cartel is my invention, but I took inspiration from Curtis 'Cocky' Warren, an English gangster and drugs trafficker who was formerly Interpol's Target One and was once listed on The Sunday Times Rich List.

In 1992, Warren smuggled 907 kilograms of cocaine into the UK. He was arrested, but the case had to be abandoned, and after release he told HM Customs agents, "I'm off to spend my £87 million and you can't touch me."

In 1995, Warren owned casinos in Spain, discos in Turkey, a vineyard in Bulgaria, land in the Gambia and had money stashed away in Swiss bank accounts. He could have retired rich, but decided to continue importing drugs.

In 2007, Warren was arrested for drug smuggling and in 2009 was sentenced to 13 years imprisonment. He was released in November 2022 and is now a free man. As I write this, he is 61 years old.

Tiger Bait

Thanks for reading 'Tiger Bait'. It would help no end if you could leave a review on Amazon.

This is book 8 in my Luke Sackville Crime Series. If you read it as a standalone, I invite you to look at the first seven books: Taken to the Hills, Black Money, Fog of Silence, The Corruption Code, Lethal Odds, Sow the Wind and Beacon of Blight.

Want to read more about Luke Sackville and what shaped his career choices? 'Change of Direction', the prequel to the series, can be downloaded as an ebook free of charge by subscribing to my newsletter at:
sjrichardsauthor.com

Acknowledgements

First, I have to thank my wife Penny for her help and support while I write, as well as for her constructive feedback on my first draft.

As always, my beta readers provided fantastic feedback. Thanks to Chris Bayne, Deb Day, Denise Goodhand, Jackie Harrison, Sarah Mackenzie, Allison Valentine and Marcie Whitecotton-Carroll.

Thanks also to my advance copy readers, who put faith in the book being worth reading.

Yet again Samuel James has done a terrific job narrating the audiobook, while Olly Bennett designed yet another tremendous cover. 'Give me a scary van in the woods', I said, and he did a great job.

Last but not least, thanks to you the reader. I love your feedback and reading your reviews, and I'm always delighted to hear from you so please feel free to get in touch.

Tiger Bait

MR KILLJOY

Beware the bearer of false gifts

Luke Sackville's Ethics Team is stretched to breaking point across several investigations, little realising that one man links them all.

Narcissistic, cunning and ruthless, Mr Killjoy is reaping the rewards of cybercrime, and is indifferent to the fact that his victims are being driven to despair and beyond.

Luke connects the dots and begins to home in, but as the villain is cornered he strikes out and none of the team is safe.

Mr Killjoy is the ninth book in the series of crime thrillers featuring ex-DCI Luke Sackville and his Ethics Team.

Out 5th August 2025 - Order your copy now

mybook.to/mrkilljoy

ABOUT THE AUTHOR

First things first: my name's Steve. I've never been called 'SJ', but Steve Richards is a well-known political writer hence the pen name.

I was born in Bath and have lived at various times on an irregular clockwise circle around England. After university in Manchester, my wife and I settled in Macclesfield before moving to Bedfordshire then a few years ago back to Somerset. We now live in Croscombe, a lovely village just outside Wells, with our 2 sprightly cocker spaniels.

I've always loved writing but have only really had the time to indulge myself since taking early retirement. My daughter is a brilliant author (I'm not biased of course) which is both an inspiration and - because she's so good - a challenge. After a few experiments, and a couple of completed but unsatisfactory and never published novels, I decided to write a crime fiction series as it's one of the genres I most enjoy.

You can find out more about me and my books at my website:
sjrichardsauthor.com

Printed in Great Britain
by Amazon